HEART STARTER

REBELS OF RUSHMORE BOOK THREE

MICHELLE HERCULES

INFINITE SKY PUBLISHING

Editor: Hot Tree Editing
Proofreading: My Brother's Editor

Photography: Lukeography
Model: Benjamin Ahlblad

Paperback ISBN: 978-1-950991-67-9

1

SADIE

I BLINK my eyes open and don't know where I am at first. Then I hear a faint and constant beeping sound, which draws my attention to the machine to my right. It's monitoring my heartbeat. Fragments of memory rush through my brain, and then I remember being at the pub with my teammates after we won the championship game.

There were some wankers at the pub, drunk out of their minds. They followed Anika and me when we left, and then... *fuck*. The flash of a steely blade, the white-hot pain in my side.

"Sadie, darling. You're awake." My mother moves into my line of vision, face scrunched in worry, making the lines on her forehead deepen.

"Apparently. I could be dreaming though," I croak.

"Even heavily sedated, her sarcasm is intact. She'll live, Mum," my brother Dominic pipes up from somewhere in the room.

"Piss off, Dom," I grit out and try to sit up. A sharp sting flares in my side. "Bloody hell."

"Sadie, you can't move. You'll open your stitches."

Mum fiddles with the bed's control panel, raising the back until I'm in a comfortable sitting position.

"How is Anika?" I ask.

Her gaze narrows, getting darker with anger. Mum is usually a mellow person; she rarely gets aggravated, but when she does, you'd better pray you're not the one in her path of wrath.

"Distraught, naturally. She came to visit you yesterday. Brought you those flowers." Mum points at the vase with white lilies, my favorite.

"And the motherfuckers who attacked us?"

"In custody."

A wave of relief washes over me. "Good."

"Yes. But what were you thinking, Sadie? Jumping in front of someone carrying a knife? You could have been killed."

Anger bubbles up my throat. "What was I supposed to do? Stand aside and let them stab my best friend instead?"

Something like remorse flashes in my mother's eyes. She steps back, and then Dominic walks over to take her place next to the bed.

"Come on, Mum. Let Sadie rest before you lay on the guilt-trip," he says with an easygoing smile, but his eyes are serious.

I must have scared them to death. The knowledge makes me feel guilty, but I don't regret my actions.

"I called your father," she tells me, and in a flash, I'm as rigid as a board.

"Why?"

"Sadie." Her tone is reproachable. "He loves you. You really ought to let go of your resentment."

I clench my teeth so hard it hurts my molars.

"What did he say?"

"He wanted to come see you."

"What? No way." The heart monitor starts beeping faster, picking up on my distress.

"I told him there's no need," Mum adds quickly.

I sag against my pillow, feeling the tension whoosh out of my body. I can't handle seeing Dad on top of everything else.

"And he just accepted that, right?" I can't help the bitterness that seeps into my voice.

Mum and Dominic trade a look, and immediately the small hairs on the back of my neck stand on end. Bad news is coming my way.

"He did on the condition that you attend college in the US, like we agreed when your father and I...." She looks away.

"You can say divorce, Mum. It's been twelve years. And I told you I didn't care about your agreement. I don't want to study in the States. Dominic didn't."

He puffs his chest out. "That's because I'm a genius and got into Oxford. Don't be a hater. Besides, I know what you're saying is pure rubbish. I've seen you staring at Rushmore's brochure for ages. Their football program is legendary. You'd be a fool to pass up that opportunity."

I try to cross my arms, but it hurts when I move. I settle for pouting like a five-year-old. "They call it soccer over there. I can't take them seriously when they don't use the correct name for the sport."

He rolls his eyes. "Yeah, sure. Let's go with that horse-shite excuse."

Mum hits him on the chest with the back of her hand. "Dom, language."

He scowls. "What? Sadie can drop f-bombs and I get told off when I use 'shite'?"

I smirk. "You didn't almost die."

He sticks his tongue out at me like he's a little boy, not a twenty-year-old man.

He's not lying though. John Rushmore does have a wicked

football program. It's why—despite my protests—I applied. As much as I want to stay mad at my father and piss him off, I can't do so at the expense of my future.

"I can't make that decision right now," I say, just to be difficult. "I'm still recovering from getting shanked, for crying out loud."

Dominic's lips curl into a knowing grin. "California, here we come, babe."

I shake my head, struggling to keep my scowl. "You're delusional."

He knows me too well. There was never a doubt that I'd go to Rushmore, but protesting until the end is how I roll. I'm too stubborn to acknowledge defeat.

DANNY– A month later

My heart is about to burst from my chest when I skid to a halt in front of Coach Clarkson's office. He called me in even though we don't start preseason training for another week. I had a shift at Three Dudes Smoothies and ended up staying past my shift due to the crowd, so I had to race here.

I knock on the door, still breathing hard.

Shit. He's going to think I'm out of shape.

"Come in," he says.

"Hey, Coach. Sorry I'm late."

He turns his gaze away from his computer screen and frowns. "What in God's name happened to you?"

I remove my uniform hat and wipe the sweat off my forehead. "We were busy at work today, and then I had to ride my bike. My car is in the shop."

He swivels around in his chair and bends over to retrieve a

bottle of water from his mini fridge. "Here. I can't have you passing out on me due to dehydration."

"Thanks, Coach."

I twist off the cap as I take a seat. Then I pretty much inhale the whole water bottle in the blink of an eye. I was parched.

"Do you need another one?" Coach asks with the hint of a smirk.

"I'm okay. Thanks."

"All right, I won't keep you waiting. You must be wondering why I asked you to see me before preseason training starts."

"Yeah. I'm not in trouble, am I?"

Worry has been consuming me since I got his call. I'm on a sports scholarship, which is the only reason I can afford to attend Rushmore. If that went away, I don't know what I'd do.

"No, of course not."

"Nothing wrong with my grades?"

"Your grades are fine. You're probably the best student on the team. Really, Danny, relax."

I sink against the back of the chair as relief sweeps over me.

I had been obsessing about this meeting, much to Andy's amusement. He says I stress too much. I do, but only about things that matter. My status on the team is one of the things I worry about. It's my ticket to a better life. He experienced what it was like to be in my shoes for a hot minute, and he almost lost his mind. But I've lived in constant survival mode my whole life.

"Okay, so why am I here? Do you need something from me?"

"I want to talk about the NFL. Have you ever considered going pro?"

My heart suddenly speeds up, and my tongue gets stuck to the roof of my mouth. After a moment, I reply, "Yeah, of course. Isn't every kid's dream to play in the NFL?"

He chuckles. "True. But in your case, it could become a reality."

"How so?"

He furrows his eyebrows again. "Danny, come on. Surely you know you're one of the best quarterbacks we've ever had on the team."

"Troy was pretty good too. Honestly, I'm only trying to fill his shoes and not mess up, sir."

I'm not only saying that because Troy is one of my best friends. He legit kicked ass during his time as the Rushmore Rebels' quarterback.

"Troy was good, but he lacked focus and ambition. I suspect his heart wasn't one hundred percent in the game. You, on the other hand, have a fire I haven't seen in all my years of coaching. When Troy got injured, you hit the ground running. If it hadn't been his senior year, I'd have benched him in favor of you."

I'm at a loss for words.

"Wow."

Coach laughs. "Another great quality you have. Humbleness. You're not cocky, and you always put the team above your own interests. I appreciate that. But, son, this year, I want to see you shine."

"Yes, sir."

"A buddy of mine is a scout for the NFL. He saw your tape, and he was impressed. He's interested, which means other recruiters will soon be as well. However, if you want to give the NFL a shot, you have to train harder than before, be focused solely on the game and your academics. No excessive partying, no distractions."

"I want to make the NFL happen, sir. I'll do anything. No parties, no distractions. You tell me what I need to do, and I'll do it."

He nods. "That job of yours. I assume it's only during the summer?"

It wasn't, but I can't tell Coach I was planning on keeping my job at Three Dudes Smoothies for as long as I could. I want him to know I'm committed to the goal. So what if I have to live on a tighter budget? I've made do with less before.

"Yes, sir."

"Good. Well, that's it for now. Enjoy the rest of your summer break."

"Will do, sir. And thanks for the opportunity."

He shakes his head. "Don't thank me, Danny. You've earned it."

2

SADIE

I'M bleary-eyed when I push my trolley through the arrival gate of LAX and search the crowd. In the end, Dominic didn't come with me. He got the internship he'd been vying for, and I couldn't ask him to drop that to accompany me on this trip, only to be a buffer between Dad and me.

It's easy to spot my father in the sea of people. He's taller than most, and he always wears a baseball hat with his school's logo on it. I haven't seen him face to face in three years, and our online calls have been sparse. I simply never had much to say to him. Now I'm back to my home country—a place I never wanted to leave to begin with—and it feels surreal. I'm not sure if I belong here anymore.

He has a tentative smile on his scruffy face as he walks over. "Hi, Sadie."

"Hey, Dad."

He circles around the trolley with the clear intention to pull me into a side hug, but he stops abruptly and asks, "Is this okay, or are you still healing?"

It's hard to school my face into neutral. I don't like to talk about my battle wound. I thought I was fine when I was in the hospital, but when I returned home, my brain decided having PTSD was the way to go.

"It's been six weeks. I'm fine."

He hugs me awkwardly, and I can't help the stiffness of my body. Mercifully, he steps back fast.

"Let me help you with that."

He takes the trolley from me, which was acting like a shield. With that gone, I can increase the distance between us. I can't stray too far, though, or he'll notice. I clutch the straps of my backpack tighter while I pretend to people watch.

"How was your flight?" he asks.

"It was good. The seat next to me was empty."

"I love when that happens. Did you manage to sleep?"

"Couldn't. I was too wired."

"Nervous?"

I glance at him, frowning. "About what?"

"New school, new teammates."

I shrug. "It's not like this is my first rodeo moving across the ocean and starting from scratch."

He falls silent after that, which is what I wanted. The jab was intentional. Before my parents' divorce, Dad and I were close. I was your typical daddy's girl. Mum decided to move back to England after the split, and Dad agreed with giving her full custody of me and my brother. I begged to stay and live with him. I didn't want to move to a country I knew nothing about, save that it rained a lot. And according to my six-year-old mind, Mum was to blame for breaking up our family. She was the one who wanted to move back to her country. Naturally, things were way more complicated than that, but still, I resented my father for not fighting for me.

The sun has yet to set in California, but back in London, it's way past my bedtime. I can't wait to crash into a bed, any bed.

"I bought In-N-Out Burgers if you're hungry." Dad offers me a paper bag once we're in the car.

I was determined to keep up with the grumpiness, but a grin unfurls on my lips. "I haven't had one in years."

Eagerly, I take the bag from him and dive in.

"I remember you and Dominic ate so much the first time, you both had a tummy ache."

I wish Dad would stop reminiscing. Those were the happy days before the implosion of our happy family, and there's no point in dwelling there.

"I want to ask if you changed your mind about staying over for a couple of days, and give us a chance to catch up."

My stomach twists into knots, forcing me to stop chewing for a moment. "Nope. I haven't changed my mind. I'd like to get settled in my dorm room as soon as possible. Preseason training starts in two days. Besides, I think it's best if we keep our relationship on the down low at campus. I don't want to be treated differently because my father coaches the American football team."

"It's just called football, honey."

"No, *I* play football." I shove a fry into my mouth.

I'm only saying that to annoy him. I obviously know the difference in terminology.

"I like your accent. It's cute."

"I hope it'll help me get laid as much as it helps Dominic whenever he comes to visit you."

"Sadie!"

"What? Americans love a British accent."

It's hard to keep a straight face when Dad is redder than a tomato.

"I thought you had a good head on your shoulders," he grumbles.

"Will you relax? I was just taking the piss. I have no intention on dating. Football will be my only focus."

"And your classes too."

I roll my eyes. "Sure, and classes."

"We need to go shopping for cars. Any model you have in mind?"

Tension sweeps over my body. I forgot that owning a car is a must in America. I hate to drive mainly because I suck at it.

"Nope. Anything will do."

"Okay. I'll start looking online and then send you links."

"Brilliant."

"Are you sure you want to go to the dorms now?"

I nod. "Yeah, I might as well get settled. I've already emailed my roommate and told her I'd be moving in today. It's all arranged."

"Okay, Sadie. If that's what you want," he says, resigned.

I look out the window, not feeling an ounce of satisfaction in getting my way.

Since I only brought two suitcases and a backpack, getting settled in my minuscule dorm room took less than five minutes. I didn't unpack, just shoved my suitcases under the bed. Dad didn't linger, for which I had to thank my roommate, Katrina Montana, an extremely enthusiastic girl from my original hometown of Austin, Texas.

As soon as my father left, she started talking a mile a minute. "I'm so excited to finally meet you, Sadie. I had no idea your father was the football team's coach. You know what that means, right?"

"No idea." I flop on my bed, trying to give her a clue that I'm bone-tired and in no mood to chat right now.

"You'll get access to all the cute boys on the team." Her voice rises to a shriek.

"I guess. I don't really care, to be honest. I'm here to play football, not chase jerseys."

"Well, you'll be chasing jerseys anyway. I mean, when you play soccer, you're technically chasing jerseys."

Oh God. She's one of those Miss Smarty-pants girls. I pull a pillow over my head and groan.

"Are you okay?" she asks.

"Please don't take this the wrong way, but I'm super tired. It's been a long day."

"I'm so sorry. Of course you are. You probably want to take a nap before the party."

I pull the pillow away from my face and lean on my elbows. "What party?"

"The preseason party at the Red Barn. It's a jock thing. You don't know? The girls' soccer team is always there."

Ugh. I've received a few emails from Vanessa Castro, the team's captain, which I ignored. I was not in a good place emotionally. I was afraid she'd mention the attack in them. Now I know it was stupid to be so cowardly. I hope my radio silence didn't shine a bad light on me; I don't want to be perceived as a liability to the team.

"I've been traveling all day. I'm sure I was invited and just missed the email."

"Yeah, I'm sure. What time do you want me to wake you?"

All I want is to sleep until tomorrow, but now I have to do damage control. If this is a preseason kickoff party, my presence is a must.

"Whenever you're ready to go. I need a ride anyway, as I haven't gotten around to getting a car yet."

"Sure. Will do."

Katrina leaves the room, and not a second later, I pass out.

3

DANNY

"EARTH TO DANNY. HELLO!" Andy snaps his fingers in front of my face.

"What?" I glare at him.

"Please don't tell me you're still worried about your car."

I had to park in a heavy pedestrian traffic area, and knowing how drunk everyone gets at parties on campus, I wasn't happy. The last time I drove, a few idiots used the hood as a make-out spot and left a big dent behind. So the truth is, I *am* still stressing, but if I confess, Andy won't stop bugging me.

"No," I lie.

"Where was your head, then? I've been talking to myself for the past five minutes."

"So the usual for you, then?" Paris pipes up with a smile on his face, joining us in the small space we carved out in the jam-packed area.

"Bite me, Paris," Andy retorts. "Flying solo tonight?"

Andy's question erases Paris's amusement in a flash. "No,

Lydia stopped to chat with some old friend from her high school."

"I'm shocked she has friends," Andy mutters before he takes a large sip of his beer.

Paris doesn't reply. Either he didn't hear it or he's choosing to ignore Andy's comment. He knows his longtime girlfriend is no one's favorite. He's a pretty chill guy, friendly and outgoing. The little I've seen of his girlfriend suggests she's the opposite, but I won't join the hate bandwagon based solely on first impressions.

I take a sip of my beer—the only one I'm drinking tonight—as I scan the crowd. The Red Barn preseason party is one of the most popular events on campus, and it's bursting at the seams with people. Most in attendance are part of an athletic program or a Greek. Last year, I got totally trashed. It was my first college party, after all. But after my convo with Coach Clarkson, I'm one hundred percent dedicated to not letting Rushmore's social life deviate me from my goals.

"Where's Jane tonight?" Paris asks Andy.

"She has a game out of town. She'll be back tomorrow."

Paris drops his jaw, widening his eyes in an exaggerated surprised expression. "And you let her go?"

I snicker when Andy's spine goes taut and he clenches his jaw in displeasure. "What are you insinuating, buddy? I trust my girlfriend completely."

"Gee, relax. I'm just busting your balls. It doesn't feel great, does it?"

Andy grumbles before chugging his beer. Since getting together with Jane, this is his first big college party without her, and I can already tell he's in the mood to get wasted, which sucks for me. Drunk Andy is a fucking pain in the ass.

Despite there not being enough space to walk from one side to the other in the open room without using elbows to make way, I can still see distinct division lines among the crowd.

Everyone is hanging out with their own teammates, groups, or cliques. However, that will change as the evening progresses and alcohol consumption increases.

Not far from us, I spot the girls from the soccer team. They're cool chicks, drama-free, and focused as hell on their game. It's no surprise they're at the top of their league. The same can't be said about their counterparts. Rushmore's men's soccer team not only sucks but also their players are mostly dicks, especially their captain, Nick Fowler.

I catch sight of him making his way to Vanessa Castro, the captain of the women's soccer team. He gets into her personal space and whispers something in her ear. It's obvious by her body language that she's not happy about the proximity or whatever Nick has to say.

"Shit. The douche king has arrived," Andy sneers.

Paris follows his line of sight. "What the hell is that weasel doing?"

He stands to his full height, body tense all of a sudden. Paris is a beast, the tallest player on our team and as strong as a bulldozer. He seems ready to run interference, but Vanessa doesn't seem to need his help after all. She says something to Nick that sends him away scowling. Unfortunately, he's coming in our direction now.

When he's within earshot, Andy speaks up. "Need some aloe vera for that burn, Nick?"

His expression turns murderous, but he quickly covers it up with an arrogant smirk. "Don't know what you're talking about, Rossi. Vanessa and I were chatting about the upcoming season."

"Not what it looked like from here," Paris replies, his tone harsh and cold.

Nick's eyebrows arch. "Sounds like you're jealous, Andino. Does Lydia know about your other interests?"

It's Murphy's Law that Lydia would show up just in time to hear Nick's comment.

"What other interests?" She loops a possessive arm around Paris's waist.

"Nothing, babe. Come on, let's get a drink. The air here has gotten rotten."

He steers her toward the nearest bar before Nick can get another malicious comment in.

"You're such a dick, Fowler." Andy glowers at the douche.

Like the idiot he is, Nick steps into Andy's space. "Oh, I'm a dick, huh? Do you think I'm afraid of you, Rossi?"

Andy has already curled his hand into a fist, and I can see things are about to turn bad in the blink of an eye. Nick's buddies from the soccer team are already striding our way. *For fuck's sake.* I toss my cup to the floor and get between Andy and Nick, pushing the jerk back.

"Get lost, Fowler," I tell him.

"Make me, Hudson," he grits out, bringing his ugly mug inches from my face.

Knowing full well that if I get into a fight, Coach will have my head, all I can do is swallow my anger and not fall for Nick's goading.

Suddenly, Puck and Paris are there, pulling Nick off me. His buddies lose their bravado and hang back. It was stupid of them to think they could take on Andy and me, and suicidal to face off against Puck and Paris, the Rushmore Rebels' linebackers.

"Get lost, Fowler. You're stinking up the place." Puck shoves the jackass toward his friends.

Shaking with anger, he points a finger in our direction. "This isn't over."

I rub my face, annoyed as fuck that the asshole managed to get under my skin. I wish I could have made a pancake out of his face.

"I can't believe you got into a fight, Paris," Lydia complains loudly.

"I didn't get into a fight. I helped avoid one," he retorts, sounding annoyed, which is a surprise. He always treats his girlfriend as if she's breakable.

"Why did you have to meddle?" she continues.

"Are you serious right now?"

I hear the frustration in his tone, which reminds me of how I used to sound by the end of the only serious relationship I've ever had.

Not wanting to witness Paris and Lydia argue, I turn to Andy and Puck. "Let's get another drink."

"Fuck. Let's." Andy leads the way.

It's impossible to walk side by side, so I end up following Andy and Puck. But a hand on my arm stops me in my tracks. I put my game face on despite the fact that I don't feel like socializing with strangers now. Only, the person staring at me is not unfamiliar. Gwen, my ex-girlfriend, is standing there with a big smile on her face. I have to blink twice to make sure I'm not seeing things.

"Gwen?"

"Hi, Danny."

My heart is pounding fast, and not in a good way. The end of our relationship wasn't amicable. It was ugly, and it made me swear off serious relationships for the next decade or longer.

"What are you doing here?" I ask, on edge.

Her smile wilts to nothing. "I didn't come here to follow you, if that's what you're worried about."

I'm still in shock from seeing her here, so it takes me a moment to process her words.

"What do you mean, come here?"

"I transferred to John Rushmore."

I feel the blood drain from my face. *She didn't follow me, my ass.*

"You transferred to the school I go to and you expect me to believe it's a coincidence?"

She drops her hand from my arm. "I don't care what you believe, Danny. I've always wanted to come here, but I didn't in our freshman year because of you. But why shouldn't I attend the school of my dreams to spare your feelings?"

I scoff. "Trust me. My feelings are fine. The question is, are yours?"

She watches me through slitted eyes. "Yes, Danny. I've finally moved on. You don't have to worry about me anymore."

She seems hurt by my question, and despite the shit she made me go through in our senior year in high school, I feel guilty.

I sigh. "Listen, I'm sorry, okay? It's been a shitty night, and the last person I expected to see here was you. I'm glad you're at your first-choice school."

"Thanks. Well, I'd better get back to my sorority sisters."

I watch her disappear into the crowd, but the foreboding feeling still lingers in my chest. *Damn it.* I sure hope Gwen is telling the truth about why she transferred here. I glance around, trying to find the guys, but the crowd has swallowed them up. *Whatever.* I need fresh air more than I need a beer.

When I finally manage to get outside, I keep walking until I'm back in the parking lot. Hell, it's clear that what I really want is to go home. I pull my cell phone out and text Andy. He can ride back with Puck or Paris. No sooner do I get near my car than I notice one of the taillights is busted and my bumper is crooked and bent.

Fucking hell. Someone rear-ended my car, and now there will be hell to pay.

4

SADIE

"SADIE, WAKE UP." Someone shakes my shoulder, but instead of doing what they want, I roll on my side and pull the pillow over my head.

"Sadie! You said you wanted to go to the party."

Finally, my dead-tired brain recognizes Katrina's voice. I'm tempted to tell her I've changed my mind, but I suffer from major FOMO. If I don't go, regret is going to make me her bitch tomorrow.

"I want to go," I mumble as I try to open my eyes, but it seems Mr. Sandman poured superglue over my eyelids. They feel heavy and stuck together.

"It doesn't look like you want to."

"I do. It's just my body that has other ideas. I can't even open my eyes."

"Should I do something to help?" she asks.

"Like what?"

"I don't know. Throw cold water at your face?"

"If you do that, I'll punch you in the throat."

Katrina gasps, and because I don't have a visual of her, I can't tell if her indignation is fake or genuine. I push the pillow aside and manage to open one eyelid. "I'm kidding. I'm not a psycho, you know?"

She laughs nervously and waves her hand. "Oh, I knew that."

Sure, sure. I'd better watch what I say to Katrina. She seems to be the oversensitive type. I've been told on multiple occasions that I have an abrasive personality, which is true. I've made people cry without even trying.

I push my covers out of the way and throw my legs to the side of the bed. A yawn sneaks up on me, and it takes me several seconds to be able to close my mouth again.

"How long do you need to get ready?" Katrina asks, bouncing from side to side.

Gee, I wish I could steal some of that nervous energy. It's better than this damn lethargy.

"It depends. How do I look?"

"Do you want an honest opinion or the polite answer?"

"Honesty always. The quickest way to get on my shit list is to be fake with me."

"Okay. Well, you look like a cat chewed on you for days and spat you out."

I jump off the bed, rubbing my eyes. "A shower is in order, then. I'll need twenty minutes."

"Twenty minutes?" Her eyebrows shoot to the heavens. "It takes me at least an hour to get ready to go to school. Just doing my hair for tonight took me half an hour." She points at her perfectly arranged curls.

I smile. "I'm not fussy about my looks. Not aiming to impress anyone." Blush spreads through Katrina's cheeks, and I sense I said the wrong thing. "I just want to focus on my career for now," I amend.

"So that's what you want to do? Play soccer professionally?"

"Yes. It's been my dream since I started playing in the wee league."

"Wee league? Isn't wee a Scottish word?"

I chuckle. "Yeah. My neighbors growing up were from Scotland. I picked up a few things from them."

She tilts her head to the side and narrows her eyes. "If you were given the chance, which national team would you pick? England or USA?"

I thought I knew the answer to that. Back in London, I never considered another alternative besides playing for England. But I'm back in the States now, and their national team is the best in the world. What athlete wouldn't want that?

"I never stopped to think about it," I lie. "Well, I should get going or we'll never leave this room."

OKAY, it didn't take me twenty minutes to get ready. It took double that, but only because I wasted precious time looking for bathroom shit in my suitcase and my favorite pair of jeans.

Katrina was shocked that I planned on leaving the apartment without drying my hair first. I did put makeup on because I'm not anti-beautification. I might not be interested in dating anyone, but this is my first social event at this school, and I don't want anyone thinking I'm a troll.

I guess I *do* want to impress people.

As we walk out of the dorm building, I can feel excitement in the air. Classes haven't officially started, so right now, only people in the summer program or athletes here for preseason training are in residence. I follow Katrina to her car in silence, distracted by my surroundings. I was so knackered when I arrived and keen on getting rid of Dad that I didn't really pay attention to anything.

The buildings are a little disappointing. They're bricks

without anything appealing to them design-wise. I should be glad the interior is clean though. I've heard horror stories of student dorms back in England.

Katrina stops abruptly and points at a silver Honda Accord. "That's my car."

"Okay?"

She offers me the key. "Here, you need to drive."

"Why?" I stare at her hand as if she plans on killing me with that key.

"I had a few pre-party drinks while you took your nap. I shouldn't get behind the wheel."

"But the party is on campus. What's that, a five-minute drive?"

I'm freaking out that she wants me to drive. I barely passed my driving test back in London, and also, we drive on the other side of the road. I'm bound to run over someone or collide with another car.

"It's not five minutes, and it'd be irresponsible to drive. I'm drunk, in case you couldn't tell."

I want to say, *"How was I supposed to tell? I've just met you, and I was barely conscious for most of the time."*

"Ugh. Fine. I'll drive, but only if you promise not to judge me if I drive like an arse."

"Arse." She giggles. "I love your accent."

"Yeah, it's brilliant. I'm still waiting for your answer."

She arches her eyebrows as if she already forgot what I said earlier. "Oh, don't worry. I won't make fun of you. I promise."

Like an idiot, I automatically open the wrong door. Yeah, that bodes well. Katrina doesn't make a comment though. Either she's keeping her promise, or she's too drunk to notice.

The positive side is that her car is automatic, so I don't have to worry about shifting gears with my left hand.

The first minute of the drive is the worst. I'm nervous and queasy. It gets better after a while, and there isn't a lot of traffic at this hour. I begin to relax, only to regress to a panic state when we get near our destination. Way too many drunk pedestrians walking in the middle of the road and not a parking spot in sight.

"Keep your eyes peeled for a place to park," I tell Katrina.

"Ah, man. I had no idea it would be this busy already. We might have to park farther back."

I choose a random lane, because at this point, it'd be sheer luck to find anything. It turns out it was the wrong choice, and this one is a dead end. Bloody fantastic. I have to make a T-maneuver to get us out of here, which wouldn't be a big deal if the space wasn't tight as hell and I didn't have an audience.

"Why don't you get us out in reverse?" Katrina asks.

"I guess I could."

I had already started to get the car turned around, but going in reverse would be easier. I switch gears again—at least I think I do—and press the gas pedal, but instead of going backward, the car lurches forward, and I bump into the vehicle parked in front of me before I can stomp on the brake.

"Shit!"

"Oh no," Katrina mutters.

I back up a little and then get out of the car to inspect the damage, trying my best to ignore the group of jackasses lingering nearby and now laughing at my expense.

"Who had the bright idea to let women drive?" I hear one of them say.

My face is burning, but I refuse to acknowledge those arseholes. I'm also more preoccupied with the damage I caused. The taillight is busted and the bumper bent. Bloody hell. Whoever owns this car will be pissed.

"Do you know whose car this is?" I ask Katrina.

"No idea."

"Oh well. We can't just stand here and wait for the owner to show up. Got a piece of paper and pen?"

"Yeah. One sec."

She hands me a Post-it notepad and a Sharpie. I jot down my name and email address, then shove the note under one of the windshield wipers.

"Shouldn't you also put down your cell phone number?" Katrina suggests.

I glance quickly at the idiots who are still watching us with interest. I wouldn't put it past them to read the note. I definitely don't want those dumbasses to have my phone number.

"Better not. Email will be fine."

"What are we going to do now?"

I give Katrina a droll look. "What do you think? After this ordeal, I need a bloody distraction. We'll find a parking spot, and then it's party time, babe."

5

DANNY

My blood is boiling as I stare at my car. I even checked underneath the windshield to make sure the person responsible didn't leave a note. Nope. The asshole just took off, hoping I'd never find out their identity.

"Danny, my man. What's up?"

I look over my shoulder and find a freckled kid holding a red Solo cup.

"Someone hit my car and bailed."

He whistles as he assesses the damage. "Dude, that sucks."

"Do you have any idea who could have done it?" I ask with zero hope that there were any eyewitnesses.

"No, man. I just came out for some fresh air."

And pot, if the stench wafting from him is any indication.

"I know who did it," someone else pipes up.

I turn toward the guy's voice. "I'm listening."

"It was a blonde chick. She had a British accent. Hot as sin but as blind as a bat. I still can't believe she managed to bump into your car."

There are a ton of pretty blondes at the party, but I doubt many have a British accent. However, I can't talk to every single girl who matches the description in order to find the culprit.

"Do you happen to know her name or the car she was driving?"

"Uh, I think she was driving a silver sedan, maybe an Accord? Don't know her name though. Never seen her before."

Great.

"Hey, I've heard the soccer team got a new player from England," the freckled guy chimes in. "I actually saw her talking with Vanessa Castro not too long ago."

"No shit. Thanks, man. That helps."

I head back to the party, ready to confront this new girl who thought it was okay to damage my car and get away with it. Who does she think she is? I thought English people were supposed to be the epitome of good manners. Apparently not.

I'm so worked up by the time I get back to the party that I ignore anyone who attempts to say hello. I spot Andy and Puck first, but I'm in no mood to talk to them either. They'd probably try to calm me down, which is the last thing I want. I'm pissed, and I need to yell at someone.

I push my way through the crowd, going in the direction I last saw Vanessa, hoping she didn't head someplace else. She's still there and, what do you know, speaking with a pretty blonde who is gesturing exaggeratedly with her hands. Vanessa says something that makes the blonde laugh like she doesn't have a care in the world. I clench my jaw hard and march in her direction.

Vanessa notices my approach first. She turns to me and smiles, giving me an opening to address her new teammate. I've been mulling over what I was going to say to her on the way here, but when she looks at me, I forget my spiel. The guy describing her wasn't wrong. She's hot all right. But that's not what's making me tongue-tied. I honestly don't know what it is about her that has rendered me speechless.

"Hey, Danny. I thought you left," Vanessa chimes in.

"I was going to, but someone rear-ended my car." I turn to the blonde. "You don't happen to know anything about it, do you?"

Her pretty blue eyes widen. "That was *your* car?"

"Yes," I grit out. "Does it matter? You damaged it and left."

"Uh, what's going on here?" Vanessa butts in.

"Oh God. I messed up. I had an issue with the car's gear and crashed into a vehicle that was parked nearby. But I left a note. You didn't get my note?" Her voice rises to a pitch. She sounds sincere, but I don't really know her. She could be lying to save face.

"There was no note," I reply.

"I tucked it under the windshield wiper."

"That's the first place I looked."

She shakes her head. "I'm not lying. I swear."

"Are you saying someone simply got rid of your note? To what end?"

"I don't know. There were some drunk wankers nearby."

"Danny, come on. If Sadie is saying she left you a note, she left you a note," Vanessa intervenes.

Damn it. I'm letting my emotions get the better of me. I'd usually give the other person the benefit of the doubt. This evening has just been a clusterfuck of bad surprises.

"Fine. Don't believe me if that's what you want to do," Sadie retorts. "I'll give you my information again. Get your phone out."

I was ready to apologize, but her bossy tone rubs me the wrong way. *Why am I suddenly the bad guy here? There was no note!*

"Really? No 'please' or anything?"

She narrows her eyes. "What exactly do you want from me?"

"Maybe a fucking apology, for starters?"

"I said I was sorry."

I scoff. "Uh, no you didn't."

"I said it in the note."

"And we've already established I never got your note."

"Jesus Christ." Vanessa throws her hands up in the air. "Can we please move on from the note that wasn't there? I swear to God, if you two become a thing, this is the worst meet cute ever."

Sadie and I wince at the same time and turn our attention to Vanessa.

"Are you mental? We're not going to become a thing," Sadie retorts, then turns to me. "No offense."

"Ditto," I reply curtly, not understanding why her comment annoyed me.

Even if I hadn't sworn off romantic relationships, she'd be the last person I'd date. Yes, she's gorgeous, and don't get me started on her accent and raspy, sexy voice. But her attitude spells trouble. I've dated one crazy chick already; don't need to repeat that same mistake twice in a row.

I need to get the hell out of here as quickly as possible. Phone out, I glance at her. "Number?"

"I haven't gotten around to getting an American number yet." She takes my phone from my hand even though I didn't offer it to her. "But I'll give it to you anyway. You can WhatsApp me."

Not wanting to sound like an ass, I bite my tongue and don't complain about her rudeness.

"Here." She returns my phone.

I glance quickly at the information she wrote before pocketing it again.

"And for the record, I *am* truly sorry I busted your car," she continues.

She's remorseful, that much I can tell—or she's an amazing actress. I'd try to make her feel less guilty about the whole deal, but I swallow my words of reassurance. I guess tonight, I'm not a nice guy.

"I'll let you know how much you owe me."

SADIE

My heart is still beating like a mad drum a minute after Mr. Too Hot to Handle stormed off.

"That was intense," Vanessa says. "I've never seen Danny so angry like that before."

"He's never met me before. I have a reputation. I can aggravate the most patient people in the world."

She cocks her head to the side and watches me closely. "Are you saying you're like the bee that stung Ferdinand?"

"You can't possibly be implying that the huge football player is a peaceful flower-sniffing bull."

"How did you know Danny was a football player? I thought you just landed and didn't have a chance to learn anything about our school."

Shame makes my cheeks warm. I'm glad it's dim here. I wasn't completely honest with Vanessa about why I didn't check her emails. She knows I got hurt, but she doesn't know how, and I'd like to keep it that way.

"Just a hunch. He has the physique." I shrug.

"Danny is one of the good guys. Super chill and humble. Actually, most of the guys on the football team are nice, even the cockiest ones like Andy Rossi."

No surprise there. Dad wouldn't tolerate rubbish from his players. I don't make a comment though. Vanessa knows who my father is, but I don't want to remind her.

"If you'd arrived earlier, you'd have had the displeasure of meeting Nick Fowler, the captain of the men's soccer team. He's a dick with a capital D. Obnoxious and a perv."

"So basically a total creep."

"Yep. I don't hate a lot of people, but he's one of them. Fucking asshole." She takes a large sip of her drink and then continues. "I'm sorry. I shouldn't have been so candid about my opinion of him."

I shake my head. "Don't apologize about that. If you have a list of wankers I should avoid, send it my way."

"You betcha. I'm glad you could make it tonight despite the drama."

"Me too. I shouldn't have driven my roommate's car. I'm not a good driver, and I'm not ashamed to admit it."

She snorts. "I'm glad we don't need your talents behind a steering wheel. We want you for your skills on the field. You're good to play again, right?"

I grimace. "Yeah. I've been cleared to practice. It wasn't a big deal, just a superficial wound," I lie.

My new coach is the only one who knows the extent of my knife injury and how I got it. I don't want anyone else on the team to know I was attacked.

"That's good to hear. You probably need to work extra hard to compensate for the time you were recovering. I'm sure Coach Lauda already talked to you about that, but as the captain, it's my job to reinforce the message. We worked fucking hard to get where we are."

Whoa. Straight to business. I'm not mad though, just surprised.

"Sorry if I'm being too blunt," she continues.

"No, don't apologize. I appreciate your honesty. I abhor people who beat around the bush. Your directness is refreshing. And don't worry, I have no intention of being a deadweight to the team. I don't do anything half-arsed. No time for losers and all that."

She smirks. "Nice Queen reference."

"Queen songs make the soundtrack of my life."

Vanessa laughs and then asks, "Where's your roommate, anyway?"

I glance around me, and sure as shit, Katrina is not in the vicinity.

"I'd better go look for her. She said she'd been drinking since God knows when."

"Good luck."

The moment I'm alone in a sea of strangers, I rehash the argument I had with Danny. I came across like a jerk, even though I didn't mean to. And I was in the wrong to begin with. I did smash his car. But he put me on the spot and accused me of being a liar. It triggered my self-defense mechanism, and the bitch came out.

Of course, the altercation had to happen in front of Vanessa. I can't have the captain of the team thinking I'm a liability. I'm an acquired taste—I have enough self-awareness to know that. So I have to be extra careful, let them get to know me slowly. Unleashing the full Sadie Clarkson hurricane on them too soon will only blow up in my face.

6

SADIE

I SPENT the entire weekend agonizing about my first day of preseason training. Besides Vanessa, I only met a couple of the girls last Friday before I had to haul Katrina back home. If I couldn't tell she was drunk on the way to the Red Barn, there was no mistaking her drunken state when I finally found her at the party. She couldn't even stand up straight; I had to practically drag her to the car.

I made sure to set my alarm clock an hour earlier than my usual wake-up time. I simply couldn't arrive late on my first day. Anxiety kept me up all night, so the alarm wasn't needed in the end. I was wide awake.

I still don't have a car. Dad was busy all weekend prepping for work today and only sent me a few links. The options all looked fine to me. I'm not fussy about what car I drive.

The training field isn't far from my dorm building, so I simply jog there. It's a good warm-up. I'm surprised when I find Vanessa in the locker room, already in practice gear.

"Wow, I can't believe you beat me here," I say in greeting.

"Coach Lauda wanted to talk to me about the season before the rest of the team arrived."

"Oh."

I turn around and look for the locker with my name on it. One of the topics of the conversation was probably me. I'm the new recruit recovering from an injury, after all. I've spoken with Coach Lauda a few times online before I flew over, but I haven't met her in person yet.

"She told me you're aware we have two strikers already. Melody McCoy and Joanne Barnes."

"Yeah, I'm aware. But she said she'd let me play during a portion of the second half depending on my performance during training."

I'm not conceited when I say I was the star of my former team. But I *am* worried my performance won't be the same. Six weeks without playing is way too long. I don't voice my doubts out loud though. I sure hope Coach keeps her promise, because that's all I need, a chance to prove I should be starting the game. I've seen a few tapes. McCoy and Barnes are good, but I'm better—or *was* better.

No, Sadie. You can't think like that.

"Don't worry though. This is Melody's senior year. You'll have plenty of time to show off your skills. Just be patient."

"I'm a team player. I'll do whatever is best for the team."

"I'm glad to hear that," Coach Lauda pipes up from outside her office.

Wearing a tracksuit in dark green with our team's logo embroidered on the chest and a determined glint in her eyes, she's the epitome of a badass coach. Her short blonde hair and businesslike stare remind me a bit of Coach Sue Silvester from *Glee*.

"Good morning, Coach," I say.

"Good morning, Sadie. I'm happy to see you're here bright and early. You're sweaty. Have you been running already?"

"Yeah, I jogged here. No car yet."

"Nothing wrong with a good cardio to begin the day. There are three new girls starting today besides you. Two are freshmen like you, and the third is a sophomore transfer from Florida. You might have met them at the mixer last Friday."

I almost giggle at her use of "mixer," but I manage to swallow my amusement down. Glancing at Vanessa, I catch her trying to hide a smirk.

"No, I didn't stay long at the party," I reply.

"You'll meet them today. Vanessa will show you around before we start." She returns to her office and shuts the door.

Despite the circumstances surrounding my admission to John Rushmore, Coach Lauda was clear that she wanted me on her team. I'm not a favor Dad had to call in. From the get-go, I knew she had a no-bullshit attitude and didn't play favoritism. All she cares about is having the best players on the field and winning games.

Once I change clothes, Vanessa shows me where everything is in the locker room plus the showers, and by the time she finishes her tour, some of my other teammates have arrived. The three newbies—Charlotte, Phoebe, and Steff—are standing close together and looking a little uncertain about themselves. Super easy to tell they're fresh meat. I made sure to learn who they were before coming here, because as the newest people on the team, we have to stick together. I'm sure there will be some kind of hazing to welcome us to the Rushmore Ravens.

Tessa and Gabi—who I met at the party on Friday—are also already here, way less chatty this morning. They barely look awake. I say hello to them, and they grunt and nod in reply.

"Hi, I'm Sadie." I wave at Charlotte, Phoebe, and Steff.

"Nice to meet you, Sadie. I'm Charlotte," the shortest of the group replies.

What she lacks for in height, she makes up for in solid

muscle. Her kicks can turn a ball into a missile. She's a midfielder. In high school, she alternated between center midfielder and attacking midfielder. Vanessa usually plays the latter, and she's damn good at her job.

Phoebe and Steff proceed to introduce themselves, and then the conversation veers toward the Red Barn party. Since I didn't have a jolly good time like everyone else, I choose to simply listen.

Steff is the transfer from Florida. I couldn't find out in my research why she transferred, but I'm sure I'll learn that soon enough. She's a keeper, but despite being new to the team, there's a good chance she'll be starting. Her nickname at her previous school was The Wall because getting through her was almost impossible. I'm glad she's on my team.

And finally there's Phoebe, the girl with the multicolored hair. She plays defense. While Steff and Charlotte chat away, Phoebe remains quiet like me. It's hard to get a read on her.

A minute later, Melody walks into the locker room, acting like she's a bloody rock star. She even has sunglasses on. She says hello to everyone in a cheerful tone, and then she spots our little group.

"Oh, you're the new blood. Welcome to the team." She pushes her shades up and stares at me.

"Thanks," I say.

"I heard you're a striker. I can't wait to see what you got."

"Melody holds the record for most goals scored in the championship two years in a row," Gabi pipes up from across the room.

"That's awesome. I'm looking forward to beating that record." I smile from ear to ear.

Melody's grin fades, and her eyes flash with annoyance.

Oooh, the claws are already coming out. If there was a record for bringing the worst out in people, I'd win it.

"You'll have to actually play in a game to score," she replies sweetly and then walks to her locker.

Vanessa comes over and whispers, "Why did you have to poke the bear with a short stick?"

"I didn't realize we had wild animals among us," I joke, earning chuckles from my companions.

She rolls her eyes. "Antagonizing Melody the first time you meet her was not smart, Sadie. She's fiercely competitive and has a mean streak."

"Oops?"

"Yeah, joke now. Don't come crying to me later." She walks away.

"Vanessa is right. I should know," a cute brunette with short hair says. "I'm Joanne Barnes." She shakes my hand in a businesslike manner. "Welcome to the team."

"Thanks."

I'm not sure if Joanne was joking or not, but it's unlikely their advice will scare me off. If Melody is mean, then I'm her 2.0 version. Maybe I should have played nicer until I get the lay of the land, but what's the fun in that? And a little competition among teammates is healthy. It keeps us on our toes. It's not like I'm showing off my scary side yet. This is just letting them get to know me slowly.

After Joanne heads over to her locker, Charlotte asks, "So, any guesses as to what our welcoming prank will be?"

"No bloody clue," I reply.

THE THREE MUSKETEERS AND I—THAT'S what I started calling Charlotte, Phoebe, and Steff—couldn't guess what our welcome to the team hazing was, and our imagination had been wild. After practice, we were more than ready to hit the showers and go home, but it wasn't meant to be.

Our wonderful teammates let us shower in peace, but when we were all fresh and wearing clean clothes, they turned us into oversized chicken tenders ready for the fryer. First came the egging, and I tell you, being hit by dozens of eggs at once hurts. And I'm certain Melody aimed most of her attack at me.

After the first coating was done, it was time for the flour part. And for the grand finale, we have to go back to our dorm rooms in a walk of shame from hell. The mix of egg and flour formed a disgusting coating over our bodies, which is turning hard as we trudge under the hot California sun.

"I thought I was prepared for the prank, but this is a nightmare," Charlotte moans.

"I have egg and flour everywhere, even in my ears," Steff joins the cryfest.

"And it itches like crazy," Phoebe adds.

"Well, it could have been worse," I say.

"Worse than this?" Steff's voice rises an octave.

"We're not bleeding."

A heavy silence descends on our group. I glance at the trio and find them looking at me with their jaws hanging loose.

"What?" I ask.

"What exactly did you think they'd do to us?" Charlotte asks.

I shrug. "Well, they could have whooped our arses, for starters."

"Jesus, is that what they do in England?" Phoebe asks.

I open my mouth to reply, but the sound of a car approaching distracts me. I glance over my shoulder and grimace when I notice the vehicle is slowing down. It's one of those open Jeeps that fuckboys like to drive, and that seems to be exactly who is behind the steering wheel.

"Good afternoon, ladies." The driver smiles at us, exulting cocky attitude and amusement. "Need any help?"

For a second, I suspect he's from the soccer team until I notice the guy riding shotgun.

Bloody hell. It's Danny, looking like a damn Greek god with his blond curls shining under the sun. And here I am covered in junk.

"If by help you mean a hose down, sure," I say, trying my best to avoid making eye contact with Danny.

"Sorry, don't have enough water here to get all that gunk off you. But even if I did, I wouldn't meddle in the Ravens' affairs. Vanessa would have my balls."

"You could give us a ride," Charlotte pipes up.

The driver twists his face into a scowl. "Are you crazy? And let you guys mess up my car? Hell no."

"So did you just stop to laugh at us?" I ask, annoyed.

"I stopped because Danny-boy here asked me to." He points at his friend, and like an idiot, I shift my attention to him.

I can't guess what he's thinking since he's wearing sunglasses and has a poker face on, but I feel oddly exposed.

"Is that so? Did you want to make sure I hadn't skipped town?"

Danny scoffs. "I wanted to make sure you were all right. Clearly you are."

"Yep, we're all fine and dandy here. Run along now." I wave my hand impatiently.

I expect him to scowl, but he laughs instead, shaking his head. "I'll call you later, Sadie. Come on, Andy. We've been dismissed."

"See you later, alligator." Andy waves at us and then accelerates away.

I keep staring at their car while I wrestle with my emotions. *Why didn't Danny bite my head off? Or better yet, why did I want him to?*

"What was that all about?" Charlotte asks.

I blink fast, peeling my eyes off the road. "Nothing."

"It didn't sound like nothing," Steff chimes in. "When did you meet Danny Hudson?"

"It's a long story." I resume walking.

"It's a long trek back to the dorms." Charlotte nudges my elbow.

Bollocks. I guess there's no escaping rehashing the stellar beginning of my new life.

7

DANNY

"You've been holding out on me, Danny-boy," Andy says as soon as we leave Sadie and her teammates on the side of the road.

"I don't know what you're talking about."

"You never said the girl who crashed into your car was one of the Ravens."

"How is that important?"

He shrugs. "I guess it isn't important. But that accent of hers? That's hot."

"Dude, you have a girlfriend."

"I just said her accent is hot. That doesn't mean I want to bone her. Jeez."

I snort. "Yeah, that'd fly well with Jane."

"Jane knows I'm one hundred percent devoted to her. Besides, I'm not telling her, I'm telling *you*, in case you want to do something about it."

"Do what exactly?" I turn to him, glowering now.

He shrugs. "The tension between you and that girl was

obvious. I couldn't really tell if she was pretty thanks to all that crap covering her, but I'm going out on a limb here that she has a face to match that voice."

I clench my jaw tight and look at the road ahead. I'm annoyed now for a myriad of reasons. The main one is that Andy was able to guess what was going on with me during only a few minutes of conversation. The second reason is that I *do* find Sadie attractive to the point that I haven't been able to stop thinking about her. As soon as I take care of my car repair, I have to avoid her at all costs. She's a distraction I don't need.

"Really? You're not going to say anything?" Andy continues.

God, he won't leave me alone now.

"The only thing I want from Sadie is money to repair the damage she did to my car. That's all."

"So when you said you'd be completely focused on football this season, did you mean you would turn into a eunuch? That's not healthy, man."

"I didn't say that."

"Okay... then why are you so bent out of shape because of my comment? I didn't say you should date the girl."

"Why are you interested in my love life all of a sudden?" I ask.

"Dunno. Maybe payback for all the times you butted in mine."

"You should thank me that I did."

"Yeah, yeah. You did me a solid, and I'm never going to forget that. But anyway, when are you planning on taking your car to the garage?"

"Whenever you're free. The sooner the better."

Andy shakes his head. "No can do today. I've got to see Jane."

"I'll ask one of the guys, then."

"Why don't you ask Sadie to give you a ride? She's the one responsible for the damage, right?"

I roll my eyes. "Will you quit trying to matchmake me with that girl?"

"That's not what I'm doing, but whatever."

If I tell him the reason why I want to spend as little time as possible with Sadie, Andy will never drop the subject. So I pull up my phone and text Paris to check if he's available. His reply comes a minute later. He's busy today, but he can do it tomorrow. Waiting another day wouldn't be too bad if I hadn't promised Mom to run some errands for her. I can't drive around LA with a busted taillight. Getting a fine is not in the budget. The sooner I get my car fixed, the better.

Hell, if I can't get a ride with anyone today, I can always take the bus back to campus.

Immediately, I feel better that I have a plan that doesn't involve Sadie in any way.

SADIE

I've been back in the dorms for an hour, and it took me that long to wash the egg and flour paste off my body and hair. I'm ready to veg out in bed and watch TV when Dad calls me.

"Hello?"

"Hi, kiddo. How was your first day at training?"

"Good. We got pranked."

"You did? How bad was it?" he asks.

"Mild compared to what I was expecting. I'm glad it's out of the way."

"Do you have plans for dinner? I thought I'd take you out. Any place you want."

I could eat, but I'm not ready to spend a couple hours alone with Dad yet. I don't know what I'd say to him. Maybe if there was someone else there to be a buffer, it'd be better.

"I'm knackered, to be honest. I was planning to go to bed early."

"Oh, of course. And you're still not over your jet lag, I bet."

"Yeah, right. Not over it yet."

"Right. Well, I got something for you."

"Oh, what is it?"

"A car."

"You got me a car?" My voice rises to a shrill.

"It's nothing fancy. It's a Toyota, a good car. It has low mileage, and I got a deal."

He's rambling, which is not something I remember him doing before. He must be nervous. I'd been so caught up in my awkwardness around him that I never stopped to consider that this situation must be strange for him too.

"That's cool, Dad. When are you dropping it off?"

"As a matter of fact, I haven't picked it up yet. But I can take you there now, and you can drive back to campus."

Instant sweat dots my forehead. "How far is the dealership?"

"Not far at all. Fifteen minutes or so."

I swallow the huge lump in my throat. "Do I have to take the highway?"

"Yeah. What's the matter, honey? You have your driver's license, right?"

God, I'm acting like a ninny.

"Yep. But.... Never mind. When can you come over?"

"I'm two minutes from your building."

"Okay, I'll see you soon."

I WAS SO nervous about the prospect of driving on my own on the highway that I barely cared about the awkwardness of being alone with Dad again in a moving vehicle. I'm glad he kept the chitchat to a minimum.

Now with key in hand and standing next to my new car, my heart is beating so fast and hard, it feels like it might burst out of my chest at any second. I'm queasy too, but I try my best to hide my nervousness from Dad.

"What do you think, Sadie?" he asks me, not hiding his satisfied grin.

"It's lovely." I clutch the key tighter in my hand.

"We're all set here. You can follow me back to campus."

"Yeah, that's a good idea. Getting lost in LA is not my idea of fun times."

He nods and then walks toward his car. I slide behind the steering wheel, trying my best to keep my body from shaking. While I wait for Dad, I glance over the dashboard to learn where everything is. Then I fix the side mirrors and adjust the seat.

A minute later, Dad pulls up next to me and nods.

All right, then. Here we go.

My hands are sweaty from holding the steering wheel too hard, and when we enter the highway, my stomach is twisted so tightly it hurts. I thought following Dad would be the best idea, but I quickly realize that making sure I don't lose him in the heavy traffic while trying to avoid a car wreck is stressing me the fuck out.

I freak out for a second when I lose visual of Dad's car, and I almost end up colliding with the dickhead who cut me up. I should have honked, but pressing on the brakes seemed more important. When I finally manage to switch to a faster-moving lane, I can't find Dad's car anywhere.

Shit. Did he take an exit?

I should have kept my phone handy so I could call him. There's nothing for it now. I have to get off the highway, grab my phone, and use Google maps to find my way back to campus. The international roaming fee is going to be murder, but this is an emergency.

My phone rings. It must be him wondering where I am.

The next exit leads me to an industrial area where most of the buildings are warehouses. There's less traffic here, which helps with my nerves. I turn toward the commercial building that has a parking lot and stop in front of an old car repair shop.

I'm just about to fish out my phone from my purse when the last person I expect to see here walks out of the building: Danny Hudson. He must have brought his car to get fixed.

"You have got to be kidding me," I mumble to myself.

He doesn't see me as he walks right next to my car. Instead, he veers toward the street.

Wait. How is he getting back to campus?

Before I can overthink it, I get out of the car and call his name.

He stops and looks over his shoulder, eyes going wider as he sees me there. "What are you doing here?"

"I got lost," I reply as I walk over.

Don't know why I feel the need to move closer to him. It's like he's the sun or something and I'm a cold planet in need of his warmth.

For fuck's sake, Sadie. What kind of rubbish are you thinking?

"You got lost," he repeats as if he doesn't believe me. "So, are you saying Andy didn't tell you I'd be here?"

I squint. "Who's Andy?"

He shakes his head. "Never mind."

"Anyway, I assume you dropped off your car to get it fixed?"

"Yep."

He shoves his hands in his jeans pockets, pushing the waistband lower and revealing a strip of golden skin. I want to be able to say my eyes didn't linger there for a second too long, but I'd be lying.

"How are you getting back to campus?" I ask after I force my eyes to look up again.

"The bus."

"God. Aren't they bloody awful here?"

"They aren't that bad."

"Well, I can take you back. I pulled over to pull up Google maps, but having you to give me directions would be easier."

He seems unsure for a hot second.

Damn, did I make such a terrible first impression that he doesn't even want to accept a lift from me?

"I suppose you owe me a ride back home." He cracks a tiny smile.

I'll take that.

As we walk back to my car, I ask, "Why were you taking the bus anyway? Couldn't find a friend to give you a lift?"

"I need my car fixed ASAP, and everyone was busy today."

God, way to make me feel even guiltier. Though to be fair, I don't think he's doing it on purpose.

Distracted by his presence, I once again veer for the wrong side of the car

"Oh, do you want me to drive?" he asks.

I pull my hand from the door handle with a jerky movement. "Bollocks. I keep doing this."

Pure amusement dances in his blue eyes now. "*Should* I drive? I mean, you don't have the best track record."

A part of me wants to take him up on his offer, but hell, I'm too proud to let a dude drive my car because I'm afraid.

"Ha ha. Very funny."

I circle around the car and pretend I'm not a bundle of nerves inside. It's much harder than I thought though. I didn't count on Danny taking so much space inside the vehicle. It's not because of his size—the car is roomy. It's his presence that seems to take over everything. He doesn't make it any easier when I can sense his eyes on me.

"What?" I whip my face to his.

"I was wondering if you know how to start the car." The upturn of his lips tells me he's teasing me.

"I'm beginning to regret offering you a lift," I mutter as I turn on the ignition.

"I'm not." He laughs.

My phone rings again, and I finally remember Dad. *Shit.* Where's my purse now?

Danny leans forward and then lifts the accessory from the floor. "Are you looking for this?"

"Yeah. Thanks."

The ringing stops. It was indeed Dad calling. Not willing to disclose my father is Danny's coach, I text him instead of calling back. Then I shove my phone back in my purse and toss it to the back seat.

"Is everything okay?" he asks.

"Of course. Why wouldn't it be?"

He snickers. "You seem awfully tense."

I clench my jaw and swallow the retort on the tip of my tongue. His mocking comments are better than the angry ones I received when we met. I was never one to care much about what strangers thought about me, and yet I don't want Danny Hudson to think I'm a bitch.

Ignoring him is hard, but if I can keep my cool during a penalty kick that will decide a championship game, I can drive with him by my side.

Mercifully, he doesn't tease me any more after and only opens his mouth to give me directions. When he's not being a pain in the arse on purpose, he has a calming effect. A few minutes into the drive is all it takes for my anxiety to melt away.

"Did the mechanic give you a quote for the repairs?" I ask.

"Yeah. Five hundred should cover it."

Not too bad. I thought it would cost more.

"Hey, I can give you cash right now."

"You carry that much money on you?"

"Well, I don't have it with me. It's in my dorm room, you know, left over from my trip."

"No, I don't know."

He sounds prickly all of a sudden, so I chance a quick glance at him. He's looking out the window with his jaw locked tight.

Did I say something wrong?

"Anyway, if you have time, we can make a pit stop at my place and I'll pay you."

"Sounds good."

Does it though? How come I have the impression he's angry at me again?

8

DANNY

I SHOULDN'T HAVE LET Sadie's comment about money get to me. I know five hundred bucks is not a lot for most of the students here at Rushmore. And she's a foreign student, which means she must not be lacking in the finance department.

It's so damn stupid. I never had a problem with my friends being richer than me. Why am I feeling so small that Sadie didn't even bat an eye when I told her how much she owed me for the car repair?

Like a total grump, I follow her in silence to her dorm room. She must have picked up on my mood change because she doesn't try to make conversation. This is for the best. I was trying to avoid the girl anyway, and now that we're about to settle the car issue, there won't be any reason for us to hang out.

Then why the hell do I feel so gloomy about it? I have this stupid feeling that I'm going to regret the way I'm acting the moment she drops me off.

She stops suddenly in front of a door and says, "This is me. Hmm, there's a sock on the doorknob though."

"We probably shouldn't go in."

She turns to me, piercing me with her beautiful blue eyes. My heart seems to lurch forward.

Fuck me. I can't be having visceral reactions for her—or any other girl, for that matter. I promised Coach no distractions, and Sadie would be one with a capital D.

"Wait. So the sock thing is for real? She's in there with someone?"

I shrug. "I don't know what kind of rules you guys have, but in most cases, that's what it means."

"Blimey, we didn't talk rules."

Sadie presses her ear against the door and furrows her eyebrows. "I don't hear anyth—" She jumps back suddenly. "Scratch that. Katrina is definitely busy."

Her face is bright red now, and she won't meet my eyes. I can't help the laugh that bubbles up my throat.

"What's so funny?"

I shake my head. "Nothing."

She glares at the door. "This sucks. What am I supposed to do? Wait out here in the hallway until she's done?"

"You could hang out at my place."

Shit. I can't believe I just said that. Didn't I just acknowledge that Sadie would be a distraction I don't need?

"Are you sure? I don't want to impose."

"Yeah, it'll be fine. I'm sure Lorenzo will appreciate the extra company."

"Who is that?"

"My roommate's brother. He's twelve."

Sadie's mouth makes a perfect O, drawing my attention to her full lips.

Stop staring, you idiot.

"And he lives with you on campus?"

"Yeah. It's a long story."

She glances at her door once again and sighs. "All right. Let's go."

"Gee, could you at least pretend going to my place isn't a burden?" I half joke. I'm a little annoyed, if I'm being honest with myself.

"Oh, you got it all wrong. I'm not upset that I have to hang out with you. It's just... well, I was looking forward to taking a nap. I haven't adjusted to the time difference yet, and today at practice was brutal."

I remember Sadie's walk of shame, and that brings a broad smile to my face. "Ah, yeah. I can imagine."

She narrows her eyes. "You're picturing me covered in all that gunk, aren't you?"

I try to convey an air of innocence by widening my eyes. "Me? Of course not."

"You're lucky you don't have any aspirations of becoming an actor."

Grinning, I reply, "Nope. Not at all."

"I'd never take you gambling either."

"I'm not a gambler, so I'm totally unfazed by your remark."

She cocks an eyebrow. "Really? You've never gambled in your life?"

I narrow my eyes. "Why do I have the impression that's a loaded question?"

With a shrug, she walks away from her dorm room. "It wasn't. I'm just making conversation."

"Okay."

Our gazes lock, and for a moment, neither of us moves. The air between us becomes heavy, almost as if there's a magnetic field trying to push us closer.

The spell is broken by the loud voices of strangers approaching. I look away first, glancing in the direction of the noise. Two girls are walking over, and when they notice me, giggles follow.

Sadie snorts next to me before she strides down the hallway toward the exit. I follow her, matching her stride. I chance a look at her face. She seems annoyed. Did she get jealous? The notion should raise a red flag in my head. I barely know her, after all, and she has no reason to act territorial. But instead, I'm feeling idiotically pleased about it.

"Are you hungry?" I ask to fill the silence.

"I could eat."

"There's an awesome diner not too far from here."

She peeks at me, smirking. "I hope that's not a roundabout way to ask me out on a date."

I scoff. "Please. If I were asking you out, you'd know."

I expect her to be offended by my remark, but instead, her grin broadens. "Brilliant. I don't have time for dating. But oddly, I don't mind your company."

Surprisingly, I chuckle. "Ditto on both counts."

We hop back in Sadie's car, and I give her directions to the diner. She grabs her phone and texts someone before driving though.

She catches me staring and says, "I asked Katrina to let me know when her visitor is gone."

"Smart."

I consider texting Andy to ask if he wants to join us, but I scratch that idea fast. He'll give me too much grief over Sadie, and I don't want him trying to play matchmaker.

It's getting close to dinnertime, and the parking lot is beginning to fill up. Odette, the waitress who always waits on Andy and me, smiles when she sees me walk in. Her shrewd eyes notice Sadie right away, which only makes her grin wider.

Great. I bet she thinks I'm on a date.

"Hi, Danny. I haven't seen you in a while."

"I've been super busy," I lie.

That's not the main reason. Eating out is simply not in the budget, which really doesn't explain why I suggested bringing

Sadie here. Date or no date, I don't expect her to pay since it was my idea. I have manners.

Odette grabs a couple of menus and leads us to my usual booth in the far corner. I try to ignore the stares that seem to follow Sadie and me. In my head, I'm cursing. It won't take long for the rumor mill to churn and for Andy to find out I brought Sadie here.

Once we're seated across from each other, Odette hands over the menus and takes our drink orders. We both ask for water.

Sadie opens the menu and asks, "What's good here?"

"Everything is good. It depends on what you're in the mood for."

She looks up. "Would you think I'm weird if I order something from the breakfast options?"

I smirk. "Sorry, sugar. That boat has sailed. I already think you're weird."

Twisting her face into an exaggerated scowl, she leans back and says in a thick British accent, "I beg your pardon?"

Laughter shakes my entire frame. "I'm just yanking your chain."

"So you don't think I'm weird."

"I don't know you well enough to have come to that conclusion. All I know is you're a terrible driver."

Her jaw drops. "Rude!"

"Not a lie though."

I watch her closely. I'm joking to mask the fact that I'm attracted to her. But this all could blow up in my face.

Sadie's expression remains serious for a couple of beats until the corners of her lips twitch up.

"Bloody hell. It's definitely not a lie. I'm dreadful behind a steering wheel. Didn't have many chances to practice back home."

"Where is back home, anyway?"

"London." She drops her eyes to the menu again. "I think I'll have pancakes with eggs and bacon."

I don't miss the quick change of subject. If she doesn't want to talk about her life before coming here, I shouldn't pry. But I'm damn curious.

I scan the offerings in front of me and decide on the half sandwich and small soup combo.

"What are you having?" she asks.

"Something light. I can't pig out or Coach will have my balls."

A shadow crosses Sadie's eyes, and her lips pinch together. I can see the difference this time. She's not pretending. What did I say that caused that reaction? She might not be weird, but she's certainly a mystery.

"How do you like Rushmore so far?" I ask.

She shrugs. "It's all right, I guess. I haven't been here that long. I flew in on the day of the Red Barn party, actually. I can probably blame the jet lag for that unfortunate event with your car."

I smirk. "Sure, let's go with that."

"Do you know when your car will be ready?"

"By the end of the week. They're busy at the garage."

"That's shite." She pauses and nibbles on her lower lip for a second. "I can give you rides while your car is being fixed. I mean, if you dare, considering how appalling my driving skills are."

I don't answer right away. Instead, I take a large sip of my water to buy time. I don't want Sadie to drive me anywhere, though not because she sucks at driving. I simply can't afford to spend more time with her. She beguiles me like no one ever has before. I can honestly say no girl has made me more curious, more interested from the get-go, and I'm not simply talking about her looks. Something about her speaks to me on a deeper level.

I should say, *"Thanks but no thanks."*

"Are you sure you're up for it?" I ask instead.

Clearly my mouth is a rogue agent now and is disregarding all my logical arguments.

"I wouldn't have offered if I didn't mean it. It's self-serving too."

"Oh?"

"I feel bloody guilty about it. So if I add driving you around as my penance, it will probably help with my heavy conscience."

"Maybe, or it could double your guilt when you kill me in a car wreck."

"Oh my God." Her voice rises an octave. "What a terrible thing to say."

I reach over and cover her hand with mine. "I'm just kidding. You're so easy to tease."

Sadie tenses a little as she drops her gaze to our joined hands. I realize my mistake then and quickly pull back.

Note to self: no touching, even if it's innocent.

Odette stops by our table just in time to diffuse the awkward moment. She takes our orders in a businesslike manner, but before she walks away, she gives me a meaningful glance and then winks.

Fucking hell. So it starts.

I'll have to do some serious damage control before we leave. I can't have Odette believing Sadie is my date. She means well, but she loves to gossip.

"I'm not easy to tease," Sadie replies to my earlier comment. "I'm just... I don't know, trying not to assume people are like me."

"I don't follow."

"Your comment that I could kill you in a car wreck. That's something I'd totally say because I'm savage like that."

I lean against the back of the booth seat. "Are you saying I'm a savage?"

Her eyebrows arch. "Oh no. That's not what I'm saying at all." She shakes her head and then rests it in her hand. "You see what I'm saying though? I just offended you without meaning to."

"You didn't offend me. That was also a joke. Told ya you're too easy to tease."

She looks up, narrowing her eyes to slits. "All right, Danny Hudson. It seems I've been holding back with you for nothing. You can obviously take whatever I have to dish out."

"I never said I couldn't."

She presses her index finger over her lips. "Hmm. I wasn't sure. I mean, you were pretty mental at the party."

"Only because someone had wrecked my car and not left a note."

"I left a note."

I give her a droll stare. "Really? Are we going to start the note debacle again?"

She smirks. "Better not, huh?"

Odette returns with our orders, and I'm thankful the service here is fast. Keeping myself busy with food will give me time to reset the thoughts in my head. I'm feeling out of my depth with Sadie, and I don't like it one bit.

My eyes are on my soup when a moan escapes her lips. The sound seems to shoot straight to my cock, making it twitch. *Damn everything to hell.* I shove a spoonful of hot soup into my mouth, burning my tongue in the process. Anything to stop the sudden awakening happening in my pants.

"This is real good nosh," she says. "Do you want a bite?"

I glance up, finding her offering a piece of maple syrup–drenched pancake to me.

Why is the idea of Sadie feeding me so damn erotic? Am I

missing pussy that much? No, that's not it. I wouldn't be reacting like this with anyone else, that much I know.

"I'm good, thanks."

"Your loss." She shoves the piece of pancake in her mouth, not caring that it is obviously too large.

"You eat like a dude," I say, and I don't know why.

She swallows before replying, "No, I eat like a person who didn't realize they were starving. This is not a date anyway, so I don't have to pretend to be all prissy. Although, I've never done that before."

"You've never gone out on a date or pretended to have manners?"

"Both. And for the record, I *do* have manners. But I also have an older brother."

"Ah, mystery solved." I swallow another spoonful of soup. "How come you've never dated before?"

"Seriously? Teenage boys are gross. Besides, I was too busy with football. I'm not saying I've never snogged or shagged anyone. I'm not a blushing virgin, for crying out loud. I have needs."

Fuck, how did I wind up talking about Sadie's sex life? I'm trying to ignore how attractive she is, and the mental pictures popping in my head are not helping.

"Hi, Danny." An annoyingly sweet voice that makes my skin crawl draws my attention away from Sadie.

I glance up and find Gwen standing near our booth. Two other girls wearing sorority hoodies are flanking her.

"Hey," I reply, cold enough that she won't miss the hint.

Her eyes turn to Sadie, who has not slowed down inhaling her food on Gwen's account.

Shit, I think I already love this girl.

What the hell am I thinking?

"We have to stop meeting like this," Gwen continues.

"Yeah, for real."

Sadie raises a questioning eyebrow at me. Hell, I hope she doesn't decide to play the ten-thousand-questions game once Gwen leaves.

"Are you going to introduce me to your friend?" Gwen asks through clenched teeth.

For fuck's sake. She's acting like she did at the end of our relationship.

"The name is Sadie. And if all you wanted was an introduction, you should have said so. I will sign a napkin if you want, but I draw the line at selfies."

"Why would we want your autograph?" one of Gwen's friends asks. "Are you famous or something?"

"Oh, you don't know who I am? How refreshing." Sadie smiles. "I knew coming to America was the right decision for me. Grammy didn't really think so. It was hard to convince her, especially after the whole scandal with Harry and Meghan. The poor thing was brokenhearted."

"Wait. Are you implying the Queen of England is your grandmother?" The girl's voice turns high-pitched.

I'll be damned. She's actually buying Sadie's bullshit.

"Of course she's not related to the queen, Carol. Come on," Gwen retorts, but I detect a hint of uncertainty.

Sadie shrugs. "Believe me or not, I don't bloody care. Now, if you don't mind, bugger off and let us get back to our dinner."

"That was rude," Gwen replies.

"No ruder than you stopping here and acting like Danny owes you anything."

Wow. When Sadie said she was holding back with me, she wasn't kidding.

"Are you going to let her talk to me like that?" Gwen turns her ire on me.

"Did she say anything that wasn't true?"

Gwen's friends trade a glance that looks a lot like third-degree embarrassment. Her face is bright red when she storms off and walks out of the diner.

I should be relieved she's gone, but I'm rattled. My hands are shaking when I break my sandwich into pieces. I can't believe I let her get to me like that.

"Dear Lord. That was pleasant." Sadie sticks a piece of crispy bacon into her mouth.

I don't offer a comment; instead, I shove a piece of bread into my mouth and chew on it with excessive force.

"You don't need to tell me who that was, even though I can guess," Sadie continues, clearly unfazed. "We all have a past that we wish stayed in the past."

"What's yours?"

She doesn't answer until she chews and swallows her food, all the while keeping her eyes locked on mine.

"Maybe I'll tell you one day."

9

SADIE

By the time Danny and I finished having dinner, Katrina had already texted me back, so instead of hanging out at his place, I simply dropped him off. I didn't think spending more time with him after we bumped into his crazy ex would be enjoyable anyway. The encounter messed him up, which obviously made me uber-curious to know what their deal was.

I'm completely beat when I finally walk into my dorm room. Katrina is watching a movie on her laptop with her headphones on. I inspect my bed to make sure she didn't use it as an extension of hers. She's burning a scented candle by the window—probably to mask the scent of sex.

Ew. Fucking gross, now that I think about it.

She glances up and pulls her headphones off. "Hey, you're finally home."

"I was here sooner, but the room was at full capacity."

I take off my jeans and then jump under the covers. I don't want Katrina to see my scar, so I keep my T-shirt and bra on. I used the restroom before I got here, and there's no chance in hell I'm going back out to brush my teeth. I'm too exhausted for that.

"I'm sorry about that. It wasn't a planned hookup."

This is where I should ask who the lucky guy was, but I honestly don't care to hear the story right this second. My eyelids are heavy, and all I want is the sweet oblivion only my pillow can provide.

"Fine. But I think we should establish a schedule of when we're allowed to bring guests. I had a full day, and I was planning on going to bed early."

"Totally. But I heard your evening wasn't a total bust."

"What do you mean?"

"You were spotted having dinner with Danny Hudson," she says way too chipperly.

"He was with me when we found the sock on the doorknob."

"What?" she shrieks. "Were you hoping to score a hookup yourself?"

"Will you tone down the excited poodle behavior? He came by to grab the money I owe him for his car repair. We decided to kill time at the diner. That's all."

"Really? So it wasn't a date?"

"No, it wasn't a date. You can stop planning our wedding now." I roll onto my side, giving my back to her, hoping she'll cease with the inquisition.

I can't believe she already knew I was with Danny tonight. Blimey, gossip travels fast here.

"Too bad. I heard you bumped into his ex," she continues, ignoring my blatant sign that I want to go to sleep.

Shite. She had to go mention something that'd pique my attention. I roll onto my other side so I can see her face.

"We did. She was a nightmare."

"I'm not surprised. I heard from a girl who is rushing her

sorority that she forbade any of her sisters to even look in Danny's direction."

"She sounds like a psycho. Poor bloke."

"For real. But anyway, nothing for you to worry about, right? I mean, you said you weren't interested in boys."

"Nope. Still haven't changed my mind." I yawn heavily. "I'm going to sleep now. I'm destroyed."

"Okay, sweet dreams." She puts her headphones back on.

I try to get comfortable again, but even returning to my favorite sleeping position doesn't help me. My body is tired, but my mind is now whirring nonstop.

I wasn't lying when I said I wasn't interested in boys. They can be such a nuisance.

So why is Danny living rent free in my head?

IT TOOK me a while to fall asleep last night, and it was equally hard to get out of bed this morning. My internal clock is still wonky. I skip breakfast and, bleary-eyed, trudge toward the school. I didn't bother brushing my hair, just simply pulled it back into a messy ponytail. I couldn't tell someone what clothes I'm wearing if they asked me. It's only when I'm a block away from my building that I remember I actually own a car now and don't need to walk.

Bollocks. I can't believe I forgot. I'm having way too many Bridget Jones moments for my liking.

I turn around, and on the way to my car, I debate if I should stop to grab coffee somewhere. I could use some caffeine.

My phone rings when I slide behind the wheel. I don't recognize the number showing on my WhatsApp, and for that reason, I almost reject the call. Then I realize telemarketers wouldn't be calling me on the app.

"Hello?" I say, suppressing a yawn that sneaked in.

"Hey, good morning, Sadie."

"Who is this?" I grumble.

"It's Danny."

My pulse quickens, and in an instant, I'm wide awake. It seems Danny Hudson is better than coffee.

"Hey. Hi, I'm sorry, I didn't recognize your voice."

Shite. I sound like an idiot.

"It's okay. I hate to do this last minute, but I was wondering if your offer to give me a ride still stands."

"Of course. Do you need one now? I'm about to drive out of my parking lot."

"No, I'm going to practice with Andy. I need a ride later today. What time are you done?"

"Around three. Where do you need to go?"

"I gotta run an errand for my mother. I wouldn't ask you if it wasn't important."

Taking Danny on an errand run means spending more than just a few minutes with him. I'm not sure I should be doing that. He's already taking up too much space in my mind.

I could offer to lend him my car. I wouldn't have to play chauffeur, but then he might think I'm avoiding him.

Blimey. Why am I having such a hard time with this?

"Sadie? Are you still there?"

"Yeah, sorry. I spaced out for a moment. I didn't have coffee yet. Where am I picking you up? At your place?"

"Uh, probably easier to swing by the field. I'll be done with practice around the same time as you."

"Okay. Sounds good. I'll see you later, then."

"Thanks a lot, Sadie. I appreciate it."

"No worries."

It's not until I end the call that I see the problem with the logistics. What if my father sees me when I come by to pick up Danny? Would he think I'm messing with one of his players just to get to him?

Hell, it's too late to change plans now without sounding like a dimwitted fool.

Shoving all my concerns related to Danny to a dark corner in my mind, I drive to practice. I managed to avoid boy drama throughout school back in London; I won't fuck it up now when being the best on the field matters the most. I have to make up for lost time while I was recovering and prove to Coach Lauda that I shouldn't be benched.

Despite getting out of bed later than I planned, I'm one of the first ones in the locker room. None of the Three Musketeers are there, only Joanne and Vanessa, who are already in training gear. Both are covered in a sheen of sweat.

"Hey," I greet them.

"Morning, Sadie," Joanne replies.

Vanessa simply stares at me with a grin. *What does she find so amusing?* I choose to ignore it for now.

"When did you get here?" I ask.

"An hour ago," Vanessa answers. "We wanted to get a cardio session in before today's training."

"I should have done the same, but getting out of bed this morning was almost impossible."

"Someone keeping you up at night?" Vanessa raises an eyebrow.

I roll my eyes. "Ugh. For fuck's sake. Not you too."

Joanne glances between Vanessa and me. "What did I miss?"

"Sadie went out on a date with Danny Hudson last night." She laughs. "I knew I saw sparks when you guys were at each other's throats."

Joanne's eyes widen. "Sadie got into an argument with Danny? How is that possible? He's the most mellow football player I've ever met."

I point at Vanessa. "First of all, that wasn't a date." Then I turn to Joanne. "And you're wrong if you think Danny doesn't have a temper. You should have seen his reaction when his ex showed up."

Both Joanne and Vanessa watch me with renewed interest, making me regret my big mouth.

"Oh, don't stop there. Tell us more, tell us more," Vanessa sings to the tune of the *Grease* song.

"Now you're just taking the piss."

I give my back to them to shove my duffel bag in my locker.

"We're not making fun of you," Joanne pipes up. "Well, at least *I'm* not."

"There's nothing to tell. She acted like Danny still belonged to her, all jealous. He wasn't amused."

More of our teammates join us, effectively killing the conversation. I hope the subject dies for real. This is only the first week of preseason training and I'm already headlining gossip. I don't want to be known as Danny Hudson's date, hookup, whatever. I'm here to make a name for myself, not be arm candy to a football player.

10

DANNY

I'M DRYING my hair with a towel when Andy bumps his shoulder with mine.

"You were on fire today, bro."

"Thanks. It was a good day."

"Keep it up and nothing will stop us this season."

"That's the plan." I grin.

"Did you find someone to take you shopping today?"

I grimace, not keen on telling Andy who is giving me a ride.

"Ah, man. You didn't?" he asks. "You know I'd lend you my car if I didn't have to take Lorenzo to the dentist."

I shake my head. "I know. Don't worry though. I found someone."

"Oh yeah? Who?"

"Sadie," I mumble, purposely avoiding making eye contact.

"Come again?"

"Why are you surprised, Andy?" Puck butts in. "Danny was spotted having a romantic dinner with her last night."

I glower at him. "I hardly consider eating at a diner having a romantic dinner."

"You went out on a date with the hot English chick and didn't tell me?" Andy's voice rises.

"For fuck's sake, it wasn't a date," I growl. "A guy and a girl can hang out together without leading to anything sexual."

"Sure, if they're related. Even so, sometimes not even blood relation stops that." He shrugs.

"Ew. Can you please spare us your impure thoughts, infidel?" Puck retorts.

"Bite me, altar boy."

Puck jumps forward, ready to wrestle Andy into silence, but Andy was prepared and danced out of Puck's reach. Now that they're occupied with their stupid antics, I finish getting dressed without interruption and slip out of the locker room before they remember me.

On my way out of the gym building, I text Sadie to let her know I'm ready. She replies saying she'll be here in a minute, but she's obviously just around the corner, because I barely have time to slide my phone back in my pocket before I see her car approach.

She stops right in front of me. When I open the car door, loud music pours out, a pop beat I don't recognize.

"What are you listening to?" I ask by way of greeting.

"Oh, Boyzone."

"Boyzone? What is it, some new boy band?"

She laughs. "No. They're old school. Like popular in the '90s and early 2000s. My friend Anika put together a playlist on Spotify that includes only the top British songs from the last decades. She demanded I listen to it regularly so I don't forget home."

"I don't know if that's nice of her or if she's trying to torture you a bit."

She laughs. "Probably both."

"What's this jewel of the UK charts called, anyway?"

"'Picture of You.' Come on. It's not that bad."

"It'd probably be more tolerable if it was a smidge less deafening."

"Okay, okay."

She lowers the volume until we can actually carry on a conversation without having to resort to shouting.

"Thank you."

"Where are we going?" She puts the car in drive again.

"Ikea. I'll give you directions."

"Seriously? You're making me suffer through an Ikea shopping experience?"

"Come on. I thought girls loved buying shit for their dorms."

She shakes her head. "Not this girl. But it could have been worse."

"Oh yeah? What would you consider worse?"

"Going to a home improvement shop."

I chuckle. "You're lucky. Not today."

The cheesy song ends, and it's followed by another oldie. This one, at least, I've heard before, but I can't name the band or song.

After a while, I ask, "How was practice?"

"It could have gone better. I woke later than I planned and didn't have a chance to go for a run beforehand."

"You're hard-core dedicated to soccer, aren't you?"

"Yeah. I want to go pro."

"Me too."

She pulls her eyes from the road for a second. "You're that good?"

"Why do you sound so surprised?"

"I'm not surprised you're a good player, although I haven't seen you play yet. I just thought getting drafted to play in the NFL was as hard as winning the lottery."

She's not saying anything I don't know, but the reminder makes me less confident that it's an achievable goal.

"Coach Clarkson seems to believe I have a chance," I reply meekly.

"If he said that, then it must be true." Gone is the levity from a second ago, her voice suddenly cold and tight.

"He could be wrong though. But I'll give my all to make it happen."

"He's never wrong, at least not when it comes to football."

I frown. "How do you know that about my coach? Do you know him?"

"Bloody hell," she mutters and then falls silent.

"Sadie?"

She lets out an audible sigh, her shoulders sagging forward. "Okay, I didn't want anyone to know this, but, uh, your coach is my dad."

I stare at her without blinking, frozen as I process her words. "Coach Clarkson is your father?"

"Yep."

"I knew he was divorced, but that's about it."

She lets out a humorless laugh. "I'm not surprised. Why would he talk about the children he so easily gave up?"

I open and shut my mouth, but no word comes forth. I've always seen Coach Clarkson as a father figure. I can't reconcile that with the image of a man who walked out on his family.

"Are you saying he abandoned you and your mom?"

"No. My parents got a divorce, and then he let my mother take us to England."

"I'm sure it wasn't an easy decision to make. He was probably trying to avoid a custody battle."

Sadie's nostrils flare, and she's holding the steering wheel so tight now that her knuckles are white.

"And that's the reason I didn't want to tell anyone Coach Clarkson is my dad. I know his players idolize him."

"I'm sorry, Sadie. I clearly know a different man than you do."

"Yeah, clearly. Can we please not talk about him?"

"Of course." I look out the window, feeling conflicted about this revelation for more reasons than one.

It was already bad enough that I was letting Sadie reel me in. Now that I know she's Coach Clarkson's daughter, she's not only a terrible idea, but she's completely off-limits. I can't even dream about getting involved with the coach's daughter, especially knowing their relationship is rocky. I won't jeopardize my rapport with him, or my future, because of a girl, no matter how alluring I find her.

"What exactly do you need to buy at Ikea?" she asks after a few minutes of uncomfortable silence.

"Bookshelves."

"That's it?"

"Yeah. Mom is a bookworm, and she has a bad habit of hoarding novels she's already read. She had an old bookshelf that finally collapsed, and now all her books are scattered around her small apartment. She's been nagging me to buy her a new one for weeks."

"Couldn't she have waited a few more days until you got your car back?"

"Probably, but I know training will only get harder as the preseason progresses. I might as well go now before Coach trains us within an inch of our lives."

She falls silent again, and I realize I shouldn't have brought up her dad.

"And that's the last time I'll mention him. Promise."

She laughs. "God, you can mention him to me. He's your coach, after all, and a big part of your life. If we're going to be friends, I don't expect you to edit him out of conversation."

My stupid heart latches onto the "friends" bit of her speech and rejoices. Damn stupid muscle.

"So that's where this is going? Friendship?"

"Am I not driving you to bloody Ikea?" She glances at me, sporting a smirk.

"Sure, but I thought you were doing this to ease your guilty conscience."

"Nah. I'm only doing it because I like you."

"You like me?" I try not to sound too eager and fail.

"Down, boy. I like you as a friend. Don't get any ideas."

I scoff to hide my humiliation and disappointment. Friend zoned. I can't say it doesn't hurt.

"You think too much of yourself. I have zero interest in dating you. It's nothing personal. I just can't get distracted."

"We're on the same page, then. Besides, you're not my type."

"Ouch. Tell me how you really feel, why don't you?"

She winces. "Sorry. I did warn you I was savage. My tongue is a lethal weapon."

Hell. She had to go and mention her tongue. Now I'm thinking what kissing her would feel like. I bet she tastes sweet and dangerous. It's almost as if after I learned she's forbidden fruit and she doesn't want me, she became even more irresistible.

I have to stop this stupid shit. If I were any smarter, I'd say forget being friends. But I'm not, and if all I can get is Sadie's friendship, it's better than nothing.

11

SADIE

I'm glad the cat is out of the bag, but at the same time, I'm peeved that Danny was so quick to defend my father. He acted exactly how I expected one of my dad's players would, and it pissed me off. I can't blame him though. He didn't know what it was like for me when my entire life fell apart.

I can't believe I told him we should be friends. This has disaster written all over it. Despite what I told him, he *is* my type—or at least I think he is. I'm not sure. I've never been so at ease with a guy before, and maybe that's doing my head in. The good thing is, he isn't interested in dating me—or anyone—either. We have that in common, so maybe this experiment of being friends with a bloke won't blow up in my face.

After another fifteen minutes driving on the highway, which went better than I expected, the blue and yellow Ikea building finally looms on the horizon. The car park is half full, which makes me wonder if people don't have any jobs. It's the middle of the afternoon on a weekday, after all.

"You'd better pray it's not a zoo inside," I tell Danny once I park the car.

"Ah, where's your sense of adventure?"

"Never had one."

"Somehow, I don't believe you."

He gets out before I can offer him a retort.

For the sake of keeping the peace and also not revealing too much about myself, I let his remark go.

We take the escalator up to the showroom, but since we know exactly what we're here for, I look for the sign pointing to the store area. Danny veers in the opposite direction.

"Where are you going?" I ask him.

"I don't know what kind of bookshelf I need yet."

I groan. "Great."

To my surprise, he throws his beefy arm over my shoulders and pulls me against his side. "Come on, Sadie. It'll be fun."

Alarm bells sound in my head when a ripple of desire travels down my spine and butterflies I never felt in my tummy before spring awake. Being this close to him is wreaking havoc in my body, but I'm too stunned to do anything besides bask in his warmth.

"We'll see," I reply weakly.

He steps aside in the next moment, releasing me from his embrace. I let out a breath of relief, but at the same time, I miss his proximity.

Note to self: no more getting close and personal with Danny Hudson if I want to keep my sanity.

The problem is that now I'm too aware of his presence, and the damn insects in my belly are still throwing a rave.

To distract myself from my problematic reaction to Danny, I focus on the knickknacks on display. Maybe I should buy something for my dorm room after all. My bed could use some colorful pillows, and a pinboard would be nice.

I stray from Danny when I find something that catches my eye in the home office section. It's a print of a picture of London in black and white with only the two-decker bus in color. I stare at it for a moment while I decide if it will work on my wall.

"Do you like that?" Danny stops next to me.

"Yeah. I know it's cheesy, but it's also cool."

"You should buy it, then."

"It might be too big."

"If it doesn't work, you can return it."

Wrinkling my nose, I say, "That means coming back here. No thanks."

I pivot around Danny and walk away from him and the picture. I should just stick to my original three items: a couple of pillows and a pinboard. I find one that will fit above my desk and promptly grab it. A second later, Danny pries the board from me.

"I'll carry this."

"There's no need to be chivalrous. You're not trying to get into my knickers, remember?"

He raises an eyebrow. "Do you think that's the only reason a guy would do something nice for a girl?"

I shrug. "Basically."

He laughs, shaking his head. "I don't know if I should be offended or sad for you."

"Hey! Don't you dare feel sorry for me."

"Fine, I'll stick with feeling deeply hurt, then."

I nod. "That's better. I always prefer when I'm inflicting pain on blokes."

"Even your friends?"

"Truth be told, I've never had a guy friend before. But if you ask any of my girlfriends back home, they'd tell you I'm not one to spare their feelings either. I'm too blunt for that."

"I don't mind brutal honesty as long as you can take as much as you can dish out."

"I've got thick skin. Don't worry."

We spend the next ten minutes looking at various

bookshelves in the showroom until we get to where they're all displayed together. Mercifully, Danny doesn't take long to decide which one he wants. He takes a note of their model number and where they're located in the pickup area. We head downstairs, and on the way to the big warehouse, I wind up grabbing more items for myself than I intended.

"I thought you weren't one of those girls." Danny chuckles.

"Shut up. These are all basic necessities."

"Pillows are a basic necessity?"

"When they brighten my sleeping space, yes."

"Maybe you should grab some succulents too." Danny points at the miniature plants in cute vases.

"Oh God, no. They'd be dead in a week."

He stops offering comments as we continue to the warehouse. Then I try not to ogle him too much as he loads the large boxes in our trolley. It's pretty hard not to notice the muscles straining against his T-shirt though. The boy is damn gorgeous.

Curse football players and their top-shape physique.

"I think that's it," he declares as he turns and catches me staring. A broad smile splits his face. "Are you okay there, Sadie?"

I blink fast, trying to clear my mind of its lust-induced fog. "I'm hunky-dory."

"Hunky-dory." He chortles. "I don't think I've ever heard anyone our age say that before."

"I like to be different."

His eyes seem to shine with appreciation, making my face feel hot. "Okay, then."

He pushes the trolley forward, but I lag behind, still pissed that I let him see me drooling over him and also confused about that loaded glance.

"What are you doing back there? Checking out my fine ass?" he teases.

I snort. "Your arse is not that fine."

"So you *were* checking it, then?" He laughs.

I walk faster to catch up and, in retaliation, pinch his waist.

"Hey! What was that for?"

"Punishment for being a bellend."

"A what?"

I sigh. "A dickhead."

"How does stating the obvious make me a dickhead?"

"When it's nothing but a bold lie."

"Fine, Sadie. From now on, I'll pretend you don't find my tush appealing."

"Good," I say, then immediately realize my error.

Danny smirks but refrains from commenting.

When it's time to pay, I try to cover the cost of everything since I owe him money, but he doesn't let me pay for the bookshelves.

"What difference does it make how the money is spent?" I ask.

"Huge difference," he replies, and that's the end of it.

He then veers for the line where you can arrange for transportation.

"I think those will fit in my car, Danny."

He eyes them with a frown. "I'm not so sure."

"We should try anyway. If they don't fit, we'll come back."

"Okay."

We return to the garage, and after some maneuvering and a few cursed words, the boxes are in and the boot is closed.

"Told ya," I say.

"You don't need to gloat. I'm not a macho man who doesn't believe women can be right. I know better."

I snicker. "Your mother obviously trained you well."

He grins while his eyes fill with pride. "She did."

I'm not sure what it is about his look, but my chest feels warm and fuzzy all of a sudden.

12

DANNY

I WASN'T EXPECTING the bookshelves to fit in Sadie's car, so when I approach my mother's humble apartment building, a sense of shame takes hold of me. I don't know why I don't want her to know that I don't have a lot of money. Maybe it's stupid male pride.

Sadie doesn't bat an eyelash at the faded paint on the building or the yellowed grass and sad-looking garden at the front. When she gets out of the car, she does glare at the stairs leading to the second floor with her hands on her hips though.

"Please tell me your mother's apartment isn't on the top floor."

I circle to the back of the car and open the trunk. "I can't say that."

She looks over her shoulder, glowering. "You suck."

"Come on. It'll be great exercise. You were upset you missed your morning run. This ought to compensate for it."

"Breaking my back is not how I envision leading the Ravens to victory."

"Leading the Ravens? Does Vanessa know you're vying for her position as the team captain?"

She waves her hand dismissively as she walks over. "I don't want to be captain, but I do want a starting position. Melody McCoy thinks she's Megan Rapinoe, and someone needs to knock her off that pedestal."

"Ah, naturally. Because there can't be two queens on the field." I smirk.

Instead of backtracking, Sadie smiles wickedly. "Of course not. There can be only one."

My eyebrows arch. "Please tell me that was an actual *Highlander* reference and not a coincidence."

"You can't drown, you fool, you're immortal!" she replies, trying her best to sound like Sean Connery as Ramirez.

I throw my head back and laugh from the belly up.

"Blimey, I didn't know my Sean impression was that bad."

I wipe tears from my eyes. "It's actually spot on. I'm laughing because... well, I don't even know."

Deep down, I do know the reason. I've never met a girl who was into classic '80s movies, especially that particular one. My laughter wasn't from amusement but a rather pleasant surprise.

She shakes her head. "You're such a confusing boy. Come on. These boxes won't get themselves up those steps."

She nudges me out of the way and slides the top box off the trunk.

"It'll be easier if we carry the boxes together," I suggest.

"Are you implying I can't lift one by myself?"

"Not at all, but go on, try."

She narrows her eyes at me, and I sense she's taking my comment as a dare. Bending her knees, she lifts the box using her core strength and legs. But getting the box off the ground was the easy part; balancing the long board is what I predicted would be hard. Sadie staggers back as she tries to find her equilibrium, bumping into me.

"Watch it," I say through a suppressed laugh.

"If you laugh, I swear I'll do more than just pinch you."

I grab the end of the box. "Stop being stubborn and let me help you. I know you're strong, but there's no reason to make your life harder just to prove a point."

She moves forward to hold the other end of the box. "Fine, Hudson. You win."

We trudge toward the building and then up the stairs, carrying all the boxes up first before I open the front door and bring them into the apartment. As usual, the scent of baked cookies hits my nose. Mom always has them around when she knows I'm coming by. What she doesn't know is that I never eat everything she makes. If I did, I'd be a round little pig. Instead, I bring her treats to school and share them with my classmates or teammates.

"This is cozy," Sadie remarks. "Is your mum not home?"

"No. She's at work."

After all the boxes are inside the apartment and propped against the wall, Sadie glances around the room. "Where do you want the bookshelves to go?"

"Oh, we don't need to put them together now."

She gives me a droll stare. "I bet you were planning on assembling them right away. Two can get the job done faster than one."

"Are you sure you're up for it? I think I've already abused your friendship too much."

"Abuse away. I always prefer to have people indebted to me instead of the other way around."

"Is that so?"

"Yep. So they can't say no when I call asking them to help me bury a body."

"Jesus, Sadie. You have a twisted mind."

She sticks her tongue out at me, and all the blood in my body seems to whoosh south. This cannot happen. It's the second time in less than an hour that the urge to push Sadie against the wall and claim her mouth hits me. I need to reset my brain somehow.

"So, where are they going?"

I point at the wall where several book towers are lined up. "There. I need to make room first so we can set up the working area."

With Sadie's help, I move the furniture around. It's a small living room, so there isn't much space to work with. In the end, I have to carry the coffee table to the kitchen so we can spread out on the floor. It takes an hour to get all the bookshelves up, and we manage to do it without cursing at the furniture, or worse, bleeding all over Mom's rug.

"Done. Finally." I wipe the sweat off my forehead with the back of my hand.

"Not quite. What about all those books?"

"It's probably better if we let my mother organize them as she prefers. I'm sure she has a system."

"Fair enough."

"I'm parched. Do you want something to drink?" I head for the kitchen.

"Yeah. Water, please."

I fill a tall glass with cold water from the fridge and hand it over to Sadie, brushing the tips of her fingers with mine during the transfer. I've never believed in romantic nonsense such as sparks, but as we both drain our glasses of water, it does seem that the air around us is crackling with electricity. Maybe I shouldn't have locked gazes with her while I was drinking, and I most definitely should have looked away after I set the glass back on the counter.

"So, what now?" she asks.

I'm so caught up in the fight between reason and desire going on in my head that I totally misunderstand her question.

"What now what?" I ask in a high-pitched tone. Shit. My heart is racing.

"Do you have any other chores you'd like my help with while I'm here?"

Fuck. It seems only *my* mind was in the gutter. I'm glad I didn't do something stupid.

"No. We're all done. We should be heading back to campus."

No sooner do I say that than the sound of a key turning announces Mom's arrival.

Hell and damn. I wasn't planning on making introductions today. Probably never, if I'm being honest. Mom has always been able to tell what I'm feeling at any given time. If I don't control my emotions around Sadie, Mom will know I have the hots for the coach's daughter. She was never a fan of Gwen and was secretly hoping I'd find a new girlfriend soon. I don't need another matchmaker. Andy is bad enough.

"Danny, I didn't think you'd be here today. Isn't your car in the shop?" She walks over and then stops when she spots Sadie. "Oh, hello. I didn't know Danny had company."

Sadie steps forward, extending her hand. "Nice to meet you, Ms. Hudson. I'm Sadie, Danny's friend from school. I gave him a ride today."

"Oh, how nice of you. You can call me Martha." She smiles as she shakes Sadie's hand, then turns to me. I can see the glint of curiosity shining in her eyes.

"I owed him the favor considering I'm the reason he doesn't have a car."

Mom's brow furrows. "I don't follow."

"Sadie was the one who wrecked my car," I explain.

"Oh." Mom's eyes grow larger. "Well, it's still nice of you to offer."

"She also helped put the bookshelves together," I add.

"She did?" Mom's eyebrows arch slightly. "Well, thank you, dear."

"You're home early," I say, trying to divert her interest on Sadie.

"Slow day at the office today, and Dr. Francis is out of town."

I turn to Sadie. "Mom works at a plastic surgeon's office."

"Cool. You must be busy all the time, huh?"

"Oh yeah. Everyone in this town wants to look younger, better, or different. So, what brings you to LA?"

"Sadie's Coach Clarkson's daughter," I blurt out thanks to nervous agitation.

I look at Sadie, trying to convey that I'm sorry about my outburst. She shakes her head as if to say I'm the worst.

"Really?" Mom asks. "I didn't realize Coach Clarkson had kids. But you have an accent."

"Yeah, I've lived in London since I was six, after my parents split. I would have gone to uni there, but my parents had a deal that I'd come back to attend college in the US."

That's way more information than she volunteered to me in the car. Maybe she's telling Mom all that to avoid questions she isn't keen to answer.

"Well, we have to go now to try to beat traffic," I butt in.

"It's already too late for that, hon. Why don't you stay and have dinner?"

"Eh...." I can't think of an excuse to refuse, but I know I don't want to subject Sadie to my mother's inquisition.

"Oh, I can't stay," Sadie replies. "I promised I'd take my roommate out tonight. Maybe another time."

Mom's face falls. "Oh, that's too bad. Thanks for driving my son around and for helping him with the bookshelves."

"It was my pleasure," Sadie replies through a beaming smile.

Before we rush out, Mom shoves a bag of cookies into my

hand and also Sadie's. By the time we make it back to her car, she's already on her second cookie.

"I thought you had dinner plans. You're going to spoil your appetite eating all that."

"I don't have dinner plans. I only said that because you looked so pained. I figured you didn't want me to hang out with your mum."

Shit. That's what she thought?

"Sadie, you got it all wrong. I was just trying to protect you from her billion questions. I'm sorry I told her who you were."

"I didn't mind that. It's the truth, after all."

She stops in front of her car and offers me the keys. "Do you mind driving back? I'm knackered."

"Not at all."

Our fingers connect again, and I try not to react to it. I should have learned my lesson when I pulled her into a side hug back at Ikea. She felt too damn good in my arms, which means I have to keep my distance and avoid all contact, even innocent ones like this.

"Since I'm driving, maybe I should pick the music this time?" I ask once we're both inside.

"Sure. Go ahead. I'm curious about what your musical tastes sound like."

"I like a lot of different styles."

"I'm the same. Don't judge me through my friend's choices."

"Oh, it's already too late for that."

She rolls her eyes but refrains from replying.

I pick a random radio station and drive away from my mother's building. We don't speak for several minutes, but this time around, the silence isn't uncomfortable. When traffic slows to a stop, I glance at Sadie. Her head is propped against the window. She's sound asleep. Glutton for punishment that I am, I stare like a creep until some asshole honks behind me.

I see then that the line of cars has moved and I had been holding traffic.

Mom was right; it was too late to avoid rush hour, and it takes me an hour to get back to campus. Instead of driving to my place, I head to Sadie's building instead.

"Sadie." I shake her arm lightly. "We're home."

She blinks her eyes open, looking a little confused. Her gaze is unfocused as she stares at me, but when she looks out the window, her body seems to tense.

"You drove to my place, not yours."

"You were passed out. I didn't want you to have to drive back alone when you're that exhausted."

"How are you getting home?"

"I'll figure it out. Don't worry about me."

"Take my car."

My eyes widen. "What? No. How are you getting to practice tomorrow?"

"I can jog there. Seriously, it's no big deal."

I shake my head. "No, I'll pick you up. What time do you have to be there?"

"Six. Is that too early for you?"

Yes, but I don't tell her I don't need to be at practice until eight.

"Not at all. I'll see you tomorrow, then. And thanks for the ride and everything."

She leans across the gap between our seats and kisses me on the cheek. My breath catches.

What the hell is she doing?

"What's that for?" I ask when she returns to her side.

"That's my thank-you for today. I had fun. See you later, alligator."

She's out of the car before I can recover. In fact, it takes me a full minute to finally snap out of my paralysis and drive away.

I'm so fucked.

13

SADIE

I WAS tired until I decided to play dead from the neck up and kiss Danny on his cheek. My lips were still tingling by the time I slipped into my dorm room. Lucky for me, Katrina wasn't around, and I didn't have to make small talk while freaking out that I fancy Danny way too much and I really, really want a snogging session with him.

I can't allow myself to fall for a boy, especially one of my dad's players. That'd be more stupid than getting into the path of a knife.

I prop my new pinboard against the wall and then toss my new pillows on the bed before changing into my pj's. Once under my covers, I try to get comfortable, but now I'm too wired and can't relax.

You're just horny, Sadie.

Ugh. How did I let Danny sex me up like that? He wasn't even trying. God, I'm such a twat.

Well, there's nothing for it now. I have to get rid of this pent-up sex drive or I'll jump Danny the next time I see him. I send

Katrina a WhatsApp message to ask when she thinks she'll be home. I don't want her to burst in when I'm playing with my toys.

She replies that she'll be back in a few hours and to not wait up.

Wasn't planning on it, sugar.

I get out of bed again and pull my suitcase from under the bed. *I really need to finish unpacking.* After a minute rummaging through the mess of clothes, shoes, and other junk, I finally locate my stash of toys, which I had the foresight to put in a small pouch just in case some nosy airport employee decided to check the contents of my luggage.

I want fast relief because I do need to sleep, so I choose my favorite toy, a bullet that can make me come in less than a minute.

But tonight it seems my body refuses to cooperate, and my faithful device is not doing the trick. *Goddamn it, Danny. You'd better not have ruined me for my toys.* I close my eyes and remember how he made me feel when he hugged me briefly, how his cheek felt against my lips. Then my imagination runs wild, placing him in my room. In my head, he kisses my neck and touches my body with his big hands. I pinch my nipple through the fabric of my shirt and arch my back when I finally feel the tendrils of pleasure build between my legs.

When I climax, I pretend it's Danny between my legs, pumping into me and fucking me into oblivion. I may have said his name out loud.

Blimey, I didn't realize I had it that bad for him.

I do need to find a way to get him out of my head. In hindsight, getting off while thinking of him is not the best way to do it, but at least I'm relaxed now. I'll figure out how to stop wanting him tomorrow.

THE SOUND of someone knocking on my door disturbs my peaceful dream. I groan, hiding my head under the pillow and hoping whoever is bothering me will go away.

"Sadie? Are you there?"

Fuck. That's Danny.

I jump out of bed as if I've been electrocuted. *What's Danny doing at my door at this hour?* Katrina's bed is empty, so she must not have made it back home yet.

I hurry to open the door, tripping over my duffel bag's strap and colliding with the door.

"Ouch!"

"Jesus, what was that?" he asks.

I open the door with a jerky movement, not caring about how I look. If he's here, there must have been an emergency. It takes me a second to notice he's fresh out of the shower. His curls are still damp, and he smells soapy.

"What happened?" I ask.

His eyes widen when he sees me there, standing in all my just-out-of-bed glory. I must be quite the sight.

"Uh, you told me you had to be at practice at six. It's a quarter till," he says, smirking.

"What?" I shriek. "It's morning already?"

"Yeah."

"Bloody hell." I pivot around and try to find my phone in the dark.

"Uh, should I wait in the car?"

"No, you can come in. It's fine. I'll change in the bathroom. Would you mind hitting the light switch? I can't see a damn thing."

The sudden brightness makes my eyes burn, but when I get used to it, I regret not sending Danny to wait in the car after all. My room is a fucking war zone.

"Better?" he asks.

"Uh, probably not."

He steps around my stuff, looking at everything with curiosity. "What happened here?"

"I was too tired last night to tidy up my room." I yank the cover off my bed so I can at least straighten it and accidentally send my bullet flying right into Danny's hand.

"What do we have here?" He looks at the pink device, fighting to keep a straight face.

My cheeks are burning as I reach for it. "Give me that."

I step back fast, clutching my bullet tightly, while Danny is watching with mirth shining in his eyes.

"Quit looking at me like that."

"Like what?" he asks innocently.

"Like this is amusing to you."

"I can't help that it is."

"Shut up. This is the most embarrassing moment of my life." I bend over to grab the little pouch from the floor, but I forgot to zip it closed last night and, in my haste, end up spilling all my toys onto the floor. "Shite!"

"Whoa. That's quite a stash. You weren't kidding when you said you had needs."

"I take it back. *This* is the most embarrassing moment of my life."

I keep my gaze down, hiding my face behind my hair as I quickly shove everything into the container and out of sight. Then I drop the pouch in my luggage, close it, and slide it back under the bed. When I finally rise from my crouch and dare to look at Danny again, he still has a shit-eating grin on his face.

"What?" I cross my arms over my chest.

"Nothing. Maybe I should wait in the car and give you time to recover."

"Recover from what?" I snap, even though I know exactly what he's saying. I just told him I was embarrassed.

"Uh...." He rubs the back of his neck while his cheeks turn pinker.

Ha! I managed to turn the tables on him and I wasn't even trying. It doesn't make me less mortified, but at least I'm not the only one feeling uncomfortable as hell.

"Just sit down and wait for me. I'll be back in a few minutes."

I grab the first pieces of clothing I can find in my dresser drawer plus my toiletry bag and then rush out of my room. I usually take a shower in the morning, but since I'm already late, I just brush my teeth and wash my face. I try not to cringe too much at the state of my hair. It's good that Danny saw me at my worst. I need him to remain in the friend zone at all costs. It'll be easier if he perceives me as one of the guys and not at all attractive.

I return to my room in less than five minutes and find Danny browsing on his phone. He looks up when I enter, no longer red-faced.

"Ready?" he asks.

"Yeah."

He stands up, and the room becomes much smaller suddenly. He's a tall guy, over six feet, with wide shoulders. But it's not the size of his frame that makes it feel like the place has shrunk. It's his presence that gives the illusion. He's everywhere.

His eyes shift focus to something over my shoulder, so I turn to see what caught his attention.

"Do you need help putting that up?"

"Oh, the pinboard? Nah, I just need a nail and a hammer."

"Do you have those tools?"

"No."

He chuckles. "Okay. I'll bring them next time."

"Next time?" I arch my eyebrows.

He shrugs in a cute, boyish way, and my insides turn into gummy bears.

Danny Hudson must have a horrible flaw, and I need to find out what that is before my attraction to him gets out of hand.

"We're friends, aren't we?"

"Yep. Let's go already before my roommate decides to show up and get the wrong idea about us."

"She didn't spend the night?"

"It doesn't look like it."

My intention of avoiding gossip becomes moot when we encounter several people in the hallway, either heading out or going to the bathrooms. Danny and I earn curious glances, which only sets my teeth on edge.

In the car park, he veers straight to the driver's side but stops suddenly when he realizes his mistake. "Eh, you probably should be driving since it's your car."

"It's fine. I'm not fully awake yet."

I slide into the passenger side before more people see us together, pulling the hoodie over my head.

"Cold?" he asks me.

"Yeah."

"If you weren't late already, we could stop to grab coffee."

My stomach growls at the prospect of the warm and delicious caffeine treat, but I can't indulge.

"Maybe next time. I'm sorry I wasn't ready. I forgot to set my alarm."

"No worries. I didn't mind coming up to your room."

"I bet you didn't," I grumble.

He laughs. "You know, girls have it much easier. You have all those cool toys. I have to make do with my hand."

I sink farther into the seat. I just pictured Danny wanking off, and that makes my core throb. My memories of last night come to the forefront of my mind, making my face feel hot again. I'm glad the hoodie is hiding it. But instead of changing the subject, I make it worse.

"That's not true. What about blow-up dolls?"

"Have you seen the size of those? It's not like I can hide them under my pillow."

"There's also this device made out of silicone or something that's supposed to replicate a woman's vagina. Dudes say it feels almost like the real deal."

Danny groans. "Sadie, stop talking about sex toys."

"You started it."

"Well, now I want to stop," he grits out, almost as if he's in pain.

"Why?" On a hunch, I drop my gaze to his crotch and see the huge bulge his sweatpants can't hide. *God have mercy.* "Oh. Sorry."

He tries to fix his pants in a way that it's not obvious he's sporting wood. Of course I have to open my big mouth again.

"It's fine. I get that guys can't always control what their wieners do."

"It would help if you'd stop staring at it," he grumbles.

I look out the window, covering my mouth and trying to suppress the laughter that bubbled up my throat. I fail.

"Stop laughing, Sadie. This isn't funny."

The giggles take over, and I can't stop.

"I'm sorry, but you have to see the humor in this situation." I wipe the tears from the corners of my eyes. That's how hard I'm laughing.

He grins. "Fine. It was funny. I'm glad we're friends. I'd be double mortified if you were a girl I was trying to score with."

My heart constricts in my chest at his reminder that he isn't interested in me. But I can't complain. I was the one who set the rules, after all.

14

DANNY

GETTING Sadie out of my head after the sex toy convo was hard. I kept imagining her playing with them, which left me in a state of semi-arousal in the most inappropriate moments. I couldn't even look Coach Clarkson in the eye. What would he think about me if he knew I was lusting after his daughter?

Mercifully, Andy didn't give me a hard time about Sadie, even after I revealed she was Coach Clarkson's daughter. I have to thank Jane for that reprieve; whenever she's around, Andy only has eyes for her.

In an exercise of self-restraint, I manage to keep my contact with Sadie to a few messages here and there throughout the rest of the week. I felt tempted to invite her to hang out, but that wouldn't help me at all. In just a few days, she managed to get under my skin. It's crazy how much I miss her already, and I barely know her.

Friday morning, I get a call from the garage to let me know the car is ready. The damage was more extensive than their first assessment, so the repair cost was more than five hundred dollars. The knowledge made me consumed with guilt, which is nonsense. Sadie wrecked my car, after all. But I still avoided telling her until the last minute, right before Andy was getting ready to give me a lift.

I send her a message on WhatsApp. She doesn't answer, and a moment later, I get a call from a number I don't recognize.

"Hello?"

"Hey, Danny. It's me. Sadie."

"Whose phone is this?"

"Oh, I finally got a US number. You'd better save it in your contacts. Anyway, I'm calling to ask if you need me to drive you to the garage. Then I can pay the bill."

I glance at Andy, who's eating a snack in the kitchen. I should tell Sadie I don't need a ride, but I would still need to swing by her place to get the money. It'd be easier to just let her drive me there instead of bothering Andy.

"Yeah. Sounds good. What time do you think you can be here?"

Andy snaps his head in my direction, frowning.

"Ten minutes tops. Does that work?"

"Yeah."

"Okay, see you soon."

"Who was that?" Andy asks after I put the phone away.

"Sadie. She's taking me to the garage."

His lips curl into a knowing grin. "Is she now? You sure enjoy spending time with the coach's daughter."

"Shut up, man." I flop on the couch and turn the TV on.

Not satisfied, Andy walks over and sits next to me. "I get the appeal. Forbidden fruit always tastes better."

"Oh yeah? Was that why you went after Jane?"

My comment erases the mirth off his face in an instant. "You know it wasn't like that with Jane."

"Fair. Just like it isn't like that with Sadie. We're just friends."

"Uh-huh. Sure. I'll pretend I believe you."

"I'm not kidding, Andy. So stop with the cupid shit, all right?"

"Are you saying if the opportunity presents itself, you're going to hook up with someone else at the Pike party tonight?"

I scoff. "Shit. Is it tonight? I forgot about it."

"Yeah, it's tonight, and you're going."

"*I'm* going? What about you and Jane?"

"Nah, we're staying home tonight. Gotta make up for the time she was away."

"What about Lorenzo?" I ask.

"He has a sleepover. Everything is arranged. All I need is to get rid of you for a few hours."

"Gee, way to make me feel good about being your roommate."

"Come on. It's not like I'm asking you to find a place to crash tonight. Just do me a favor and don't come home before midnight."

Before I can reply, I receive a text from Sadie saying she's downstairs.

"Fine. I'll go to the stupid party." I get up and head for the door.

"Maybe Sadie wants to go," Andy chimes in before I walk out.

"Right. Whatever. See you later."

Like I'd ask her to come to the party with me. Maybe I *should* hook up with someone just to stop obsessing about her.

As soon as the idea enters my head, I reject it. I don't want to sleep with a random girl.

Outside, I search for Sadie's car. She must not have parked near the building's entrance.

"Hey, Danny," a female voice says from behind me.

I turn but haven't the faintest clue who the girl is smiling at me.

"Hi."

"Are you going to the Pike party tonight?"

I'll never get used to people acting like I owe them information about my life. Popularity was never my goal. I just want to play football.

"I'm not sure yet."

She steps closer and places her hand on my arm. "I hope you do."

A loud honk makes her jump back. We both turn to the street. Sadie just stopped in the middle of the road. Her passenger window is down, and she's leaning closer to it.

"Hey, lover boy. Get in here," she says.

My face splits into a broad smile. My reaction is not for this random chick's benefit. I'm genuinely happy to see Sadie. Too happy, actually.

Settle down, stupid heart.

"Is that your girlfriend?" the girl asks.

"Sure," I reply absentmindedly and rush to Sadie's car.

She takes off before I have the chance to put my seat belt on.

"Whoa. What's the hurry?"

"I was blocking traffic."

"There was no one behind us." I click the seat belt in place.

"Well, I don't want to get stuck in traffic. Katrina invited me to a party, and she wants to doll me up. I have no idea what that entails or how long it will take."

"Are you talking about the Pike party?"

"I don't know. Some Greek party. I wasn't paying attention. Why? Are you going?"

"I was thinking about it." I look out the window to hide my lying face.

I don't know why I felt the need to lie to her about it when I know I'll be there. It's just a party. I'm an idiot.

"Cool. Then maybe I'll see you there. Although, considering Katrina has roped me into being her guinea pig, maybe it'd be better if you didn't go. There's a fifty-fifty chance that I'll look like a lost pageant contestant."

I laugh. "Damn. Now I have to go."

"Shite. I should have kept my mouth shut, huh?"

"Probably."

She yawns. "God, I'm so tired. The last thing I want is to go to a stupid party. But I promised."

"I hear ya. If you hadn't promised, I'd offer to hang out with you."

"What? In my tiny dorm room? Why couldn't we hang out at your place?"

"We can any other night, but my roommate has planned a romantic evening with his girlfriend, and he wants me out of there for a few hours."

"Ah, I see. So you *are* actually going to the party." She smirks.

"Well, I'm not sure yet. I was thinking of catching a movie."

"Ugh. That's sounds like a better idea, but like I said, I promised."

"I'll go to the party if that will make you feel better."

Not because I want to spend more time with you.

I can hear Will Ferrell saying I sit on a throne of lies. Shit.

"Hmm. Would I get to witness you fend off all those jersey chasers?"

I fidget in my seat, not liking where she's going with this.

"Uh...."

She laughs. "For fuck's sake. Relax. I'm just taking the piss. I don't care if you have a bazillion arse lickers all over you."

"You don't?"

She glances at me for a second. "Why should I?"

I grind my teeth, annoyed.

"No reason."

Fuck. I'm doing a hell of a job pretending Sadie and I are just friends.

15

SADIE

"WHAT DO YOU THINK?" Katrina turns my chair around and finally allows me to see her masterpiece.

My jaw drops. I don't look like me.

"What did you do?" I ask. "I look so pretty."

"You *are* pretty. I just enhanced your natural looks with makeup."

"My hair feels so luscious." I run my fingers through it. The blonde seems even lighter.

"That's the effect of brushing it." She laughs.

"Hey! I do brush my hair... on occasion."

"I know. But it's always in a ponytail."

"Of course. I'm always training. It'd get in the way otherwise."

"What are you planning on wearing?" she asks as she collects all her beauty products and puts them away.

I glance down at my favorite pair of jeans and flouncy top. "This."

She glances at me with an eyebrow raised. "Really? You don't want to wear a dress?"

"I only own one dress, and it's boring as hell. I prefer jeans anyway." I stand and go in search of my shoes.

"How about a skirt? You've got those soccer player legs. You shouldn't hide them."

I do have nice legs, but I never bothered flaunting them before. I want to look my best tonight though, and it has nothing to do with a certain someone who's going to be at the party. My pulse accelerates just by thinking about Danny. Crap.

"I suppose I could wear a skirt." I look in my drawers, remembering I already unpacked my micro jean skirt.

Anika made me buy it on a dare, but I never felt like wearing it, to be honest. It still has the tag on it. I change out of my jeans and into the skirt, then grab my Doc Martens from the closet.

Katrina scrunches her nose. "Are you seriously wearing those ugly boots?"

I press a hand over my chest. "How dare you offend my Doc Martens? They're classic."

She shrugs. "If you say so. It doesn't really matter. No one will be looking at your feet."

I roll my eyes. "I'm not going to this party in the hopes of scoring. I just want to have fun with my friends."

"And is one of your friends a tall and handsome football player?" She smiles slyly.

I watch her through slitted eyes. "Yes, Danny is one of my friends. And that's all we are. Don't get any ideas."

"So you wouldn't care if I went after him?"

A sliver of jealousy spears my chest. I can't help but glare at Katrina, even though I should be keeping my expression neutral.

"I don't care," I say through clenched teeth.

"Holy shiiit. That was the most intense death glare I've ever received in my life."

I sit on my bed to put my boots on and effectively avoid making eye contact with Katrina. "Whatever."

Boots laced up, I jump up with sudden jittery energy and reach for my small purse on my desk. I can only fit my phone, keys, and some cash, but Katrina is driving tonight, so I don't need to worry about bringing my license.

"I'm ready. Let's go."

"Eager, aren't we?" she teases.

"Yes, I'm eager to mingle with people who are not getting on my nerves."

"Gee, you're so touchy. I won't say another word about Danny. Promise."

GOOD ON HER WORD, Katrina doesn't mention Danny on the drive to the party. It seems we arrive just when the place is filling up. We follow the flow of partygoers going into the house, but soon Katrina is swarmed by her sorority sisters. Not wanting to be engulfed by that sea of high shrieks and phony smiles, I step aside and lose sight of her. My teammates said they'd come, so I pull my phone out and send a message to our WhatsApp group.

ME: I'm at the party. Where is everyone?

VANESSA: We're all the way in the back. Beware of the dicks in the kitchen.

ME: You have to be more specific than that.

JOANNE: Nick Fowler and his buddies.

ME: Don't worry. I can handle a few tossers.

I'm tempted to text Danny too, but think better of it. There are a lot of people here and we might end up missing each other, but I won't seek him out, no matter how much I want to see him.

I push my way through the throng of people until I finally reach the kitchen. There is a group of guys huddled together, filling red Solo cups and laughing about something. They look positively pissed already. I ignore them and continue toward the door to the back. One of them sees me and steps in front of it, blocking my way.

"Hello, gorgeous. Where do you think you're going?"

"Taking into account that you're not my father or anyone who matters, I don't bloody need to tell you anything. Now move."

"Burn, Fowler!" One of his friends laughs, and the others join in.

So this is the wanker Vanessa warned me about. His eyes flash with annoyance as he takes a step into my personal space. "Such a bitchy attitude for a pretty face. Don't worry, I can fix your bad manners in no time."

"Listen up, creep, because this is the only warning you're getting. Move any closer and you can forget procreation. Although, thinking about it, I'd be doing humanity a favor by ripping your nut sack off."

I can see Nick is not taking my threat seriously by the way his lips curl up in amusement. Sometimes, words aren't enough; people need to be shown you mean business. I really wasn't looking forward to getting into a brawl with anyone tonight, but hell, I'm not going to be coerced by an asshole who thinks a penis gives him the power to say and do whatever he pleases.

"Hello, party people!" a male voice shouts from behind me. "Welcome to La Casa Pike."

Nick looks over my head and twists his face into a scowl. I half turn to see who came in. There's a guy wearing a paper crown on his head with a pretty blonde who doesn't look too happy to be standing next to him.

"Hey, Leo," one of Nick's friends says. "You're out of booze, man."

"Only because you drank it all, jackass."

He staggers forward in my general direction. His eyes are glazed over, and to avoid getting pushed right into Nick, I jump aside. Leo's drunken antics distract Nick enough to allow me to shove him out of my way.

"Hey, where do you think you're going?" he asks, grabbing my arm.

In a knee-jerk reaction, I kick back, hitting his shin hard. He releases my arm and curses.

"Fucking bitch!"

"I warned you, arsehole."

I'm out the door before he can say anything else. My heart is racing as I stride through the backyard. I didn't expect such a high-intensity situation tonight. It wasn't the same, but it put me back in the evening in London when Anika and I were accosted. I hate that someone like Nick Fowler made me relive my darkest nightmare. Fucking hell.

There's a bonfire going, but I don't see any of my teammates near it. I do see Danny though, talking to some girl I don't know. I get jealous all over again, and that just adds insult to injury. This evening is turning out to be a total bust, and I'm a second from going home.

I pivot, changing my course of direction, and end up bumping into someone else I didn't care to see tonight.

Danny's ex.

"Watch where you're go—oh, it's you." Her lips twist into a malicious grin. She looks over my shoulder, probably in Danny's direction, then back at me. "Ah, it seems you've been replaced already. Too bad."

"Piss off, psycho." I push her out of my way, seeing nothing in front of me. My temper isn't rising—it's already reached boiling point. If I bump into another annoying person, I might punch them in the throat.

"Sadie! Over here." Vanessa waves at me.

I walk toward her and see she's hanging out with Melody and Joanne. No sign of the Three Musketeers.

"Jeez, what happened to you?" Joanne asks.

"I've met the dick, the witch, and now I need a drink."

"Oh my God. She's spewing bad poetry. Give her a beer already," Melody tells Vanessa.

"I'd prefer something stronger."

Melody raises an eyebrow. "Sorry, sugar. This isn't a bar. We only have beer."

"I didn't mean it like that."

Vanessa shoves a bottle of Corona in my hand. "Don't listen to Melody. Here, drink this. It'll take the edge off."

"Thanks."

I twist the cap off and take a couple big chugs, emptying half the bottle. Then I wipe off my lips with the back of my hand. Classy I'm not.

"Better?" Vanessa smirks.

"Not yet, but I'll get there. You weren't kidding. Nick Fowler is a major arsehole. I had to kick him to get rid of the wanker."

"You kicked Nick?" Joanne asks. "Where?"

"Please tell me in his junk," Vanessa pipes up.

"I got his shin. Sorry to disappoint."

I drink some more, then ask, "So this is it? We just hang out here and drink beers?"

"For now. Why? Too boring for you?" Melody retorts.

"No, I'm just wondering. There's music inside. I don't mind dancing."

Vanessa opens her mouth to reply, but then something behind me catches her attention. "Ah shit."

"What?" I turn and see the blonde girl who came with Leo into the kitchen marching in our direction.

"It's my twin sister, Heather."

"Oh."

A moment later, Heather joins us, and Vanessa asks, "What's up, sis? Got tired of your boyfriend already?"

"Leo is a jackass. Can I have a beer?" She reaches for the cooler next to Melody without waiting for an answer.

"Hold on a second, honey. This is for Ravens only. Why don't you go back to your flock?"

"Mel, come on. Let Heather have a beer," Vanessa chimes in.

"Fine."

"Thanks." Heather takes a bottle from the cooler and, just like me, drains half of it in large gulps.

"Whoa. Slow down, Heather," Vanessa says.

I'm distracted when I feel a tap on my shoulder. I turn around and stare right into Danny's eyes. The breath whooshes out of my lungs. I wasn't expecting him and therefore didn't put up my shield.

"Hey," he says.

"Hi," I squeak.

"Did you just get here?"

"Uh, no."

"Hello, Danny, how are you?" Melody says in a mocking tone that indicates she caught on to his rudeness. He didn't acknowledge any of them.

"Oh, hi, girls," he replies sheepishly, then turns his attention back to me. "You look nice. Nothing at all like a lost pageant contestant."

"Yeah, Katrina did a good job."

"I don't think I've ever seen your hair down." He reaches over to take a strand between his fingers.

Fuck a duck. What the hell is he doing?

I clear my throat. "It's not like we hang out all the time."

He drops his hand as his expression becomes more serious. "True. Well, I'd better go look for Puck and Paris."

"What? Andy and Jane aren't coming?" Vanessa asks.

"Ah, not tonight. They're still in the honeymoon phase." He shrugs. "Well, I guess I'll see you guys later."

"Sure," I try to reply, like I don't care, but I think I end up sounding a bit snobbish. *Shite.*

Once Danny is out of earshot, Joanne says, "Was that weird or what?"

"I don't know if it was weird, or he simply felt that Sadie's cold behavior was too much like Siberia," Vanessa replies.

"What are you talking about?" I look at her, genuinely surprised.

"You acted like you couldn't wait to get rid of the guy," Heather replies, then takes a sip of her beer.

"I did not!"

"Uh, you kinda did." Joanne nods.

Stumped, I glance in the direction Danny went. *Fuck. Did I mess up already?* I didn't mean to act like a cow.

"Ah, who cares? He's just another dude who thinks he's the king of the world because he has a sausage between his legs," Melody butts in.

"Danny is not like that," I retort. "Shite. I have to talk to him."

"You do that," Vanessa says, smiling from ear to ear.

I don't have time to dissect that expression. I finish the rest of my beer and head after Danny. He went back into the house already, and I can't find him that easily. It's too busy. *Come on, now. He's tall. It shouldn't be that hard.* I wind up in the main room where the DJ is set up. People are dancing to an upbeat tune that, at any other time, I might appreciate. But I'm too concerned about Danny to care.

Bloody hell. A dude is making me act like a deranged twat.

What the actual fuck? I'm doing exactly what I said I wouldn't do.

I stop in my tracks, but the crowd's motion pushes me forward until I'm right in the middle of the dance floor. I don't know how, but someone managed to ride the wave of writhing bodies while carrying a tray of shots. He stops in front of me and hands me one.

"What is it?" I take the small plastic cup.

"Tequila."

All right. I can use that. I toss the shot back, then take another cup from the tray. Why the hell not?

It doesn't take long for me to feel the effects of the drink. My body relaxes, and I forget Danny for a while. I dance and dance, losing track of time. And when "Blinding Lights" by The Weeknd starts to play, I close my eyes and let the music take control. All my problems evaporate into thin air and nothing matters besides the beat of the song. I'm definitely buzzin'.

I feel hands touching me, pulling and pushing in different directions. Even with my eyes open, I can't make out the faces of the people around. The room is spinning, and everything is blurry. Maybe I drank too much, but hell, I've never gotten that drunk after a couple shots of tequila and a beer. I decide that maybe I need fresh air and some water.

Moving through the crowd isn't as easy as before, and my legs don't seem to want to cooperate. Vertigo hits me, and I end up staggering forward and bumping into a body. Arms circle around my waist, and I'm pulled closer to a bloke who is smiling too broadly and smells of beer and sweat. I try to push him off me, but he only keeps his hold on me tighter.

"Not so fast, sugar. We have a score to settle."

"Let me go," I say feebly.

I push against his frame, but it's like my arms are made out of cotton candy. With me firmly in his grasp, he steers me farther away from the dance floor. I have no idea where he's taking me. I just know I have to get away.

"Sadie," I hear someone call out, but I can't pinpoint the direction the voice came from. Everything is so damn loud.

A second later, I'm pulled from whoever was holding me into the arms of another person. At this point, dark dots are clouding my eyesight, and I feel like I might pass out at any moment. There are shouting and angry words exchanged, but I'm too far gone to distinguish the words.

Then my legs seem to vanish from under me, and everything is pitch black.

16

DANNY

When I saw Sadie being dragged by Nick Fowler, I knew something was wrong. She'd never associate with that jackass. The moment I got close and saw her condition, anger like I'd never known surged through me, making me see red. I wanted to punch the asshole's face into a pulp. Sadie was barely conscious.

But I couldn't get into a fight with him while he had Sadie trapped under his arm.

Good thing I wasn't alone.

While I pried her from his grasp, Paris got into his face. If some of the frat boys hadn't come in to intervene, I'm sure he'd have done what I wanted to do myself. They dragged Nick away, preventing a fight that would cost us big-time.

Now Sadie is passed out in my arms, and I don't know what to do.

Paris turns his attention to her, still breathing hard from the altercation.

"She's out cold," I tell him. "I don't know what happened. She was fine when I talked to her earlier."

"Was she drinking?"

"She had a beer in her hand."

Paris peels her eyelid back. Being premed, he's more qualified to figure out what's wrong with her than I am.

"Her pupils are dilated. You said she was fine. How long ago was that?"

"I don't know. Maybe an hour."

He rubs his face. "I don't want to make you even more worried, but I think she was drugged."

"What? Are you sure?"

"I'm almost positive."

"I should take her to the emergency room, right?"

"Danny?" Sadie asks in a small voice.

"Sadie, honey. Are you okay?"

Her eyes are only half open and unfocused.

"I can't feel my body. Where am I?"

"We're still at the party."

"What party?" Her eyelids begin to close again.

"Maybe you should take her to the hospital," Paris tells me.

"What? Why?" she asks in a high-pitched voice.

I don't like how people are staring at us, so I move toward the front door and don't answer her until we're outside. Paris is right behind me.

"What did you take, Sadie?" I ask.

"Two shots of tequila, I think."

"Do you remember who gave you those shots?" Paris asks.

"No."

"Shit. There could be more people affected," he says as he stares at the house.

"Go back and tell Puck and the others to keep an eye out for possible victims," I tell him. "I'll take Sadie to the emergency room."

"I don't need to go to the hospital," Sadie insists. "I just need to sleep this off."

"Sadie, I think you've been drugged."

"Roofied?"

"We don't know."

"I can't go back to the hospital, Danny. Please don't take me back. Please," she begs, twisting my insides.

"Don't take me back," she said. What does that mean?

"If she was given a roofie, the effects should wear off between sixteen and thirty-five hours," Paris explains. "If you keep an eye on her, she should be fine."

I glance at her, and agony rips through me. Her eyes are shut again, but I can see the streak marks the tears left on her cheeks.

If I find out who gave her those shots, I'm going to kill him.

Paris returns to the party, and I head to my car. People stare at us, and I know tomorrow the gossip mill will be running wild with crazy stories. Not important right now. My only concern is to make sure Sadie is okay.

Afraid she'll throw up if I lay her down in the back seat, I place her in in the front and buckle her seat belt. Her head lolls forward, heavy and almost lifeless, making my heart twist painfully with worry.

During the drive, I make the decision to go back to my place. I don't know her roommate, but I can't rule out the possibility that she might bring back company.

I hope Andy and Jane are done with their evening activities. Both will have a myriad of questions if they see me carrying an unconscious girl into the apartment, but I can deal with them later.

There's no sign of the lovebirds in the living room, and the apartment is quiet. Hopefully they're asleep already.

Walking softly, I make a beeline to my room. I'm glad I tidied up earlier and got rid of the mountain of dirty clothes scattered everywhere. Carefully, I lay Sadie on my bed. Her short skirt has hiked up to her hips, giving me a view of her black underwear. Damn. I feel like a pervert for accidentally looking. I have to cover her.

I head out to grab a blanket from the living room, and when I get back, I find Sadie leaning over the side of the bed, making retching sounds.

"Shit." I rush to her, skidding to a halt before I step over the mess she left on the floor.

"I'm so sorry, Danny. I couldn't run to the bathroom."

I push her hair out of the way. "It's okay, Sadie. Do you think you're still going to throw up?"

"I don't know. I got vomit all over me and your bed."

"Don't worry about it. Let's get you cleaned up." I lift her from the bed and prop her up against me.

She can barely walk on her own, which makes me furious all over again. What would have happened if Nick Fowler had managed to leave the party with her?

In the bathroom, I feel torn about how to proceed. Sadie can't stand on her own, and unfortunately, there's no bathtub here.

"Do you think you can sit on the toilet for a second?"

"Yeah."

She drops like a sack of potatoes and clutches the side of the counter to keep upright while I turn on the shower.

"You got vomit all over your shirt," she says.

"It's fine."

I take it off because it seems I need to get into the shower with her anyway.

Then it hits me. I can't take off her clothes.

"Uh, Andy's girlfriend is here. Should I ask her to help you?"

"Are you mental? I don't want a stranger seeing me like this."

"You need assistance. You can't even stand up."

"Why can't you do it?"

"I don't want to make you uncomfortable."

She waves her hand awkwardly. "I puked all over your room. We passed uncomfortable five exits back."

Sadie lets go of the counter and tries to pull her soiled top up, but she topples forward instead. I catch her just before she plunges headfirst into the tiled floor.

"Careful there."

"I think you need to help me out of my clothes."

"Okay."

"I don't care if you peek. Although, I don't think I look that attractive right now."

"You're always attractive, Sadie, no matter what."

She lifts her gaze to mine. "Really?"

I shouldn't have said anything. I don't even know how the words left my mouth.

"Come on. Let's get you out of these filthy clothes."

She attempts to sit straighter, but it's clear the drug has reached its peak. I can't believe she hasn't passed out yet.

"Lean back a little. I won't let you fall."

She does as I told her and braces her hand against the counter. I pull her top up, glad it doesn't have a zipper on the back. I didn't think to check first. I was expecting to find a bra underneath, but she isn't wearing one, and I get a full view of her breasts. My face and ears burn because despite what she said, it doesn't feel right to see her topless. I have every intention of looking away, but something else catches my attention—a red scar on her side. It looks recent judging by the color.

Her words come back to me. She didn't want to go back to the hospital. Does this scar have anything to do with it?

"Are you looking at my battle wound?" she asks.

I force my eyes to return to her face, embarrassed she caught me staring. "Sorry. I didn't mean to."

"It's okay. I don't mind that you see it. I don't mind a lot of things when it comes to you. Why is that, Danny?"

I swallow hard, not knowing how to answer the question. She's pretty loopy, and I'm sure she won't remember this conversation tomorrow, but somehow, she's never been more honest. Maybe that's the drug at play too.

"I don't know, Sadie. It's the same for me too. Probably why we're friends."

Her eyebrows furrow. "Bollocks to friendship. This is way bigger than that."

I couldn't agree more, but now is not the time to discuss what's going on between us.

"We can talk about that tomorrow. Let's get you cleaned up."

I can't bring myself to remove her skirt as well, not when her comments have made me even more aware of my conflicted feelings about our relationship. I hoist Sadie up, throwing her arm over my shoulder, and then head into the shower stall. It's big enough that both of us fit in it. The water is already warm, but she still jolts when the jets hit her head.

"Ugh. Why am I getting all wet? Is it raining inside?"

"It's just the shower. You had vomit all over you, remember?"

"No."

She doesn't complain further; instead, she lets out a soft moan and rests her head against my chest, making it really hard to wash her, or ignore how her breasts are now pressed against me. I'm keenly aware how the water turned her nipples into pebbles too.

Fuck me.

I decide that just rinsing her off will have to do. There's no way

I'm lathering her with soap. I shut off the water and then dry her off with a towel. Sadie finally passes out on me then. I lift her up, cradling her like a baby with the towel covering her upper body, and return to my room. It stinks of vomit, reminding me of the mess I still have to clean up. She did get some on my bed, so I set her in my chair, then quickly change the sheets and wipe off the floor.

Sadie is snoring by the time I finally put her into bed. Even with her makeup all smeared, she's so beautiful that I can't help but stare at her for a moment. My chest feels tight suddenly, like I can't breathe.

A soft knock on the door draws my attention away from her. I'm not surprised to find Andy and Jane standing outside my room. I did make more noise than I intended when I took my dirty sheets to the laundry and started the machine.

"Hey, guys," I say.

"Is everything okay?" Jane asks.

"Yeah. Sorry if I woke you."

"We weren't sleeping." Andy tries to peer over my shoulder into my room. "Got company there, Danny-boy?"

"Yes. But it's not what you think."

"Oh?" His eyebrows arch.

"Since you're going to find out tomorrow morning anyway, I may as well tell you now. I've got Sadie here. She took something she shouldn't have, and I thought it was best to bring her here to keep an eye on her."

"What do you mean, she took something she shouldn't have?" Jane asks, her eyes growing rounder.

"Paris believes she was roofied."

"What?" Andy's voice rises in anger. "Please tell me we know by whom."

His fury rekindles my own, but I put a damper on it. Getting bent out of shape now won't help me. My focus tonight is taking care of Sadie.

"No. But I left Paris and the rest of the guys to investigate when I left the party."

"I can't believe that happened. It's horrible. What if other girls were drugged too?" Jane says.

"The guys were keeping an eye out for other possible victims," I reply.

Jane hugs her middle, looking distressed. Andy pulls her into a side hug and kisses her temple. "Don't worry, babe. The Rebels won't let anyone get taken advantage of."

She nods and then asks me, "Where are you going to sleep? In the living room?"

"I want to stay nearby in case she pukes again, so I'll just sleep on the floor."

"Dude, we have sleeping bags. Hold on."

Andy disappears down the hall.

"I'll grab some extra blankets and pillows," Jane adds.

A minute later, they return with their items. Jane also grabbed a couple bottles of water, which hadn't occurred to me. They head back to Andy's room, but not before they make me promise to call them if I need anything. I close the door but keep it unlocked, then set everything down by the end of the bed and go check on Sadie. She seems fine, and her breathing is steady.

I sit next to her for a moment and brush her damp hair off her forehead. I probably shouldn't have dunked her under the shower. What if she catches a cold because I made her sleep with wet hair?

Shit, I'm an idiot. Maybe I can dry it off a bit more with a towel.

I begin to slide off the mattress when Sadie murmurs my name.

Her eyes are still closed though. She's probably dreaming.

"Don't go, Danny. Don't leave me alone."

"I'm not going anywhere, sweetheart," I reply, even though I don't think she's really talking to me.

I forget about the towel and lie next to her for a moment. I had every intention of moving to the floor in the next minute, but when my eyes begin to shut, I tell myself I'll relocate in a second.

Should have known it wouldn't happen.

17

SADIE

My mouth is as dry as a desert and tastes like a dead animal has been rotting inside for weeks. Every muscle in my body hurts, and the pounding in my head makes me wish for a swift death.

What the hell happened last night?

When I finally manage to open my eyes, I don't recognize the room I'm in. I'm also naked from the waist up, and there's a towel bunched around my waist. But what makes my pulse skyrocket is the muscled arm across my stomach.

Fuck. What did I do?

I turn my head and only see a mop of blond curls at first. *No. No. No*. Did I sleep with Danny last night? I don't remember anything. The last bit of memory I have is dancing by myself at the party.

I try to push Danny's arm off me slowly without waking him, but my movements are lethargic, and I feel weak as hell. I only manage to move him an inch when he stirs and pulls me closer to him. My heart wrestles with the meaning of this gesture. On one hand, if I did sleep with Danny, it's because I finally accepted that we're more than friends. But on the other hand, the reason why I wanted to keep things platonic between us has not simply disappeared.

I'm totally freaking out and don't know what to do.

There's nothing for it. It seems I can't escape without waking him, and I probably should find out what exactly happened last night. Running away won't make my problems vanish.

I shake him. "Danny, wake up."

He groans and then turns his face to mine. His eyes only open halfway, still clouded by sleepy fog. A couple of beats later, they fly open, and faster than lightning, he pulls not only his arm off me but his entire body in a movement so sudden, he ends up rolling off the bed in the process.

Shite. That doesn't bode well.

Pulling the towel up to cover my tits, I lean on my elbow and ask, "Danny, are you okay?"

He sits up and looks at me, startled. "Sadie, I'm so sorry. I didn't mean to fall asleep next to you."

Relief washes over me. He wouldn't be saying that if we had shagged last night. At least I don't think he would.

"What the bloody hell happened? Why am I in your room and half naked?"

His expression contorts into a grimace. "You don't remember anything?"

Fear makes my heart feel tight in my chest. "The last thing I remember is dancing for a bit."

He begins to get up but stops mid-motion, drops his gaze to his crotch—I'm guessing—and then returns to his sitting position on the floor.

"Do you mind throwing me a pillow? I'm only wearing boxer shorts."

"And I'm only wearing my skirt."

"Only because you puked all over your shirt last night."

Shame makes my face erupt in flames. I lean back, sinking against the pillow and closing my eyes. "Shite. I got too drunk, didn't I?"

"That's not what happened."

Danny's voice comes from a different place in the room, so I open my eyes. He decided to get up in the end, and I get a perfect view of his fine ass. His boxer shorts leave nothing to the imagination. I know this is the worst possible moment for it, but the sight turns me on.

Why am I getting horny during one of the most embarrassing situations of my life, and when I'm feeling like crap to boot?

"What happened then?" I ask, wincing when I notice the yearning in my voice.

I hope he didn't.

He grabs a pair of sweatpants from his drawer and puts them on too fast. This situation must not be easy for him either.

With a grim expression on his face, he walks over, holding a T-shirt. "Put this on. I'll turn around."

"You probably already saw them anyway."

And something else too. My scar.

"Well, it couldn't be helped last night." His cheeks become pinker.

Damn. Embarrassment is too cute on him, and it's turning my insides into mush. Also, how unfair is it that Danny looks like a fucking god with bed hair, while I probably look like a witch? I'm afraid to look at my reflection in the mirror.

Brat that I am, I drop the towel before he can turn around just to see his reaction.

"Sadie!" He pivots, crossing his arms. "Can you please not make this harder?"

"Why is it harder, Danny?" I tease, but I do want to know.

"You were drugged last night," he blurts out.

I'm not sure what I was expecting him to say, but it definitely wasn't that. The blood seems to freeze in my veins, and I'm unable to string a sentence together.

I. Was. Drugged.

The words seem to ring in my ears, drowning all other sounds. I feel sick all of a sudden, and not wanting Danny to see me throw up again, I jump off the bed, still topless, and rush to the bathroom. Kneeling in front of the toilet, I pull my hair back and puke whatever is left in my stomach. It turns out there isn't much, but I keep retching as if my body wants to expel not only the drug from my system but also the fact that it happened.

My eyes are teary when I finally fall on my arse. I'm too tired to even pull my legs up and hug them.

"Sadie, do you need anything?" Danny asks from outside the bathroom.

"No. I just want to be alone for a moment."

"Okay. I'll be outside if you need anything."

I don't move from my spot for I don't know how long. During the time, I'm bulldozed by a myriad of different emotions. At first I'm mortified that I was drugged and needed to be rescued like a damsel in distress. Then I'm ashamed for feeling guilty that I got drugged, followed by angry at myself for allowing it to happen in the first place. Any shrink would say that's displaced anger. The only person at fault here is the motherfucker who drugged me.

I feel like crying, but the tears won't come. It's no surprise, since I don't usually cry when I'm feeling sad or angry, and rarely when I'm in pain. All I know is I can't hide in Danny's bathroom forever, so I push myself off the floor, hating how my legs shake in the process. Some arsehole turned me into a puny victim, and that makes me want to yell and break things.

A new sense of urgency takes hold of me. I have to find out everything Danny knows.

I glance at the mirror and wince. As I suspected, I look like I've been dragged through hell. My hair is a bloody mess, half of it twisted into knots and the other half hanging limp like a forgotten dirty rag. I also still stink of vomit. And Danny slept next to me. If there was ever any chance for a possible romance between us, what happened last night effectively killed it with acid.

I need a shower, pronto.

I jump into the stall, not bothering to wait for the water to warm up. I wash my hair twice, getting lost a bit in the scent that my brain has already associated to Danny. An ice-cold fever sweeps over my body when goose bumps form on my arms, despite the fact that the water has already heated up. I'm on edge, wired, and I don't know if that's a side effect of the drug or if it's my stupid body wanting Danny's cock between my legs.

I brace my hands against the wall, letting my head drop between my shoulders. *Football. That's the only thing that matters. That's what I need to focus on from now on. Not stupid parties, not friendships with impossibly good-looking guys. Just football.*

I repeat the mantra in my head as I finish washing up. The bathroom is foggy when I finally step out of the shower. In my rush, I didn't look for a towel first. There's one hanging on the peg—probably Danny's, and I'm not about to borrow it. Luckily, I find clean ones in the cupboard under the sink. As I dry off, I stare with disgust at my skirt and knickers. I can't bring myself to wear them. They also have a faint smell of puke. Great.

Wrapped in the towel, I grab my clothes and return to Danny's bedroom. He's not here, but getting closer to the now made bed, I see he left me more than a T-shirt to wear. There's a pair of girl sweatpants and a brand-new pair of undies with the tag still on.

Blind jealousy rushes through me. Did these belong to Danny's ex? I think I'd rather parade naked than wear them.

The door opens, and Danny comes in carrying a tray of food. He stops in his tracks. "Oh, I didn't know you were out of the shower already."

"Where did these clothes come from?" I ask brusquely.

"They're Jane's. Andy's girlfriend."

"Oh."

Now I feel foolish for getting all worked up about it.

He nods. "I'll just set this on the desk and let you get ready."

"Okay."

When he's on his way out, I say, "Thank you, Danny. For real."

He smiles, and my heart beats faster. *Stop betraying me, traitorous muscle!*

"You're welcome. For real."

DANNY

"How is she?" Jane asks when I return to the living room.

"I think she'll be okay."

"We probably shouldn't be here when she comes out." Jane reaches for her purse and gives Andy a meaningful glance. "Come on, Andy."

"Guys, you don't need to leave. I can talk to Sadie in my bedroom."

Andy stands from the couch despite my protest. "We have to pick up Lorenzo anyway. It's all good, bro. Go take care of your girl."

"She's not my girl," I grit out.

He smiles wickedly. "Whatever you say."

I wait until they're gone to check on Sadie. I knock first this time; I do not need to see her naked again. As much as I want to forget what I saw last night, it's hard to erase the image of her perfect breasts from my mind.

And now I'm officially in perv territory.

"Come on in," she says.

She's dressed in the clothes I left her, and I won't deny that seeing her wearing my T-shirt stirs feelings in me I shouldn't look too closely at.

"How are you feeling?"

"Really awful." She glances at the food I brought her and twists her nose.

"What's wrong?"

"I want to eat, but I'm afraid my stomach will expel anything I put inside."

"Try the Saltines. They should be okay to handle."

She nibbles on one, then immediately puts the cracker down. "What happened at the party, Danny?"

I swallow the lump in my throat, hating what I have to tell her.

"I don't know who gave you the drug, Sadie. You said someone gave you a couple tequila shots. When I found you, you were with Nick Fowler."

"What?" I shriek. "I'd never go near that guy of my own free will."

"I know that. I was so angry, I wanted to punch that motherfucker in the face. But whisking you out of the party was my number one priority. He's getting what's coming to him though. Don't worry."

Her eyes blaze with fury. "Do you think he's the one who spiked my drink?"

"I don't know. Paris went back into the party to investigate and also to see if anyone else had been drugged. I haven't talked to him yet."

She pulls her hair back. "I can't believe I was that stupid. I know not to accept drinks from strangers."

"Don't you dare blame yourself for what happened, Sadie," I say angrily.

Her eyes widen at my outburst. "Trust me, I've already given myself that spiel. I ran through the entire gamut of feelings when I was in your bathroom."

I rub my face. "I'm sorry I didn't find you sooner."

"Hey, don't you go blaming yourself for it, either. You're not my bodyguard. And why would I need one at a party anyway? Everyone should feel safe."

"You're right."

We stare at each other for a moment, and I fight the urge to walk over and pull her into my arms. She breaks the connection first by looking at her feet.

"Was I a terrible burden to you after the party?"

"Nothing I couldn't handle. Don't worry."

"Nice evasion, Danny." She looks up, her lips curled into a grin. "That means I was a nightmare."

I smirk. "Fine. If you want to know all the gritty details of what a pain in the ass you were, I'll tell you."

"Go on. Spare me nothing."

"After you puked all over yourself, my bed, and the floor, I had to stick you under the shower, hence why you weren't wearing your shirt."

"Why didn't you take off my skirt too?"

"Uh...." I rub my neck. "Honestly, I already felt guilty enough that I'd seen your breasts."

She laughs. "So what? They're just tits, Danny. Cows have them."

"Nothing like yours," I reply, exasperated.

The satisfied smile Sadie rewards me with tells me I fell for her trap. Devious woman.

"You let me sleep with a wet skirt on. And if you felt so bad about seeing me topless, you should have given me a shirt to wear."

"I covered you with the towel." I cross my arms. "Stop making me feel worse."

She shakes her head. "God, you're so easy to tease."

"You must be feeling better if you can think of ways to torture me."

She raises an eyebrow. "Talking about my boobs is torturing you? Good to know. As for feeling better, I'm not so sure. I'm not quite myself yet. There's the nausea, and I'm feeling weak as hell."

"I can take you to the hospital. They can run some tests and find out what drug is in your system."

The playfulness leaves Sadie's face in an instant.

"No hospitals. I can't deal with them."

"Does your scar have anything to do with it?"

She looks away, bracing her hands on the back of the chair. "Yes. Maybe one day I'll tell you about it, but not today."

"I'll be here to listen whenever you're ready."

"You're a good friend, Danny." She gives me a half smile that doesn't reach her eyes.

"Ditto."

"Even after I reenacted a scene from *The Exorcist* in your room?"

"Yeah, even after that."

Friends. That's all Sadie and I can ever be. I want to make peace with that, but I can't.

It seems this is going to be the lying season.

18

SADIE

UPON DANNY'S INSISTENCE, after I ate a bit, I took a nap and didn't wake up until midafternoon. Danny left my phone on the nightstand in case I needed to ask for something. The boy is too sweet for his own good, and if I'm not careful, I might fall head over heels for him. I can already feel the butterflies waking up in my belly. Hell, I'm giddy just thinking about him.

When I glance at my phone, I see a bunch of notifications stacked on top of one another on the screen. I open WhatsApp and find out that my teammates blew up our group chat. Vanessa is the one sending most of them.

Before they decide to march into Danny's apartment to check if I'm alive, I reply to all.

ME: I'm fine, still a little groggy from whatever I was given.

VANESSA: Thank heavens. Can you talk? I wanna call you.

ME: Sure.

A second later, the phone rings.

"Hey," I say.

"Sadie, I'm so sorry. Are you really okay?"

"I am. Don't worry. Danny is taking good care of me."

"Is he now?"

Bollocks. I shouldn't have let that slip out.

"Yeah. He's an angel."

She laughs. "What kind of angel? I hope Lucifer."

I rub my legs together as my mind takes a nosedive into the gutter once again. Maybe the drug made me horny too.

"Stop it. I don't want to picture Danny doing wicked things to me. We're just friends, and that's all we'll ever be."

"Why? If you like him and you're attracted to him, I don't see the problem. He's clearly into you."

I don't want to rejoice at her statement, not when he made it clear that he only wants to concentrate on football.

"We're both trying to focus on our careers. No time for relationships."

"Are you saying you're going to turn into a nun and not hook up with anyone?"

"I have toys. They'll do. Besides, apart from Danny, the quality of blokes I've been subjected to so far at this school is appalling."

"Slim pickings, I know. I'm livid that Nick Fowler tried to take advantage of you when you weren't yourself. He's an asshole through and through. I wouldn't be surprised if he was the one who spiked your drinks."

I share the same thought, but without proof, I can't accuse the tosser of anything.

"You didn't hear anything about who did it, then?"

"No. I know the guys on the football team were looking and asking questions, but that party was a fucking zoo. No one saw or remembers anything. At least we don't think anyone else drank what you did. Small blessings, I guess."

"Yeah."

"Anyway, I'm glad you're okay, and that you have a sinfully good-looking guardian angel looking out for you." I can hear the grin in her voice.

"Thanks for checking on me."

"Of course. We're Ravens. That means family in my book."

"I don't think Melody considers me family." I snort.

"Nah, she does, but she's jealous as fuck that you're as talented as she is."

"*As* talented? What the hell? I'm better than she is."

She snorts. "God, I forgot humbleness is not your forte."

"No, it isn't."

"When are you going home? Tomorrow?" she asks.

"Why tomorrow? I was planning to head back to the dorms today."

"Paris told me the drug is likely to stay in your body for thirty-six hours. I'd stay at Danny's if I were you, just in case you require his *assistance*."

I sigh. "For fuck's sake, Vanessa. Nothing is going on here."

"Yeah, yeah. Remember, I called it first. I demand to be in the wedding party."

"I'm hanging up now. Bye."

I end the call and lean back against the pillow. It's hard enough to lie to myself when I'm around Danny. It doesn't help when my friends keep reminding me that I'm the biggest pretender there ever was.

I scroll through my other messages. There are a few from Katrina. The first she sent soon after I left her with her sorority friends, asking where I was. The second one was drunken nonsense, and the last one was from this morning, again asking where I was. She didn't sound worried that I didn't go back to our shared room last night. I'm sure she assumed I hooked up with someone.

I send her a quick text so she knows I'm not missing, but there's not a chance in hell I'm telling her where I am.

There's a missed call from Dad, and I fear he somehow heard about what happened to me. My stomach coils tightly. I should call him back, but what if he knows? Is he going to get mad? Probably.

Ugh. What if he doesn't care? I don't know which is the worst scenario.

I'm freaking out while I stare at my phone.

A knock on the door jolts me out of the stupid panic mode.

"Sadie?" Danny calls.

"You can come in. I'm up."

I run my fingers through my hair, remembering belatedly that I just woke from a nap and must look like shite.

He sticks his head in first and catches me in the act of preening. I drop my hands quickly, making it even more obvious that I was trying to hide that I want to be pretty for him.

Kill me now. I want to go back to when I barely noticed boys. None of the blokes I knew in London looked like Danny though.

"How are you feeling?" He walks in and shuts the door.

My pulse accelerates. Why am I all of a sudden so aware that I'm alone with Danny in his room? It didn't affect me when I woke up in the morning as much as it is now. Maybe because I was too busy puking my guts out.

"Much better. Hey, quick question. Did you tell my father about what happened to me?"

His eyes widen. "No. Of course not."

I exhale loudly in relief. "Thank God. I can't handle any more drama about this. I just want to forget the whole deal."

My statement doesn't seem to sit well with Danny. He's scowling a little.

"What? You don't think I should move on?"

"That's not it. I understand your reasoning. I'm just pissed that someone did that to you and they're going to walk away unpunished."

I shrug. "That's life, Danny. Most of the time, the bad guys don't get what they deserve. Hoping otherwise just leads to disappointment."

"Was that what happened to the person who gave you that scar?"

All my barriers fly up in the blink of an eye. "What makes you think that scar was from an attack?" I snap.

Remorse seems to shine in his eyes. "I'm sorry. I didn't mean to assume or pry. You don't need to tell me."

"I know I don't."

Irritated, I throw my legs to the side of the bed and stand up too fast. The room begins to spin, and I find myself tumbling forward. In two long strides, Danny reaches me and prevents the fall.

"Careful there. You're not completely recovered yet."

"I feel fine. As a matter of fact, I want to go home."

"Sadie, is this because of my stupid question about your past? I'm sorry, okay? But I want you to stay."

I should insist about going home, but I can't think straight when I'm this close to Danny, when I can feel his accelerated heartbeat under my flattened hand over his chest. Actually, those are the very reasons I should go. But I'm weak, and I can't say no to him.

I step back, even though Danny keeps holding my arms. "Fine. But I need a change of clothes. I feel funny wearing borrowed pants."

"Okay, if you give me your keys, I can bring your stuff."

"I'll come with you."

"Sadie, you should rest. If your roommate is home, I'll ask her to pack your things."

I scrunch my nose. "Honestly, it wouldn't make a difference

who packs my stuff. It's still two strangers going through my knickers."

His eyebrows furrow. "I thought we had moved past the strangers phase after you puked all over my room and I saw your tits."

My jaw drops. "I can't believe you're throwing that in my face. You're such a bellend."

"Sorry if the truth hurts, sugar." He smirks.

I watch him through slits. "Are you trying to get on my bad side, Danny Hudson? I'm only weak for another ten hours or so, but after that, you don't really want to mess with me."

He flicks my nose. "You're cute when you're angry."

I'd kick his shin if I thought I could do it and not lose my balance. "Stop saying stuff guys say when they're trying to get laid."

Danny twists his face into an exaggerated scowl. "That may have been true before I saw the insides of your stomach. You ruined it for me, Sadie."

It's hard not to wince, but I think I manage not to give away how his joke upset me. I'm such a basket case. I want us to remain in the friend zone, yet I want him to secretly want me.

"Listen, it doesn't matter. If I'm to stay another night, I have to pack my own overnight bag. Besides, I don't want any more rumors spreading about me. If you show up at my dorm alone and leave with a duffel bag, people will think we're shacking up."

"Would that be so terrible?" My heart skips a beat, thinking he means the question, but then he continues. "Do you find me *that* abhorrent?"

"Absolutely. Now let's go. If we're lucky, Katrina won't be around."

19

SADIE

I DIDN'T FEEL like an A-lister being chased by the paparazzi in the streets of London when I went back to the dorms to grab my stuff. I didn't run into that many people, and I made Danny wait in the car. Spending another night at his place wasn't as hard as I thought it would be either. He slept on the couch in the living room, and I was so tired that I fell asleep as soon as my head hit the pillow.

I was back in my dorm room on Sunday morning, and mercifully, I didn't have to fight Danny on that. He was probably sick of me already.

I called Dad back since I'd forgotten to do so on Saturday. It turned out he was just checking on me, then invited me over to his place whenever I had the time. I said I would get back to him on that, which was code for "I will avoid you as much as I can." Is it horrible that I keep blowing him off? Sure. But it'll take more than moving closer to him to erase all the years he wasn't there for me.

Monday morning at practice, I feel the weight of all the

stares of my teammates when I enter the locker room. It was foolish of me to think they would have already forgotten Friday's incident. The thing is, I had already moved past that, and their scrutiny just got under my nerves.

"Can you guys piss off with the concerned looks? Like I said, I'm fine." I veer for my locker.

"The bitch is back. She's clearly fine," Melody pipes up.

"You haven't seen the bitch yet," I murmur.

Vanessa stops next to me. "I guess your sleepover was a bust, huh?"

"If you're inferring it was a bust because nothing happened, then you're correct and wrong at the same time."

"You lost me."

I give her a droll look. "Nothing happened, like I said it wouldn't, and it wasn't a bust."

"Then what's up with the foul mood?"

I close the metal door with a bang. "I don't know. I'm just on edge, like I have all this pent-up energy that needs to be released. I'm keen on a good practice game."

"Or pent-up sexual tension." She laughs, stepping away from me.

"Dude, you'd better pray you're playing on my team today."

"What were you guys talking about?" Joanne asks.

"Vanessa was being nosy." I sit on the bench to switch my shoes.

"Sadie, I want to apologize for Friday night. I feel awful that I didn't go check on you after you disappeared."

I look up. "What's with everyone feeling bad about Friday? It wasn't anyone's fault that some wanker gave me a spiked drink."

Joanne shoves her hands in her hoodie's pockets. "We still should have come after you sooner, especially with the likes of Nick Fowler at the party."

The anger that was simmering in my gut returns with a

vengeance. Nick may not have put the drug in my drink—that's something we'll never know for sure—but he didn't hesitate to take advantage of the situation, and I won't forget that.

"He'd better stay away from me if he has any sense of self-preservation."

"I heard Paris almost smashed his face," Steff says. "Pity the Pikes dragged Nick away and saved his sorry ass."

"Paris would probably get benched if he got into a fight. It's best that it didn't happen, even as much as I'd like to see Nick get an ass whooping," Vanessa replies.

A loud rumble shakes the building, interrupting our lovely convo.

"Whoa. Was that thunder?" Joanne asks.

A moment later, heavy rain pelts the windows, and the world outside looks like nightfall has come earlier. That type of storm is the kind that hurts when it hits you and makes playing football not fun at all.

Couch Lauda joins us in the common area a minute later.

"Well, it looks like this rain won't stop until the afternoon. I'm switching the schedule. You're going to do some weight lifting now."

Almost everyone groans, including me. Weight lifting is boring as hell and not what I was looking forward to. I retrieve my duffel bag from the locker and change shoes again.

"Crap. We'll get drenched walking from here to the car," Phoebe moans.

"We used to get heavy showers like this all the time in Florida. It's not a big deal." Steff shrugs.

"Sadie must be used to it too since all it does is rain in London." Joanne smiles.

"One never gets used to bad weather," I reply. "Or the cold."

No one was expecting rain, so naturally, no one had an umbrella. To be fair, I didn't carry one with me in London either because they're such a hassle. I'd rather use a raincoat.

In clusters, we run to our cars. The distance is short, but puddles have already formed on the pavement, and I manage to step in every single one of them.

The gym building is only a minute from the field, but all the parking spots near the entrance are taken. Before I head out in the rain again, I check my duffel bag, hoping I packed an extra pair of sneakers. Working out in wet shoes won't do. I sigh in relief when I see my old gym shoes in the bag. I meant to toss them out and forgot. Sometimes, having a shite memory is a good thing.

When we enter the building, I wrinkle my nose, getting a whiff of something awful.

"What's up with the wet dog smell?" I ask no one in particular.

Vanessa's eyes sweep the open room, where half the machines are currently in use. "It must be Nick."

I follow her line of vision and spot the tosser far back, standing next to a bench press while his friend goes through his reps.

"For fuck's sake. What is he doing here?" I glower in his direction.

"His coach probably had the same idea as ours." Vanessa tugs on my duffel bag's strap. "Come on. Ignore him. We're here to work out. Don't let him distract you."

Grumbling, I follow Vanessa and the rest of my teammates to the gym's locker room. It's hard to let go of my anger though. Maybe instead of weight lifting, I should take out my aggression on a punching bag.

That's exactly what I do. While my friends spread out through the gym to work on the machines, I head to one of the workout rooms where I spied a punching bag the other day I was here. There's no one here, so for a good fifteen minutes, I have the punching bag all to myself. But then a couple of girls come in, chatting too loudly, and end my solitude.

Not in the mood to listen to idle gossip, I head out and search for a familiar face. I should probably work out my legs now. I spot Vanessa and Joanne sharing a leg press machine and make a beeline in their direction. My pulse is still pumping loudly in my ears thanks to the cardio, and for that reason, I don't pay attention to what's going on in my periphery.

That's when bloody Nick decides to show up, sporting a sneer. The wanker once again blocks my path.

"I was wondering where you were, darling."

"Get the fuck out of my way," I say, loud enough to draw attention.

He grabs my arm tightly, as if he has the right to touch me. "You have to learn some manners."

"How about this for manners?" I bring my knee up, slamming it against Nick's balls.

He howls, stepping back and leaning forward as he cups his junk with both hands. "You bitch."

"What the hell is going on here?" Coach Lauda asks, looking none too happy.

"She kicked me in the balls," he moans.

"Sadie?" She looks at me, frowning but not yet glowering.

"He got handsy. Men need to understand they can't go pawing whoever they like without asking."

"You wish I touched you," he lies.

I glance around, searching for a witness that will step forward and confirm my accusation. No one meets my eye, not even the girls.

Wankers. The whole lot.

"All right, Sadie. Come with me." Couch Lauda turns around and walks away without bothering to wait.

That wasn't a request, it was an order, so I follow her quietly. My face is burning, which means it must be as red as a tomato. It's not embarrassment as some of the people staring might think. I'm red from anger.

Coach Lauda leads me to a back room in the gym, which must be used as administration slash storage. There's a small desk and two chairs. She motions for me to go in first and then closes the door. She doesn't make a motion to take one of the chairs, so I remain standing as well.

"Explain to me what that was back there."

"Nick Fowler is a dick," I say angrily.

Coach pinches the bridge of her nose. "I'm aware that Fowler is problematic, but his behavior is not my problem. Yours is."

"How is that fair? The bellend grabs my arm and I'm supposed to just ask politely for him to let go?"

"That would have been better than kicking him in the nuts. Everyone saw you do that. No one stepped forward to say he touched you first."

"Because they're all a bunch of cowards."

"Probably. But you need to understand, Sadie. Whatever you do reflects on the entire team. I can't have one of my players assaulting another student. You're a promising star. I'd hate to bench you because of a weasel like Nick Fowler."

My blood is boiling, and it's taking every bit of self-control to keep my angry retort bottled inside.

"What's going to happen now?"

"Hopefully I can smooth things over with Coach Phillips. We go way back. But you have to promise me there won't be a repeat. If you must defend yourself, make sure there are willing witnesses to confirm your story. Is that clear?"

"Crystal."

"Oh, and one more thing. Skip parties throughout the rest of preseason training."

My chest feels tight suddenly. Does Couch Lauda know about last Friday?

"Why?"

"Drinking to the point of passing out is not something I want to hear about my players."

Shame washes over me, even though that's not what happened. But I can't confess to Coach Lauda what actually did. She might want to tell my father, and that's something I want to avoid at all costs.

So I swallow my pride and let her believe the lie.

"Understood. It won't happen again."

20

DANNY

COACH CLARKSON TRAINED us harder than ever, despite the rain. By the time practice was over, I could barely walk. I welcomed the exertion though. Focusing on not slacking off, I barely had time to think about Sadie. And in the locker room, my teammates kept me occupied with their banter.

It's not until I'm riding home with Andy that thoughts of Sadie invade my mind and I can't think of anything else.

"You're awfully quiet," Andy points out.

"I'm just tired."

"A certain soccer player definitely kept you busy last weekend."

"Dude, come on. You know Sadie is only a friend."

"Get your mind out of the gutter, will you? I wasn't insinuating anything, just making an observation. Taking care of someone who is sick is draining."

"Sorry, I can't tell with you. Ninety-nine percent of the time, your comments have double meaning."

"That's true." He grins. "I guess I'm improving my ways."

"What are your plans for the evening?" I ask to change the subject.

"Jane has derby training. She also has a game next weekend if you want to come. Lorenzo is psyched about it."

I grin. "I'm sure he is. Does he still have a crush on that dark-haired player? What's her name again?"

"Oh, Scary Samantha? I don't know. He hasn't mentioned her again since Jane told him we weren't allowed to speak her name in the house."

That makes me laugh. "She's still bitter about that black eye, huh?"

"Totally. I mean, I was livid when it happened, but then I reminded her that's the nature of the game, and she can't cry when things get tough."

"You probably didn't get any sex that evening, did you?"

"Nope."

"Sadie would probably love going to a roller derby game," I say without thinking.

Andy groans. "Bro, it's really hard not to make a comment about the girl if you keep mentioning her as if she were your girlfriend."

I clench my jaw hard and look out the window. I have no one but myself to blame for that. "Hell, can't I invite a girl to a game without it being a date?"

"Yeah, but we both know you're into Sadie. If you want to insist on not dating anyone because of whatever, then it's a smart idea to stop hanging out with her."

"I know."

We fall silent for a minute or two before Andy continues. "If you want to bring Sadie to the game, I guess it'd be all right. You'll have me, Lorenzo, and I believe Jane's grandma is coming with her two boyfriends. That's plenty of buffer."

Despite my gloomy mood, that makes me laugh. "Damn it,

now I have to bring her. I can't wait to see Sadie's reaction when she meets Ophelia Holland."

"Yeah, that will be epic, I bet."

No sooner are we home and I'm back in my room than I pull my cell phone out to text Sadie. I begin to ask how her day was but decide to go with something less clingy in the end.

ME: Hey, what's up?

SADIE: Not much. Veg'ing out in my room and listening to Katrina talk about her Greek life.

ME: That sounds fun, LOL.

SADIE: Barf. But it's distracting me from the shitty day I had.

ME: What? Did your coach make you train in the rain?

SADIE: I wish she had. Something else.

ME: Come on, Sadie. You can't leave it at that.

A moment later, she calls me.

"Hey. Got tired of typing?" I ask.

"Yeah, the story is too long, and my fingers were cramping up already. Anyway, if you must know why I had a crappy day, here it is. Coach Lauda made us do weight lifting because of the rain, which I hate on most days. But then we bumped into the king of arseholes at the gym, and he acted like his usual obnoxious self."

My entire body becomes tense. The memory of him dragging a barely conscious Sadie out of the party on Friday pops in my mind, making me relive the anger all over again.

"What did he do?" I grit out.

"The usual BS. But because I exchanged barbs with the wanker, I received a reprimand from Coach. To cut a long story short, I have to train harder and stay out of trouble if I want to play in our first game."

Sadie's evasion makes me suspect it was more than the usual BS. But I can probably get the details from someone else.

"That's harsh," I say. "You can do it though. If you want, I can help you on both counts."

"What do you mean?"

"I also need to train harder. Maybe we can run in the mornings or hit the gym together."

"Hmm, that's not a bad idea. But how is that going to help me stay out of trouble?"

"I'll help you make better decisions because I'm older and wiser?"

"You did not just quote Rolf from *The Sound of Music.*" She laughs.

"Guilty. I couldn't help it. My mom got me hooked on it when I was little. I think I know most of the lines and the song lyrics by heart."

Sadie laughs harder at this, and the sound is infectious.

"You're going to make me piss my pants."

"That wasn't the intention."

"Did you burst into song at the most inappropriate moments too?"

"Yeah."

"Blimey, your dad must have loved that."

I grow quiet suddenly, not knowing how to reply to that. It's normal for people to assume I grew up with a dad, but coming from Sadie, it's a surprise. She didn't have her father around either, after all.

"No dad," I reply.

"Bollocks. I'm such a moron. I don't know why I made that comment. It was word vomit, really. I'm not that thick, I swear."

I don't know what to make of that comment. Did she guess my father was never in my life? Probably. I bet most guys she knows talk about their fathers all the time.

"It's okay, Sadie. It happens."

I could tell her I've never met my father. In fact, I do want to share that with her, but now is not the time.

"If it makes you feel better, I accept your offer to tag along when I train, despite the blatant sexist comment about helping me make better decisions."

Her joke does pull me out of my sudden funk. Very few people are able to do that when I enter my dark moods.

"Tag along, huh? We'll see about that when I leave you behind, eating dust."

She scoffs. "You don't seriously believe you can run faster than me. I play soccer, in case you forgot."

"I sense a bet coming on. Should we put a wager on it?"

"That sounds brilliant. I love entering bets when the winning is guaranteed."

"That's what the hare thought."

"The hare was a dumbass and fell asleep."

"Okay, then. Let's meet for a run in front of the library tomorrow. We'll see who's the fastest. How about five?"

She groans. "I'm already not liking this, but hell, I'm game."

I smile from ear to ear, even though I know spending more time with Sadie is exactly what I don't need.

"All right, see you tomorrow, Sadie."

I'm still sporting the goofiest grin minutes after the call ends.

I see the warning signs flashing in front of me, and I'm choosing to ignore all of them.

When I crash and burn, I'll have no one to blame but me.

21

SADIE

No matter how long I've been waking at the crack of dawn, I'll never get used to it. Some people don't even require an alarm clock after a while. I'm the one snoozing mine until I'm late. But this morning, I was up before the shrill sound disturbed my peace.

I move around on my tiptoes, careful not to wake Katrina, who is snoring softly. My phone tells me it's four thirty, which gives me plenty of time to shower and get ready. Ten times out of ten, I wouldn't bother showering before a morning run—I'm getting sweaty within minutes. But after an entire weekend of Danny seeing me at my worst, I want to look good.

Yep, I'm preening for a guy who I don't want to date.

I'm such a liar.

I want Danny so badly that it hurts, which also proves I'm a glutton for punishment. But every time I make a promise to myself to cut down on the time I interact with him, I break that vow. He's my weakness, and I don't even know how I let that happen. Sneaky little bastard must have slipped through a crack in my barrier when I wasn't paying attention—or was too distracted by the way he looks.

The bathroom is empty at this ungodly hour. I'd appreciate the lack of people and take my time if I wasn't so anxious to finish quickly and head to the library. I don't wash my hair, but I do make a point of brushing it until it shines. I'm about to put it in a ponytail, but in the end, I slip the hair band around my wrist instead. I'll put it up later.

I have dark circles under my eyes, and I wish I could put some makeup on, but that would be pushing it and beyond ridiculous. I'm already wearing my sexiest workout outfit; I don't want him to notice I tried hard to look my best.

No matter how many times I repeat in my head that Danny is just a friend, my stomach is twisted in knots the entire drive to our meeting point. The clock on my dashboard is flashing that it's five minutes to five, but when I walk over to the building a minute later, I find Danny already standing there, wearing shorts and a snug, long-sleeve shirt.

"Good morning." He smiles broadly, making his eyes twinkle under the streetlights.

My butterflies decide to wreak havoc in my belly because apparently the knots weren't enough. Or maybe the damn bugs were the ones that tied my insides in the first place.

"Morning. I can't believe you beat me here. It's not even five yet."

"I was up early."

"Same," I reply.

"You didn't put your hair in a ponytail though."

He noticed, and that makes me feel all warm and fuzzy inside. *Dumb girl.*

"Eh... I forgot."

"I like your hair down like that."

His confession renders me speechless, and a new tension develops between us. We don't speak for a while, just stare at each other as if we forgot how to string sentences together. Quickly, I comb my hair back with my fingers and use the hairband around my wrist to tie it together in a messy ponytail.

Danny clears his throat, breaking the awkward silence. "So, what are the rules of our bet?"

"Are you sure you want to do this?" I smirk.

He raises an eyebrow. "What's the matter, Sadie? Are you scared to lose?"

"No, I'm just trying to save you from the humiliation."

"Aren't you sweet? So, first and foremost, we need to establish the track."

"Right. It's a pretty straight path from here to the practice fields. How about whoever gets there first wins?"

"Sounds good. And what's the prize for the winner?"

I know Danny is a scholarship student and isn't swimming in riches, so I'm not going to be a cow and suggest we bet cash.

"How about a favor?"

His lips twist upward. "What kind?"

"It can be anything, but it has to be major, like—"

"Burying a body?" he finishes for me.

"Something like that."

"Sounds good."

We stretch first, and I try to ignore the radioactive insects in my tummy. A couple of minutes later, we're both ready to start.

"On the count of three?" he asks.

I nod, getting into position.

"One, two, three!" he shouts.

We sprint forward, going neck and neck in the beginning. Danny's legs are longer, but I compensate by being faster. However, I know not to use all my gas at the start. Instead, I save some of my energy for the final stretch. That allows Danny to take the lead. I'm banking that he'll tire out and slow down, but it's possible that strategy will backfire. The guy is a top athlete, trained by my dad.

I can't allow the distance between us to increase too much or I'll never catch up. I push my legs, loving how my muscles protest at first. It's a sweet pain that will soon fade into the background.

My guess is the distance between the library and fields is around two miles.

I'm far from winded by the time we near it. When I get a visual of the finish line, I push myself to the limit, propelled by the need to win this race at all costs. Nothing motivates me more than being at the top. I hear Danny grunt as I blow past him. I'm tempted to wave, but that type of distraction could cost me. I don't want to be like the hare from the story.

I'm a few feet from reaching the wire fence when I sense Danny close behind me. Then, in the final steps, he takes the lead.

No fucking way.

In an act of desperation, I leap, reaching the fence a second before he does. Well, not reaching, more like colliding with it. Danny was too close to me when I jumped in front of him, which results in him crashing against my back and sandwiching me between him and the fence.

My left cheek and my chest take the blunt of the impact. It hurts to the point that I cry out.

"Sadie, what the hell!" Danny steps back and turns me around. "Are you hurt?"

His breathing is coming out in bursts as his frantic eyes search my face.

"Of course I am. You smashed into me."

He touches my face with the tips of his fingers, making me hold my breath. A shiver runs down my spine from the contact.

"Wh-What are you doing?" I breathe out.

"You're bleeding."

He shows me his smeared fingers.

"Blimey." I touch my cheek, feeling the moisture too. "How bad is it? Do you think I'll need stitches?"

"Nah. It looks superficial. But we should definitely clean it up properly."

"Yeah."

My heart is still racing, but I'm not sure if it's because of the run or the close proximity to Danny.

"I'm sorry, Sadie."

"You should be. I won."

His eyebrows furrow. "That's not why I'm sorry. And you only won because you cheated."

"I didn't cheat," I retort angrily. "I won the race fair and square."

"I don't think jumping in front of your opponent counts as fair and square."

"You're just a sore loser," I grumble, pushing him to the side so I can put some distance between us.

"Oh, I think you've got me confused with yourself." He throws his arm over my shoulders, effectively ruining my plan to get some much-needed space. "Come on. Let's get that boo-boo taken care of."

"Don't tell me you have a first aid kit in your car."

"Yeah. You don't?"

"Uh, no."

"Unwise considering what a klutz you are."

"I'm not a klutz!" I elbow him in the ribs, hoping to dislodge him from my side. No such luck.

Instead, he laughs and laughs.

"Are you done?" I ask after a while.

"Sure. I concede victory to you. What favor do you want from me?"

I almost say that I want him to stop making fun of me, but that'd be a waste of my winnings. Besides, the deal was for the favor to be something big.

"Don't know yet."

"Hmm, we probably should have agreed on an expiration date. I can so picture you knocking on my door fifty years from now, all wrinkled and shit, asking me to help bury the body of someone you killed."

I try to pretend I'm offended, but I snicker instead. "That could happen. Guess you'll just have to wait with bated breath until I call to cash in my favor."

"The anticipation will probably send me to an early grave. Please don't wait fifty years."

"I can't make such a promise."

He sighs. "You have a mean streak, woman. I thought I was your friend."

"You're my friend."

"I feel sorry for your enemies."

I shrug. "Unfortunately, I can't deal with all my enemies like I want to. Society really frowns upon maiming and castrating."

"Are you referring to Nick Fowler? What did he do yesterday at the gym?"

I tense, not wanting to tell Danny for fear he'll try to play the knight in shining armor. I don't want him getting into trouble because of me.

"Nothing worth repeating, Danny. Don't worry, I can fight my own battles."

He tenses next to me and then drops his arm from my shoulder. I wanted some space, but now I feel like the distance is more than physical.

"We didn't think this through," I say.

"What?"

"We should have left one car parked near the fields."

"I assumed we'd be running back. I didn't count on you getting your face slashed by a fence."

I can tell there's no real humor in his attempted joke.

"I can still run."

Danny stops and looks at me. "Shit. You look like an extra from a horror movie."

I touch my face again, noticing it's way wetter than before. "Danny! You said the cut was superficial."

"And it is. But even those bleed a lot."

"Great." I stop moving so I can take off my tank top.

"What are you doing?"

"What do you think?" I ask mid-motion. "Don't worry, Danny. I won't flash you my tits this time. I'm wearing a sports bra."

I manage to find a piece of fabric that's not completely drenched in sweat, then use it to dry off my cheek. We resume our trek back to our cars, but the absence of the easy banter feels like a heavy cloud hanging over our heads.

Thirty minutes later, my tank top has soaked up all the blood from the shallow cut, but even so, Danny insists I get it cleaned in his car. I would have protested and insist he do it outside, but rain decides to make an appearance.

Danny is half into his car while I glare at the sky.

"What are you waiting for, Sadie? Get in. You'll get soaked."

Grumbling, I circle around the front of the vehicle and slide inside.

"What were you hoping to do? Break into song and start tap dancing over puddles?" he asks.

"Sure, let's go with that." I cross my arms over my chest.

Danny leans toward me, making me tense.

He's just reaching for the glove compartment, dumbass.

"Okay, let's start with cleaning the wound. This might sting a little."

He sprays an antiseptic solution on a piece of gauze and taps it to my cheek. This moment is too intimate, and it's making me feel all kinds of things. Like an idiot, I stare right at his face. His attention is solely on the task, but my heart is racing just the same. When he pulls back, his eyes meet mine, making breathing much harder than it already was.

"There. All better," he says in a voice that's thicker, almost if he's having trouble drawing air into his lungs as well.

Then his eyes drop to my lips, which part automatically, almost an invitation for a kiss. And God, I do want Danny to kiss me now. I inch closer, allowing myself to get pulled into his orbit. He seems to lean forward too.

This is going to happen, even though it's so stupid. We're friends. Friends don't make out in cars.

At the last second, Danny's attention moves from my lips to my cheek.

"Oh, crap. You're bleeding again. We'd better put a Band-Aid over it."

He grabs a clean strip of gauze and reaches over, but I take it from him. We were a second away from making a huge mistake. I won't let that happen again.

"I'll do it."

I tap my cheek way harsher than Danny did, and then I grab a Band-Aid from his first aid kit myself. Using the passenger mirror, I apply the bandage over the cut, trying my best to ignore the weight of Danny's stare.

"All right. I'm all patched up. I'd better get going." I open the door, avoiding making eye contact with him.

"Okay. Sadie?"

"Yeah?" Like an idiot, I look.

Yep. Still want to kiss him.

"Same time tomorrow?"

"Sure."

Bloody hell. What. Am. I. Doing?

He smiles. "All right. See you later."

I slip out, ignoring the fact that it's still raining. In a daze, I walk to my car, and it's not until I'm behind the steering wheel that I feel the significance of what just happened.

Danny and I almost kissed.

How long until we finally cross the line and everything changes?

22

SADIE

DANNY and I ran every morning during the week, but we didn't place any bets, and we most definitely kept our distance. It seems both of us realized how dangerously close we were to making a big mistake the first time, and we weren't willing to take the risk again.

Without too much proximity and definitely not touching, it was easy to push it to the back of my mind that I fancy him. By the time Friday rolled around, I was confident that I had my crush under control and, therefore, totally let my guard down. So when he asked me if I wanted to come to Jane's roller derby game Saturday, I said yes.

Now here I am, standing in front of Danny's building, waiting for him to come down. I didn't want him to pick me up because it felt too much like a date. I also didn't want to drive alone to the game. My compromise was to meet him here.

He walks out of the building accompanied by a young kid with brown hair and green eyes. He looks like a carbon copy of Andy, so it's easy to guess it's Lorenzo, Andy's younger brother.

"Hey." I wave at them both.

"Hi, Sadie. This is Lorenzo."

"Nice to meet you."

He doesn't answer right away, just stares with his jaw hanging loose until Danny pipes up, "Dude, quit staring at her like that."

A sheepish expression falls on his face, and he drops his gaze. "Sorry. You didn't tell me she was so pretty."

"Aw, thanks. You're sweet." I smile.

Danny throws me a glower. "Don't encourage him. The Casanova gene is strong in the Rossi family."

"Is that so?" I raise an eyebrow at Lorenzo.

"He's just jealous that the girls like me best."

"Quit being such a pest." Danny ruffles Lorenzo's hair in an affectionate way.

It reminds me of Dominic and how he used to do that to me all the time. It drove me bonkers. Like me, Lorenzo complains and steps away.

"We'd better go, or we'll get stuck in traffic," he says.

"Is Andy not coming with us?"

"He's already there. He drove Jane."

"Ah, gotcha."

I fall into step with Danny but choose to walk next to Lorenzo. I shouldn't even be here, because seeing Danny dressed in jeans and a casual T-shirt is worse than his running gear. And his aftershave is making it hard to ignore how my body reacts when I'm near him.

When we come close to Danny's car, Lorenzo calls shotgun.

"Come on, kid. Let Sadie sit up front."

"Oh, it's fine. I don't mind sitting in the back seat," I say.

He looks at me. "Are you sure?"

"Positive."

DANNY

The gymnasium where the roller derby game takes place isn't busy yet, and that allows us to find Ophelia and her boyfriends with ease. I'm also surprised to see Jane's dad in the audience, sitting next to Andy. As we approach their row, Ophelia spots us and waves. Her hair is bright orange today, clashing—or complementing, however you see fashion—big-time with her colorful print outfit.

"Is that Jane's grandmother?" Sadie asks.

"Yep. And her two boyfriends, Jack and Louis."

"Wait? Boyfriends as in plural?" Sadie glances at me with eyebrows arched and eyes wide.

I chuckle. "Oh yeah. You're in for a treat."

Lorenzo enters their row first, followed by Sadie, then me. This is the first time since the almost kiss incident that we're going to be in close proximity again. We saw each other every day of the week, but there's an effort from both of us to keep things planted firmly in the friend zone. I considered not inviting her to come tonight, but I have to believe I can be strong and not succumb to my urges. Mind over matter and all that.

She had to go and wear something sexy though. Those jeans of hers fit her tight ass perfectly, and the crazy asymmetric top shows peeks of skin here and there that are seriously impairing my ability to not think about kissing her.

"Hello, darlings. Long time no see," Ophelia greets us.

"Hi, Grandma." Lorenzo kisses her on the cheek.

Since Andy got custody of Lorenzo after his dad died, Lorenzo got the habit of calling Ophelia "grandma," much to her delight. It makes sense, considering everyone knows it's only a matter of time until Andy proposes to Jane.

Lorenzo says hello to Louis and Jack before taking his seat

next to Ophelia. Her sharp gaze travels past him and focuses on Sadie and me.

"Danny, you brought a date."

My cheeks become warmer. "Not a date," I say quickly.

Ophelia's smile wilts a fraction. "That's too bad."

"Not really. Danny and I can never be more than friends. We're way too competitive for that. I'm Sadie, by the way. Nice to meet you."

"Nice to meet you, darling. These are my beaux, Jack and Louis. And the grouchy man with his eyes glued to his phone is my former son-in-law, Jonathan."

The man in question raises his head upon hearing his name. "What?"

"Jane's friends arrived. I was making introductions," Ophelia explains.

He says a halfhearted "Nice to meet you" and returns to his device. The man is a workaholic, and no one really cares anymore that he's only partially present whenever he's around. At least he comes to Jane's games, unlike her estranged mother.

Introductions are made, and then we take our seats. Immediately, I feel the tension build between Sadie and me. It's like whenever we get in close proximity, our bodies create an electric spark. Or maybe it's just in my head. I chance a look at her and notice her jaw is tense. Hell, I don't want things to get awkward between us because of pesky physical attraction. I like to hang out with her. If I just could stop wanting to kiss her, it would be great.

"Have you ever been to a roller derby game before?" I ask.

"Dude, you asked me that question already when you invited me, remember?"

"Right." I rub the back of my neck, dropping my chin slightly so my long hair can hide my embarrassment.

"So, have you?" Lorenzo asks.

"No. All I know about the game I learned from Elliot Page's movie."

"Ah yeah. *Whip it*. I like that movie. It's fun."

"The soundtrack is also brilliant."

"What's your favorite song from it?"

"Let me guess," I butt in. 'Bad Reputation.'"

She smirks. "You know me too well already, Hudson."

"Don't call me Hudson. Only my teammates call me that."

Her eyebrows shoot to the heavens. "Oh, sorry. I didn't mean to offend you."

I shake my head, not knowing why I made that comment. "I'm not offended. It's just... weird when you call me that."

"Why? Because I'm a girl?"

No. Because you're a girl I want to kiss so badly, it hurts.

"You're not a guy on my team. That's why." I face forward, resting my elbows on my knees.

"It's getting busy. How long until the game starts?" she asks.

"It'll be another ten minutes, I think," I reply.

"Oh good. I have time to pee." She stands and stares at me. "May I?"

Since the row is too narrow, the only way she can walk through is if I stand too. Even so, there's literally no space between our bodies when she walks past me. Chills run down my spine with the contact, which prompts me to make a hasty decision.

"Hey, Lorenzo, wanna trade seats with me? I haven't seen Ophelia in a while."

The kid shrugs and then switches places with me.

"Hi, Danny. How is everything with you?" she asks me, smiling kindly.

"Great. Preseason is kicking my butt, but Coach Clarkson thinks I have a shot at going pro."

"Oh, that's wonderful news."

We chat a little about football and then about how Troy and

Charlie are doing in Europe before Ophelia brings up the topic of Sadie.

"So, tell me why you haven't staked your claim on that lovely girl you brought tonight."

I shift uncomfortably in my seat. "I'm not interested in dating anyone. I want to focus on football."

"Danny, you're only a sophomore. You can't simply put your life on hold like that. Besides, why does having a girlfriend mean you can't also succeed on the field?"

"Ophelia is right, son," Jack pipes up. "This whole idea that no sex helps athletes stay focused is BS."

My face and ears are in flames. I so don't want to talk about my sex life—or lack of one—with Troy's grandma and her boyfriends.

"Well, there's also a complication. Sadie is Coach Clarkson's daughter."

"Oh really? How marvelous. That just made this story so much more interesting." Ophelia claps her hands.

"Shh," Jack says. "The girl is coming back."

I turn and see that Sadie is, indeed, on her way back to her seat. She pauses when she notices the change in seating arrangement but doesn't make a comment about it before she sits next to Lorenzo and proceeds to ignore me for the rest of the game.

Lorenzo is more than happy to fill the void and talks nonstop. He explains how the game works, who the players are, even tells Sadie about his crush on Scary Samantha, to which Sadie comments that she can see the appeal.

Before I know it, the game is over and we're out of our seats, shuffling toward the aisle. Sadie continues to ignore me as she walks ahead with Lorenzo by her side. The kid is beaming with the attention. As for me, I just trudge along, feeling like a dirty dog who was kicked to the curb.

Andy catches up with me and throws his arm over my

shoulders. "What's up, Danny-boy? Feeling blue because Sadie traded you for someone younger?"

I push him off me. "Shut up, Rossi."

He just laughs. "If she's giving you the cold shoulder, it's your fault. Why did you have to switch seats with my brother?"

"I wanted to chat with Ophelia."

"Right. Well, I have a solution to your problems."

"I don't have problems."

He taps my shoulder. "Don't worry, buddy. I got you."

"Andy, for fuck's sake. I already asked you not to play cupid."

He widens his eyes innocently. "I'm not."

Like I believe the asshole.

My suspicions are confirmed when Andy shows his hand outside the building.

"All right everyone. I think Jane's epic win deserves a celebration. We're all going back to La Casa Rossi for pizza."

"I should probably go home," Sadie says.

"Nope. I'm not taking no for an answer," Andy replies and then turns to wink at me.

Jackass.

"Come on, Sadie. You have to come. We can play *Mario Kart*," Lorenzo pleads.

While Lorenzo is busy giving Sadie the puppy eyes, I'm glaring at his brother.

"You're going to pay for this," I mouth silently.

The idiot just laughs.

"Fine, I guess I can hang out for a little bit," Sadie tells Lorenzo.

Even though she's not coming because of me, my stupid heart beats a little faster just the same.

23

SADIE

It was obvious that Danny switched seats with Lorenzo at the game because of something I said or did, so I ignored him while we were there. But I couldn't keep doing that while hanging out at his place. I'm not a total bitch.

Danny leans forward and reaches for the last slice of pizza, but then he stops and looks at me. "Do you wanna share?"

"God, no." I lean back on the couch and stuff my belly out. "I look like I'm six months pregnant."

He drops his eyes to my stomach and shakes his head. "You look nothing like a six months pregnant woman. Four tops."

He takes a bite of the pizza, and gooey cheese drips down the sides. That sight should have been gross, but hell if Danny doesn't make it look sexy. His tongue darts out to capture the string of melted cheese, and I can't look away.

He turns, catching me staring. "What?" he asks with his mouth full.

I sit straighter. "Nothing. I should get going. It's late."

"What? No way," Lorenzo complains. "You promised another round of *Mario Kart*. I have to reclaim my title."

From the other side of the couch, Andy says, "Yeah, Sadie. Stay. Besides, how many beers did you drink? You probably shouldn't be driving."

I'd take him seriously if he hadn't said that with a smirk.

"I'm fine to drive," I grumble.

"Says the girl who crashed into my parked car when she was sober," Danny chimes in.

Narrowing my eyes, I whip my face to his. "Really? How long are you going to hold that over my head?"

"For as long as it annoys you." He takes another bite of his pizza.

"Teasing aside, I also think you should stay," Jane says. "Danny can sleep on the couch again, right, Danny?"

"Yep. I like the couch."

I have hundreds of reasons why staying over is a bad idea, but I did drink one too many beers. Maybe I did it deliberately, so I'd have an excuse to stay. My mind is weak when it comes to Danny.

"Fine. I'll stay. But I've got nothing on me. I have to borrow one of your shirts," I tell him.

"That can be arranged."

"Maybe you should leave some stuff here since you and Danny are such close friends." Andy smiles like a cat that ate the canary.

I want to say "Hell to the no," but it would probably offend Danny. I choose to glare at his roommate instead.

"So, *Mario Kart*?" Lorenzo asks.

"Sure, but since I'm staying, I guess I can have another beer." I make a motion to stand, but Danny puts his hand on my arm.

"I'll grab it."

He heads to the kitchen, taking the empty pizza box with

him. My eyes begin to follow him, but I catch myself in time and snap my gaze to the TV.

Lorenzo and I get busy picking our avatars and then customizing our race cars.

"Sadie, we're out of regular beer," Danny calls from the kitchen.

"What's not regular beer?"

"Cherry."

"Oh, I like those."

"How in the world did we end up with cherry beer in our fridge?" Andy asks.

"I don't know. I think Charlie brought them the last time she and Troy were here."

"I miss them," Jane says in a morose tone.

"Me too, babe." Andy kisses her on the cheek.

"Who are they?" I ask when Danny returns with the bottle of cherry beer.

"Troy is my brother, and Charlie is his girlfriend," Jane explains. "They're living in London now."

"Really? If they need suggestions on the best places to go, I'd be happy to give them some tips."

"Oh, that'd be great. I'm sure they'd love it."

"Are you ready, Sadie?" Lorenzo draws my attention back to the game.

"Oh, yeah. I'm so going to smoke your arse again."

"No chance."

We play until my fingers are numb and Lorenzo finally beats me. Andy and Jane have gone to bed already, and after a silly victory dance, Lorenzo trudges to his room. I stand and stretch my arms, eyeing the three bottles of cherry beer I drank between rounds of *Mario Kart*.

It's then that I notice Danny is also not in the living room anymore. Gee, I guess being in any type of competitive game takes all my focus.

I bring the empty bottles to the kitchen, setting them on the counter. They probably have a recycling bin somewhere, but I'm too tired now to go look for it.

On my way to Danny's bedroom, I realize I *am* tipsy. His door is open only a sliver. I have no idea what I'll find inside. Maybe I should have knocked first, but the thought only occurs to me after I've already opened the door all the way. To my regret, I don't catch Danny in the middle of changing clothes.

He's asleep with a thick book lying across his stomach. I tiptoe toward him, and upon closer inspection, I see he was reading *Harry Potter and the Goblet of Fire*. My favorite book in the series. A smile tugs on my lips.

Since there are no witnesses, I give myself permission to stare at Danny unabashedly. Giddiness takes over, and who can blame me? The boy is swoonworthy. I don't know what I love more about his face: the kissable lips, his chin dimple, or his blond curls. I sit next to him and lightly run my fingers over his hairline.

Danny wakes with a start and a second later squints. "Did I fall asleep?"

"Yeah."

"Sorry. I'll go set up my bed in the living room." He begins to sit, but I push him back.

"I'm not going to make you sleep on the couch. I'll do it."

Undeterred, he rises despite my hand pressing in the opposite direction. If he wants to sit up, I'm not going to manhandle him into bed. Although I'd love to manhandle him in other areas.

Bollocks, my train of thought is already derailing into smutty territory. Next stop, O-town.

"You're not sleeping on the couch. Don't be ridiculous."

"I'm not going to let you sleep there either. So I guess we're sharing the bed."

Oh my God. What am I saying? I can only blame my behavior on alcohol.

"Fine. If that's what you want, we'll share the bed. But if you start to hog the covers, I will push you over the edge."

Since my hand is still on Danny's shoulder, I pinch his arm.

"Ouch!" he complains.

"If you push me off the bed, I'll do to you what I did to Nick Fowler at the gym."

Danny's back turns rigid as his face twists into a scowl. His hand ends up on my leg. "That's the day you said nothing important happened."

Ah hell. Stupid drunk tongue revealing all my secrets.

"Nick grabbed my arm at the gym when I told him to get out of the way, so I did the only thing I could. I brought my knee up to his nuts. Crushed 'em."

His eyebrows shoot up, and his lips curl in a grin. "You did that? For real?"

"Yep. It's not like I hadn't warned him before." I shrug.

To my surprise, Danny pulls me into a hug, and damn it if I don't melt into his arms.

"You're the best."

"I know." I laugh.

Too soon, he releases me and gets out of bed. I watch him go with lovesick puppy eyes. He pulls a long T-shirt from his drawer and tosses it in my direction.

"You can wear this. It should look like a dress on you."

I eye the piece of clothing, loving how it smells of him. I might have to steal it. "Only because you're a giant."

"I'm not a giant, at least not compared to Paris or Puck. Those two are Hagrid wannabes."

I smile. "I love that you're an HP fanboy."

He gives me a crooked smile. "Oh yeah. I got my membership card and everything."

"What house are you? No, let me guess. You're a Hufflepuff."

He glares. "Woman, I'm offended. I'm a Gryffindor."

"Oh yeah. I get that now. Soooo proud."

He narrows his eyes. "I bet you're a Slytherin."

I jump from the bed and shorten the distance between us. "How dare you? I'm also a Gryffindor."

He pinches his lips together, trying to suppress a chuckle.

"Laugh again and you get another pinch," I say.

"Stop being so bossy, *Hermione*. If you want to brush your teeth, there's a new toothbrush in the bathroom cabinet."

Immediately, I fear I have bad breath. I step away from Danny before I say anything else.

"Cool. Thanks."

I disappear into the bathroom and look for the aforementioned toothbrush. It's not in the cabinet above the sink, so I search the drawer. I do find it, but also a box of condoms. Great, like I need another reminder that I want to jump Danny's bones.

I close the drawer with a shove, then take my time brushing my teeth. I even brush my tongue—something I never do. Staring at my reflection in the mirror, I list in my head all the reasons why I should keep it in my pants. But my tipsy brain is keen on ignoring every single item.

Bloody hell.

In a hurry to change clothes before Danny decides to check on me, I almost end up falling on my butt, trying to remove my tight jeans. I bang my elbow against the wall, which sends white-hot pain up my arm.

"Fuck," I grit out.

"Sadie? Are you okay in there?"

"I'm fine."

I change into Danny's shirt next, and like he said, it covers every bit that counts. It's still short though, so he'll get a good visual of my legs.

Why is that important?

You know why, Sadie.

God, the little voice inside my head is annoying.

When I return to the bedroom, Danny is already under the covers sans a T-shirt.

"You'd better not be naked under there."

He rolls his eyes. "Come on. I'm not a perv. If my bare chest bothers you, I can put a T-shirt on. But I usually get hot at night."

Hell and damn. I won't survive sleeping next to him.

"Just stay on your side of the bed and we'll be fine."

I slide under the sheet, trying my best to act like this is natural. I can't get comfortable to save my life though. I turn around and hit the pillow to see if it helps, all the while ignoring Danny's stare.

"Are you done abusing my stuff?"

"Yeah. Keep talking and I'll abuse you next."

"Okay."

Ah, hell. That sounded bad.

"Sorry. I didn't mean to imply I'd... well.... Ugh. Forget it." I turn on my side, giving my back to him.

"I got what you meant. Can I shut off the light?"

"Yeah."

The room turns pitch black for a moment, but my eyes remain wide open. After a while, they get used to the darkness and I can see the outline of the furniture. Danny fidgets next to me, switching positions several times.

Is he as uncomfortable as I am?

"What are you doing?" I ask after a minute of his restlessness.

"Nothing."

He grows quiet after that, yet I can't relax enough to fall asleep. He sighs after a while, and like an idiot, I turn so I'm facing him.

"What is it?" I ask.

"Nothing."

"Is 'nothing' the only word you know now?"

"Apparently."

"You sound mad. Was it the abuse comment?"

"What? No. And I'm not mad."

"I can see your furrow even in the dark." I touch the spot between his brows.

"Don't do that," he says in a voice that's suddenly thick.

"Why not?" He doesn't answer right away, and I begin to really freak out. "You're angry with me."

"I'm not angry." He turns his face to mine. "You seriously don't know, Sadie?"

I lean on my elbow and boldly trace his collarbone with my fingers. "Are you saying you like when I touch you too much?"

"Yes," he hisses and then reaches for my hand, stopping what I'm doing.

"I like touching you. As a matter of fact, I think about touching you constantly."

"Don't say that."

"Why not? It's the truth."

"Because it's taking every bit of self-restraint I have to remain on my side of the bed."

"Well, I have none left."

I roll on top of him, bringing my face inches from his. I can feel his accelerated heartbeat, I can hear his sharp intake of breath, and, most importantly, I can feel his erection pressing against my belly.

"We're supposed to stay friends."

"Why can't we be friends with benefits?" I ask softly. "You have needs, I have needs."

"You have your toys."

"You can't honestly believe my toys are anything like the real deal."

"Sadie, you know this is a bad idea. You're only saying all that because you're drunk."

I seriously didn't expect him to put up so much of a fight, especially considering his body is more than on board with the idea. But there's only so much begging I can do.

"I'm not drunk." I slide off him. "But okay, I won't ask again. Good night, Danny."

I begin to turn, but he stops me, looping his arm around my waist and bringing me flush against his body once more.

"Forget good night," he says right before he slants his lips over mine.

Oh my God. All nerves in my body short-circuit. This is not a tentative kiss. It's demanding, rough, intense, pure fire. His tongue invades my mouth, claiming me in a way I never thought possible. He pulls me on top of him again, and now that we're really doing this, I don't restrain myself. I grind my hips against his erection, teasing him until he groans against my lips. My borrowed T-shirt has bunched up, and the only barrier now between our bodies is the thin layers of our underwear.

His hands find their way to my hips, and with his fingers digging deep into my exposed skin, he takes control, setting the pace. The friction is hitting me in the right spot, making me see stars already.

"This is going to end really fast for me," I murmur against his lips.

"Fuck."

He rolls on top of me and drags his lips down my chin and neck while he plays with my tits through the T-shirt. I arch my back, an invitation for him to explore further. He pushes the fabric all the way up until my breasts are exposed.

"God, Sadie. You're so beautiful." He covers one of my nipples with his mouth, using his tongue to tease my sensitive bud mercilessly.

Moaning, I thread my fingers through his soft curls, something I've wanted to do since the first time I met him.

"Confess. You've been dreaming about my boobs for a while, haven't you?"

He releases my nipple with a soft pop, then runs his tongue over it, leaving a trail of goose bumps over my skin.

"I only got a peek, but yeah, I've wanted to do this—" He bites me lightly. "—for a while."

I take his hand and guide it between my legs. "Feel how wet I am, Danny. This is what you do to me."

He forgets my tits for a moment and stares into my eyes while his fingers slide under my knickers and then find my clit. I gasp loudly.

"It's your time to confess, Sadie. Have you fantasized about me doing this to you?" He sweeps his finger over my clit again, making my toes curl from pleasure.

"Yes."

"What else have you fantasized about?" He places an openmouthed kiss on my neck.

"Your mouth everywhere on my body, your tongue inside me, claiming me."

He makes a guttural sound in the back of his throat and leans back. "I want this gone."

I lift my arms, allowing him to get rid of my T-shirt. Still maintaining eye contact, I trace the line of his boxers.

"You know what else I dreamed about?"

"What?" he asks in a low tone, thick with desire.

I push his underwear down, freeing his erection. He hisses when I curl my fingers around his shaft.

"I want to make a lollipop out of you, lick you clean."

He reaches behind my head and grabs a handful of my hair to pull me to him. His lips crash over mine, furious and hungry. While he devours my mouth, I work his cock, sliding my hand up and down, feeling it grow even larger under my touch.

He ends the kiss abruptly and rests his forehead against mine, breathing heavily. "Sadie, I'm about to explode here. Tell me what you want."

I might have fantasized about this moment, but I really didn't plan a play-by-play scenario. Do I want Danny to come in my hand, my mouth, or inside me? Hmm, he can probably recover fast.

I lean forward and whisper in his ear, "I want to sixty-nine."

I've never seen a guy react as fast as Danny does. He flips us over, so now he's under me. I laugh at his enthusiasm.

"Shh. We don't want to wake up the entire house." He laughs.

"Sorry, I forgot."

I jump off the bed to shimmy out of my knickers. Danny gets rid of his boxers equally fast.

"Damn, you're gorgeous," I say in awe.

"No, you are." He reaches over, taking my hand. "Come here."

I kneel next to him on the mattress, lean down, and kiss him softly on the lips—or try to. We're both too horny for sweet kisses. Reluctantly, I ease back and straddle Danny, facing away from his mouth. I'm glad it's dark and I'm a little tipsy, because this position always made me self-conscious in the past.

But awkwardness has no place tonight. I'm too comfortable around Danny for that. He grips my hips, bringing my pussy closer to his face. I lick his shaft from bottom to top at the same time his tongue sweeps over my clit, making me moan like a kitten. Holding the base, I bring his length into my mouth, not stopping until the head hits the back of my throat. Danny sucks me harder in retaliation, and soon it becomes clear this is a competition to see who can make the other come first.

Bring it on, babe.

I alternate deep-throating him and licking the top of his cock while pumping him up and down with my hand. With a grunt, he sucks my clit into his mouth, making me lose my focus for a second. The bastard laughs, which only spurs me on. I double my efforts, counting on victory when he grows harder in my mouth. I didn't bank on him bringing his game up to eleven. When he penetrates me with his tongue, it shatters through the control I had over my own body.

The orgasm comes so swiftly and strongly that I have to stop what I'm doing and focus on keeping my legs from giving out. I let go of his erection and press my cheek against his thigh, curling my fingers around the sheet as the wave of the most intense orgasm I've ever had levels me to the ground.

Only when the tremors subside do I remember about Danny. But when I look, his dick is hanging half limp, and there's a whole mess of jizz around it.

Fuck. He came? When?

I roll over to the side and, leaning on my elbow, look at him. His eyes are closed, and there's a stupid grin on his face. It still feels like I fucked up.

"I'm sorry," I say.

He opens one eye. "About what?"

"I didn't finish you off properly."

He runs his fingers over the back of my legs. "I disagree."

Of course he would. He's a guy. He climaxed. He'd be happy about that. But I'm too much of a perfectionist to be satisfied with my performance.

I get out of bed and head for the bathroom, already thinking how I'm going to make up for it.

24

DANNY

In my current post-sex state of mind, I can't find it in me to worry about what Sadie and I just did. We crossed a line that was already blurred to begin with, and right now, I have zero regrets. And I also know I want more, probably tonight if she's game.

She returns to the room a moment later, carrying a towel.

I lean on my elbows. "You didn't have to do that. I can clean myself."

"The reason the mess is there is because of me. It's the least I can do."

She wetted the towel with warm water, and as she runs it over my crotch and legs, my cock hardens again, getting ready for round two.

"I'm beginning to think you didn't do it only to be nice."

Her luscious lips split into a radiant smile. "It was totally self-serving. I also brought this." She shows me the condom wrapper I didn't notice before.

My heart is thundering now, and my entire being is yearning to touch her again. Yet I ask, “Are you sure?”

She nods. “More than anything.”

I watch as she rips the foil packet open with her teeth, then rolls the condom down my length. God, I’m so turned on that I’m pretty sure it won’t take much to push me off the edge again. I’ve gone too long without sex, and Sadie just puts me in overdrive.

Like a cat in a jungle, she crawls in my direction, but I’m done letting her set the pace. I’m too hungry for her, and I need to impale myself into her heat stat. I grab her by the waist and pull her up until her pussy is flush against my cock.

“Someone is eager.” She laughs.

“I’ve been lusting after you for too long.”

“You have?” She tilts her head to the side. “How long?”

“Honestly, since the night at the Red Barn party, only I was too angry to realize it then.”

“You also made quite an impression on me that night.”

She gyrates her hips, and the tip slides right in. She’s so wet, I can sheathe myself in her with a single thrust.

“I think I’m done with talking, Sadie.” I skim my hands down to her hips, keeping her in place as I jerk upward.

She moans loudly.

As I predicted, I slide in with ease. She feels too good though, so to avoid a quick-draw move, I wait for a couple of beats, hoping I can get used to her tightness.

Leaning forward, she flattens her palms on my chest and closes her eyes. “Hell, this is.... God, I can’t even form a sentence.”

“I haven’t done anything yet.” I chuckle. “I’m trying not to explode too soon.”

“Think of unsexy things.” She moves her hips, spurring me into action.

"I don't think that'd help much," I breathe as we both begin to move faster.

Right now, I don't know who is fucking whom. All I know is my head is getting lighter, probably because all my blood has converged to my junk. But as much as I love the view of Sadie's tits bouncing as she rides me, I need more. I need to be closer, to go deeper.

I flip us around, managing to stay inside her.

"There. Much better." I silence her protest with my lips, sucking her tongue into my mouth as I pound into her without mercy.

She brings her knees up, locking her legs behind me. My cock seems to grow larger, or maybe Sadie's pussy is squeezing me more. I don't know. I've lost the ability to think straight as tendrils of desire curl at the base of my spine. The release is near; my balls are tight as hell. But I want to prolong this moment for as long as I can. I want to make Sadie come again before I surrender myself to oblivion.

She moans against my lips, becoming tense around me. The tremors come and she screams quietly, the sound of her climax muffled by my mouth. Her nails scratch my back, and the pain mixes with the built-up pleasure. I can't fight it any longer, so I don't. Grunting, I piston in and out of her, milking my release to the max. I could fuck her for eternity, if that was possible. I've never had a pussy as sweet as hers.

I don't stop moving until I sense Sadie relax under me. Resting on my elbows, careful not to crush her, I lean back. Her eyes are hooded, and she has a happy, lazy smile that I want to believe only I have the privilege of witnessing.

"Hey," I say.

"Hi." Her grin widens. "That was amazing."

"Yeah, it was."

"So worth all the yearning and sexual tension."

I bring my lips to hers for a kiss because I can't resist her. In fact, I don't know how I was able to keep my distance all this time.

"Hmm, Danny?" she whispers against my lips.

"That's my name, don't wear it out."

She smacks my arm, laughing. "You and your movie quotes."

"Come on, you gave me the perfect opening."

"I can't believe you know *Grease.* I thought only girls watched musicals."

"Remember, I was raised by a single mom. Besides, I only watched it when I was a kid, and that quote stuck in my head. I used it on my mother all the time. It drove her nuts."

"I bet. Anyway, what I wanted to say is that you should probably get rid of the condom before there's a leakage."

"Oh, right."

I pull out and immediately know we have a problem. It's wet down below.

Sadie tenses and sits up.

"Oh my God. Where did the condom go?"

I stare at my dick like a moron—my very bare dick. All that's left of the condom is a rubber ring at the base.

"Shit. It broke."

"How? Ugh. Never mind." Sadie pushes me out of her way and jumps off the bed.

She rushes to the bathroom, closing the door with a bang. I stand too and get rid of what's left of the condom. I still can't believe it broke. It's a brand-new package.

Sadie comes out a minute later, clearly not happy, and begins to get dressed.

"Are you okay?" I ask her. "I'm clean if you're worried about that."

She whirls around, looking possessed. "No, I'm not okay, Danny. I'm not on the pill!"

I wince at her outburst. "Calm down."

"Don't tell me to calm down. If I end up knocked up, it only ruins my life, not yours."

"I'd never walk out on you if you were pregnant."

"You don't get it. But how could you? You're a guy. If I get pregnant, I'm off the team. I can say goodbye to any chance of playing professionally. Nothing changes in your life."

I understand she's freaking out, but I'm beginning to get angry just the same. "That's an unfair statement. Besides, it's not the end of the world. We can get a morning-after pill."

"Just shut up, Danny. You're only making it worse. And why in God's name did you have to buy such cheap condoms?"

"That condom wasn't cheap. Maybe your vagina has thorns." The moment those words leave my mouth, I regret them. "I'm sorry, Sadie. I didn't mean it."

"Ugh! I knew I should have kept my distance from you. This is all my fault for letting hormones take control."

She's already dressed and ready to burst out of my room.

"Do you think I wanted this to happen?"

She gives me an irate look. "I'm pretty sure your dick was more than on board, and now I have a legion of your little swimmers going up to my womb as we speak."

"You're being overdramatic. Come on, I'll take you to a pharmacy so we can buy the morning-after pill."

"I'm not going anywhere with you. You've done enough."

She walks out of my room in a huff, and I follow, naturally, not caring that I'm butt naked. I can't let her get behind the wheel like this. I know she's no longer drunk, but I'd consider raving mad just as dangerous.

"Sadie, come on. You're acting crazy."

"I swear to God, Danny, if you don't stop talking, I'm going to punch you in the throat."

"Just let me put some clothes on and I'll go with you."

"I said no."

"Why are you being so stubborn? This isn't only your mistake, it's mine too."

Her eyes turn rounder, and there's a tightness in her features that looks different than anger. She seems hurt, but I didn't say anything that she hadn't already said to me.

"Dude? What's with all the noise?" Andy complains from the hallway.

I turn around. "Go back to bed, Andy."

No surprise, he does the opposite and walks over. "Why are you naked? Oh...."

The sound of the door banging shut makes me turn. Sadie ran out.

Damn it. I can't follow her like this. By the time I put some pants on, she'll be long gone.

"What happened? Why did Sadie leave like that?"

I return to my room without saying a word. Andy follows. After I find my boxers, I sit on the edge of my bed and rest my head in my hands.

"I fucked up."

"How?"

"We hooked up and the condom broke. Sadie freaked out, and you saw the rest."

Andy sits next to me. "Damn. She's not taking any type of birth control, is she?"

"No."

"The morning-after pill is super effective though, especially if she takes it right away."

"That's what I said, but she was beyond listening to me."

"Well, bitches be crazy. Now that you fucked her out of your system, it's all good. You can move on."

I let out a heavy sigh. That's what I should do, but the idea of simply forgetting her brings a sudden ache to my chest.

"What if I can't move on?"

Andy doesn't speak for a few beats, and then he lets out a whistle. "Damn, you've fallen for her, Danny-boy."

"Maybe."

He snickers. "'Maybe,' he says. Sure. Well, if you said anything you shouldn't to her tonight, there's always tomorrow to grovel."

"I suggested her vagina had thorns when she complained about the quality of the condom."

I don't know why I felt the need to give Andy more ammunition to torment me.

He throws his head back and laughs.

"I think for that one, you'll require more than one day of groveling. Probably a week."

I groan at the thought. "I know."

25

SADIE

I RAN out of Danny's apartment so fast, I almost tripped on my way down the stairs. I couldn't slow down and give him the chance to put on clothes and come after me. I'm too furious, and he should stay the hell away from me. I've already said too many things no sane person would have. I've gone berserk, and I need to calm the fuck down before I can make sense of everything.

The adrenaline cleared any remaining vestiges of alcohol in my blood. I'm painfully sober as I drive away from Danny's building. I don't know the direction of any pharmacy that's open now, but it doesn't matter. I don't think I can face the pharmacist alone. I should have let Danny come with me, but somehow, his presence would only make things more humiliating.

It's not his fault the condom broke. And I'm the one who gambled and decided to trust a rubber barrier that's not one hundred percent foolproof. I have no one to blame for this mess but me. I took out my frustration and anger on Danny, and I already regret it so much.

My hands are shaking when I call Vanessa. It's past midnight, and I'm sure she's asleep, but I have no one else to call. I can't tell Katrina; she's too much of a gossiper, and I don't consider her my friend anyway.

The phone rings four times before Vanessa's sleepy voice comes through. "Hello?"

"Hey, Vanessa. Sorry to call you so late."

"No worries, Sadie. Are you okay?"

"No. Can I come over? I need a favor. It's an emergency of sorts."

"Yeah, of course. I'll text you the address."

"Thank you."

I have to park first before I can copy the address on Google maps; I can't multitask while driving, and even if I could, I shouldn't. I'm relieved when the automated voice says I'm eight minutes away from her house. I put the car in drive and veer back onto the empty street. A minute later, Danny calls. I press the decline button. Does he seriously think I can talk to him right now? If I wanted to have a conversation, I wouldn't have left his apartment.

The ping on my phone lets me know he left a voice mail. Not satisfied, he also texts me several times. Glancing at my phone screen, I see the notifications pop up one after the other. My guilt doubles. I was horrible to him, and here he is, trying to reach out.

Finally, the robotic lady tells me I've arrived at my destination. I park in front of a small house with a cute front yard and a porch. The light outside is on, and when I exit the car, I catch Vanessa peeking from the window. She has the door open for me before I reach the front steps. She's in pj's, making me feel guiltier that I decided to bother her.

"Hey, are you okay?" She watches me intently.

I walk in and survey the small living room to make sure we're alone.

Maybe guessing my train of thought, she says, "Heather is asleep."

"Oh, I didn't know you lived with your sister."

"I couldn't talk my parents out of that one. It's okay. We both have busy schedules and don't see each other much."

"I miss my brother, but I don't think I could live with him, at least not without a referee to intervene."

"Sometimes I feel like that's what I need. But quit stalling. You woke me from a pleasant dream, tell me why."

I can't hold her gaze, so I choose to stare at the floor instead. "Can you come with me to the pharmacy? I need a morning-after pill."

Vanessa touches my shoulder. "What happened? Did someone—"

"I wasn't raped. I just couldn't deal going with the guy. He offered."

"Was it Danny?"

Blush rushes to my cheeks. "Yes, how did you know?"

"You two have been pussyfooting around each other since the Red Barn party. I never bought your friendship. I knew there was more."

I sigh. "Well, now there's nothing. I totally lost it and acted like a deranged psycho. He's probably never going to speak to me again, which is fine. This awful situation just worked as a reminder of why I didn't want to date anyone in the first place."

"I get that. Soccer is also my number one priority. There's no room in my life for boys. Too much drama, you know?"

"Yep, don't I?"

"Do you want something to drink?" she offers.

"No, I'm good, thanks."

"Okay, well, make yourself at home while I go change."

"All right."

Vanessa disappears down the corridor, and I start to browse through the picture frames she has on the bookshelf in the living room. It's mostly pictures of her with her family. In one of them, they're standing in front of the huge statue of Christ the Redeemer in Rio de Janeiro. I barely have time to look at them all before she returns wearing a pair of jeans and shoes. She kept her pajama top.

"Ready?" she asks.

"Yep. Let's go."

During the short drive, Vanessa doesn't try to get more information about the fight with Danny, and for that, I'm glad. As I'm parking the car in front of the pharmacy, another text message from him comes through. It's short and shows completely on the notification.

DANNY: I'm really sorry. Please text me back. I'm worried.

Vanessa's gaze is also down, so she must have read the message too.

"You should text him back, Sadie."

"I will. After I buy this bloody pill."

"You'll be fine. I've taken the morning-after pill before. It works."

"Deep down I know it will, but my brain acts like an arsehole sometimes. If something has a 0.1 percent chance of going bad, that's what my mind gets stuck on."

"I hear ya. Well, there's nothing for it but to go in, get the pill, and hope you're not carrying a mini Danny in your womb already."

My eyes widen. "What the fuck, Vanessa? Is that supposed to make me obsess less about this situation?"

"I was joking, but you have to admit, you and Danny would make adorable babies. Oh, what if it's twins? Can I be the godmother of one? But it has to be the smart one. I definitely don't want to get stuck with a Heather version of your baby."

My mouth is hanging open as I stare at Vanessa. "You've lost your mind."

"Hey, I'm just helping out your asshole brain. I'm sure it hadn't thought of the twin angle yet."

"It had not. But now it's taken it a step further and is showing the possibility of triplets."

"Jesus, I didn't know Danny had super sperm." She scoffs.

"Well, he had a super cock. It managed to break the condom."

"Or maybe you have a super vagina. Have you thought about that?" She raises an eyebrow.

I snort. "Danny accused my vagina of having thorns."

Vanessa laughs. "He said that? Oh my God, I'm learning a whole new side of Danny all thanks to you."

"Should we go in now? I think you've taken the piss enough already."

"Sure, but did it work? Are you feeling less anxious?"

I want to say no, that she only made it worse, but that'd be a lie. I *am* feeling better. I guess by coming up with all those crazy scenarios, she helped me realize I was creating a storm inside a glass of water.

"Yeah. Thanks for your help." I look at the pharmacy building and let out a heavy sigh. "Let's get this humiliation over with."

26

DANNY

An hour after my last message, Sadie finally texted me back to tell me she was home. She didn't mention the morning-after pill, but I assumed she got it. I didn't sleep at all last night. Instead, I kept replaying our fight and dissecting what I should have said instead of what came out of my mouth.

Restless and tired as hell, I'm in a foul mood when I finally give up sleeping and get out of bed. Everyone is still in snooze town—no surprise, since it's only five past six. I drink a glass of orange juice and stare into space for a minute.

"Fuck. It's groveling time."

I get dressed quickly and head to Sadie's dorm, hoping she's there. I have no way of getting inside her building, and judging by her radio silence, I have zero hope she'll answer my call this morning. So I wait in front of the door until someone walks out.

Ten minutes later, a dude who looks like he barely got any sleep steps out, and I slip in before the door shuts again. My heart is hammering loudly as I take the stairs two steps at a time. I have no idea what I'm going to tell Sadie, but our story can't end like this because of a fucking broken condom.

In front of her door, I knock softly at first. When I don't hear any sound inside, I pound harder and call her name.

"Hold on," a female voice says, irritated.

Not Sadie. Shit. It must be her roommate.

A disheveled short girl opens the door a sliver. Her makeup is smeared, and I can smell her rancid breath from where I stand.

"Who are you?"

"I'm Danny. Is Sadie in?"

"No. She didn't come home last night."

Fuck. I rub my chin in frustration as I wonder where she could have possibly spent the night.

"Do you know where she might be?" I ask.

"No. We don't keep tabs on each other. Can I go back to sleep now?"

"Sure. Sorry to bother."

She shuts the door in my face without another word. I can't even complain about her rudeness. I did come in at an ungodly hour. I pull up my phone and call Andy, hoping he picks up. He does so after the fifth ring.

"Danny, you'd better be dying in your room to be calling me this early."

"I'm not home. I came to see Sadie and grovel like you suggested, but she didn't spend the night in her dorm. Do you have any idea where she could have gone?"

"Maybe she went to her dad's."

There's no way she'd have gone to him.

"Probably not."

"Then I'd start calling her teammates. Start with Vanessa since she's the captain."

Duh. I'm an idiot. I don't know why I didn't think about that before.

"Do you happen to have her number?" I ask.

"Yeah. I'll text you. Good luck, bro."

He ends the call, but a minute later, he comes through with Vanessa's number. I wait until I'm back in my car to place the call; in case she does pick up the phone, I don't want anyone eavesdropping on my conversation, even if campus is currently a ghost town at this hour.

To my surprise, Vanessa answers after the second ring.

"Hello?"

"Hey, Vanessa. It's Danny. Sorry to bother you so early. I was wondering if—"

"Yeah, she's here. Sleeping now. Do you need my address?"

Wow. That was easy.

"Sure."

"I'll text you."

Before she hangs up, I ask, "How angry is she still?"

"Honestly, I don't think she was ever mad at you. But you definitely should talk. I'd suggest you stop on your way to grab coffee and some unhealthy breakfast. And since I'm being so helpful, you'd better bring me some too."

I chuckle. "Sure. I can do that. Thank you, Vanessa."

"No problem."

THIRTY MINUTES LATER, I'm standing in front of Vanessa's house. It's not far from where Troy and Charlie used to live. Last year, there was a moment when Andy considered moving into their place while they were traveling, but in the end, he decided to stay put and avoid the hassle. Jane has a room there, but she spends most of her time at our place.

I realize I'm stalling, which means the coffee is getting cold. I'm about to get out of the car when Heather, Vanessa's twin sister, walks out dressed in workout clothes. She has her sunglasses on and doesn't seem to notice me parked in front of her house. She heads straight to her car on the other side of the road. I wait until she's gone to step out. The fewer people who know about what happened between Sadie and me, the better. I hate being the subject of gossip and Sadie does too.

I text Vanessa, letting her know I'm outside. I could knock or ring the doorbell, but just in case Sadie is up already, I don't want her to ask Vanessa not to let me in. I'm banking on surprise, which could backfire. It's not like I have a lot of options though.

Vanessa opens the door and tells me Sadie just got up. She'll be out in a second, and she doesn't know I'm here.

"Thanks."

She takes the greasy bag and tray with coffee and sets them on the kitchen counter. I remain standing in the middle of her living room, feeling awkward. She grabs a random cup from the tray and takes a sip.

"They're all the same. Coffee and milk. No sugar."

"Perfect. Just how I like it."

"Do I smell coffee?" Sadie asks from the hallway, but she halts when she sees I'm in the house. "How did you find me?"

"A hunch."

She narrows her eyes and turns to Vanessa. "Did you call him?"

"No. He called me. I wasn't going to lie and say you weren't around."

"Traitor."

"You need to talk. I'm just going to drink my coffee in my room. Have fun, kids. And please don't break anything."

Sadie crosses her arms and watches her friend leave.

"I'm sorry," I blurt out. "I said a bunch of things last night that I shouldn't have. I don't believe for a second that your vagina has thorns."

Her eyes widen a fraction right before she shakes her head.

"I'm not angry about that comment anymore. I know you didn't mean it. I acted crazy, I know, and I'm sorry."

My heart fills with hope, and with that sentiment spreading through my chest, I dare move closer to her.

"Please tell me we're good, Sadie."

She drops her gaze to the counter and sighs loudly. "This isn't about the fight anymore, Danny. It's about what I want—what we both want."

"What do you know about what I want?" I ask, wary now.

She glances at me. "You want to play for the NFL. You don't want drama, and last night was nothing but drama."

"True, but it was an extenuating circumstance. I like being around you. I didn't plan on it. I didn't expect to meet someone I could potentially fa—"

"Don't say it. Please." She sounds pained, and it drives a screwdriver through my chest.

"Sadie...."

She rubs her forehead, shaking her head again. God, if that isn't a sign that I'm about to receive the biggest turndown in the history of turndowns, I don't know what is.

"I can't do this. I can't start a relationship with you, or anyone, for that matter. Yesterday, it was a condom that broke. Tomorrow, it will be a cheerleader who gets too friendly with you. I just can't deal with the drama of dating someone so visible, so popular."

"Are you kidding me? You don't want to date me because I'm popular?"

"It's not only that. Please, Danny, don't make this any harder than it already is."

I'm trembling from anger and frustration. After I swore off getting involved with someone, I had to go and fall for a girl who's more stubborn and unattainable than I thought I was.

"So that's it, then. We pretend nothing ever happened between us and we go back to being just friends."

She watches me with regret in her eyes. "I don't think staying friends is possible for us anymore. We tried, Danny, and it backfired. We should just go our separate ways."

Andy told me to grovel, and I was prepared to do that. But I can't do it. I can't humiliate myself when it's clear that what I'm feeling is one-sided.

"Message received loud and clear. I'll stay out of your way and won't bother you anymore."

I turn around and walk out, fighting the urge to look back. I don't expect Sadie to change her mind, but there's a small part of me that wonders if this end is killing her as much as it's killing me. I can't risk a peek though. If I find nothing in her gaze that shows she cares, then it will be even worse for me.

27

DANNY – Four Weeks Later

I didn't expect the first game of the season, with me being the official starting quarterback, to be as intense and challenging as this one is. We're tied, and it's now down to this last play. Andy is in position, ready to run long when I make the pass. The crowd is clamoring. My pulse is drumming loudly in my ears, but my focus is sharp.

When the time comes, it's like everything happens in slow motion, even though only seconds go by. I throw the ball hard as Andy flies across the field. He catches it in midair and lands in the end zone.

I yell, throwing my fists up in the air. There isn't enough time left on the clock to allow the other team a chance to even the score again. It's over.

I'm jostled to the side when my teammates jump on me in celebration. Howls, whistles, and claps on the back are exchanged as we walk to the sideline. The Rushmore band plays our victory song, and it feels surreal. I'm a happy motherfucker, and yet I feel something is missing.

Not something. *Someone.*

I remove my helmet, and, like an idiot, I look at the stands, hoping in vain to see her face in the crowd, even though I know she wouldn't be there even if we were still friends. She has a game herself in a couple of hours.

Andy throws his arm over my padded shoulders. "Who are you looking for, Danny-boy?"

"No one." I push him off me.

He laughs and then sprays water from the plastic bottle all over his face.

Coach Clarkson walks over, grinning, which is not something I see frequently. He's a serious man, always with a poker face on.

He shakes my hand. "Good job, son."

"Thanks, Coach," I reply in a daze. "It was a close one. I'm sorry."

"Why are you apologizing? You played a heck of a game. You should be proud."

"I *am* proud."

"Good."

"The Ravens are playing later. Are you going?" I ask out of the blue, catching Coach by surprise.

"Yeah. I wouldn't miss it."

"I'm sure Sadie will do great."

He tilts his head to the side, watching me with renewed interest. Crap.

"Do you know my daughter?"

"I met her at a mixer at the beginning of preseason training."

"Ah, of course. I haven't really talked to her much. When it comes to soccer, Sadie has a one-track mind. I'd be concerned if I wasn't the same when it comes to football." His eyes shine with pride, which makes me sad and a little envious too.

Sadie is so busy holding on to her anger about her parents'

divorce that she doesn't see how much her father cares about her. She also doesn't know how much I wish I had a father who appreciated me like that. Fuck, I'd be happy just to know who he is.

"We should head back to the locker room. Don't want to make you late for her game."

Coach claps my back and smiles.

A minute later, Andy catches up with me. "I can't believe you were digging for intel about Sadie from her father. You're hopeless, Danny."

"Piss off, Andy. I was not trying to get intel."

"You don't have to lie to me, buddy. Maybe we should check out her game, show our support for the girls."

I give him a droll look. "You're out of your mind. Nothing against the Ravens, but I'm not going to show up at Sadie's game after our last conversation."

"Sorry for suggesting. In that case, let's go out and celebrate in style. We earned it, man."

I grin. "Fuck. We sure did."

SADIE

Excited energy surrounds me as I gather around in the locker room with my teammates, all wearing our Ravens uniform and ready to kick some butt. In my case, I'm hoping I'll be allowed to touch the ball today. As hard as I trained, it wasn't enough to convince Coach Lauda to bench Melody or Joanne in my favor. I didn't want to replace Joanne because she's become one of my closest friends. Melody is another story. It isn't that I don't like her, but she is my competition, which means she must be destroyed. Yeah, it doesn't make sense. She's on my team, and this is her last year. My brain can be scary sometimes.

If my relentless focus didn't earn me a starting position, at least it helped me ignore the hole in my chest. I knew I was getting close to Danny, but I didn't realize how deep those feelings went until I cut him out of my life. Now there's an ache in my chest that won't go away, and every time I see my dad's name flash on my phone when he calls, it reminds me of Danny.

Before coming here, I checked his game score. I couldn't bring myself to actually watch the game on TV. That'd be too painful. They won by a close margin. I almost broke down and texted Danny to congratulate him but wised up at the last second and didn't. He'd probably think my text was to rub it in that they almost lost.

Coach Lauda is finishing up giving her pregame speech. I missed most of it thinking about Danny. A few more sentences and we're off to the field. I'm one of the last ones in the line out of the locker room. The crowd gathered is modest, and that's saying something. Half the stands are empty. I'm sure the football stadium was bursting at the seams. It's so unfair how some sports get all the attention and others don't, especially the ones played by women. The National Women's Soccer team winning the last World Cup worked wonders to bring more attention to us, but it still pales in comparison to male-dominated sports.

Gah, why am I so bitter? This is nothing new to me.

As I head for the bench, I hear louder shouts coming from nearby. I look up and see a small group of people, all wearing Ravens team shirts with Vanessa's number. Their faces are painted with the Brazilian flag.

"Your family?" I ask her.

She looks up. "Yeah. They're big supporters. Never miss any of my games, much to Heather's chagrin."

"Why would she care that your family comes to your games?"

"Sometimes it clashes with football, so you know, they can't see her shake her pom-poms."

Grinning, I say, "Well, cheerleading is a hard sport."

"I'm not saying it isn't. I know Heather works her butt off, but it's wasted. I mean, her entire job is to look pretty and cheer for a bunch of guys who don't need cheering. They have their fans."

"Would you feel differently if the cheerleaders were assigned to support the chess tournament? Or the debate team?"

"Those aren't sports."

"Fine. You win. Table tennis, then. Or better yet, cricket."

Vanessa wrinkles her nose. "They probably could use some cheerleaders. That sport is so boring."

"Not as boring as baseball."

She covers my mouth with her hand. "Shhh, woman. That's America's favorite pastime. We can think these things, but don't say them out loud."

The assistant coach signals for her to get ready, so she steps back, releasing me. Not much later, the game begins. I park my ass on the bench with two of the Three Musketeers, Charlotte and Phoebe. Like I predicted, Steff is where she belongs, guarding the goal. I've never sat on the bench before, and to say it's nerve-racking is an understatement. I want to shout, pace, do anything to get rid of this jittery energy. It's quite maddening. Forty-five minutes never took so long to pass, and by the time we roll into the halftime break, we're losing one to zero.

Morale is low inside the locker room, and there's no indication from Couch Lauda that she plans on using me in the second half. If we were winning, that'd be another story.

When we head back out, my mood is down to the sewers. I wanted to play today more than anything because I need the reminder that sacrificing Danny was worth it. If we lose and I don't get the chance to show my skills, it'll be a real pisser.

Dejected, I sit on the bench next to Felicia Hopkins, the goalie Steff replaced.

"Why are you so sour, Clarkson? It's not like you got shoved aside for new blood." She laughs.

"I just want to play. I can't believe you're not bitter."

"I don't have anything to prove or any aspiration of playing pro. My goal was to get a free ride at college, which the Ravens gave me. I'm a happy camper."

"I guess it's good to have low ambitions."

"Uh, thanks?" She chuckles. "Although I don't think that was a compliment."

"I'm sorry. I'm such a bitch when I'm not happy."

"Aren't we all?"

My legs are bouncing up and down as I watch the game. When the opposing team almost scores again, I jump and yell, frustrated. Couch Lauda gives me a glower in warning and then starts to shout instructions to Vanessa. A minute later, someone cuts off Melody as she's getting near the goal, hitting her leg instead of the ball. She falls hard, crying out.

"Fuck!" I run to the sideline and watch her clutch her leg while her face is scrunched in pain.

The referee pauses the game, and then our medical staff rushes to the field to check on her. A moment later, she needs to be helped off the field because she can't walk without assistance.

Couch Lauda turns to me. "Sadie, warm up."

"Yes, Coach."

I start running along the sideline while the game resumes. We're playing at a disadvantage with one less member, but I can't jump in without a proper warm-up or I'll end up pulling a muscle. It doesn't help with my nerves though.

Finally, after what feels like forever, I join my teammates on the field. There's no time for a quick convo with Vanessa because the other team has the ball and they're advancing toward our goal. Joanne has taken Melody's place as the first striker, so I fall back a little. Our defense manages to steal the ball back, and then it's counterattack time. Vanessa dribbles past one, two players, and I know she plans to kick the ball to Joanne, but she'll get swarmed by the other team's defense in a few seconds while I'm wide open with more room to work a play.

I run ahead of Vanessa, careful to stay behind at least one defensive player to avoid an offside.

"Vanessa! Over here!" I shout.

She seems to ignore me, maintaining her intention to pass the ball to Joanne, when, at the last second, she kicks the ball with her heel in my direction. I don't hesitate when I have control of the ball and kick it even though I'm outside the goal line. The ball makes a curve, going over the defense and right into the corner of the goal. Their goalkeeper had no chance.

"Yes!" I jump so high, I could have been mistaken for a gymnast.

Vanessa and Joanne run to hug me, and then we wave at the small crowd. Vanessa's family goes crazy, making so much noise that it compensates for the half-empty bleachers and the lack of a band.

My heart is beating loud as fuck, and it feels like it's going to burst out of my chest. This high, this feeling is pure gold, and for a moment, it makes all the sacrifices worthwhile.

The game isn't over yet, and I give it my all through the rest of it. In my mind, it's win or nothing. We score again, this time thanks to my assist, Vanessa sending a bazooka to the goal that not even Steff, our Wall, could have stopped.

Minutes after the game is over, I'm still riding on the euphoria of the win as I laugh and get hydrated near the bench.

I'm in mid-swallow when I feel a tap on my shoulder. I turn and find Dad standing there, smiling proudly at me.

"Congratulations, honey. You were amazing out there."

"Thanks. I didn't know you were coming."

"It won't be possible every time, but I'm glad my schedule didn't conflict with yours. I'll be here whenever I can."

Shit. I don't know what to say. Dad is the reason I got interested in sports to begin with. I didn't start to play football until I moved to England, and my reason for starting in the first place was to fill the void he left in my life.

"I'm okay with that."

He beams. For once, it seems I said the right thing, and it's like a huge weight is lifted off my chest.

28

DANNY

Our celebration is at full swing at Tailgaters, a popular college hangout not far from the stadium, when the Ravens show up. Half of the people here are underage, but since this isn't technically a bar, no one gets carded on the way in. It's the easiest thing to get a fake ID if you have the right connections and enough money though. Andy got mine as a birthday present.

Despite my commitment to not party too hard—which I didn't during preseason training—I reckon I deserve to let loose a bit. I wasn't expecting to see Sadie here though, and that immediately puts a damper on my good mood. I toss my head back and gulp down the last of my beer, trying my hardest to ignore her presence.

"Ah hell. It seems the Ravens had the same idea we did," Andy pipes up. "Are you going to be okay, Danny-boy?"

"Bite me, Andy. I can hang out with them."

But I'm hoping Sadie will give me a wide berth. She's been in my head for too long, and I'm just beginning to get over her.

Paris joins us at the high-top table, carrying more drinks. I twist the cap off my beer bottle and gulp down half in one go.

"Whoa. Easy there, buddy," Paris says.

"He's trying to drown his sorrows in alcohol. Let him be," Andy replies.

I set the bottle back on the table with a loud thud and wipe my mouth with the back of my hand. "What sorrows? You're delusional."

My eyes catch Vanessa's from across the room, and with a smile, she heads our way. I no longer have a visual of Sadie, not that I was looking for her.

"Hey, boys. I heard about your win. Congratulations," she says.

"You too," Paris says. "Here, have a beer." He offers his, which still has the cap on.

"It's okay. I was heading to the bar. Who really needs a drink is our MVP." She looks around until she sees what she was looking for. Waving, she says, "Sadie, over here!"

Ah hell. Why, Vanessa? Why?

I take another sip of my beer, and when Sadie joins us, I look at everything but her.

"Hey, what's up?" she says in greeting.

"Sadie, what do you want to drink?" Vanessa asks.

"Oh, I don't think I should be drinking. Bad memories from the last time I got trollied."

I stiffen my back and finally look at her. No, not look. Glare. *Is she for real?*

"Is that so?" I ask, not hiding my annoyance.

She widens her eyes as surprise shines in them. "Are you mental? I wasn't talking about *that* night."

Shame washes over me and I look away, finishing my beer as I do so. Fuck. Maybe I should just go home. I can't keep my cool when I'm around her, and I don't want to make a fool of myself.

A loud ruckus by the entrance of the bar draws my attention. Sadie and Vanessa turn to investigate the noise as well. A second later, I spot the cause, and if I thought the evening couldn't get any worse, I was wrong. Nick Fowler and his sycophants are here.

"Son of a bitch. Why can't we get rid of that pest?" Vanessa mumbles angrily.

"Didn't they lose their game?" Paris asks.

"Yeah, they did, which means Nick will be more obnoxious than usual."

"Let him. I hope he gives me another chance to smash his balls," Sadie replies, earning an angry glance from Vanessa.

"Don't even think about it. With Melody out of commission, we need you. I won't let you get a suspension because of that weasel." She turns to look at us. "That includes the three of you too."

"You're not my captain," Paris retorts angrily.

"No, but I am, and Vanessa is right," Andy cuts in. "As much as I'd love to teach Fowler a lesson, I won't jeopardize the team. Let's just ignore him."

"Too bad he doesn't seem like he wants to ignore us. Asshole is coming our way," I say.

I shift closer to Sadie, an automatic move. I don't know if she noticed, but if she did, at least she didn't step away.

"Well, well, if it isn't the football players trying to pluck the flowers from my garden," Nick slurs.

"What the fuck are you talking about?" Vanessa glowers. "And what's that awful smell? Did you take a dive in a cesspool before coming here?"

He shoots her an angry glance, but he's too drunk to hold the stare for too long.

"I'm saying football players have their cheerleaders. They don't need to fuck around with our girls."

"Your girls? Aren't you a delusional wanker?" Sadie retorts angrily. "Just piss off already. You're stinking up the place."

Nick takes a step toward her. "Listen here, you little b—"

I push him back. "Back off, Nick. No one wants you around. You're an embarrassment to this school's sports department."

Suddenly, Nick is yanked back by his friend. "Sorry, guys."

"Let go of me, Leonard." He tries to break free, but he's too drunk for that.

"Nick, we're leaving. If Coach finds out you were drunk and creating trouble again, you'll be benched."

"You should let him get benched. It's not like he's doing much for your team anyway," Andy chimes in.

I see the remark doesn't sit well with Leonard, but he swallows his anger and drags Nick out.

"Okay, I definitely need a drink after interacting with that mongrel," Vanessa declares.

"Blimey. Me too. He's a fucking prat." Sadie replies absentmindedly.

I notice she's touching the place where her scar is. I never found out how she got that, and now I probably never will. The thought that we've gotten so close and then so far apart in such a short span of time does my head in and also makes me unbearably depressed.

"You know what? I think I'm just going to call it a night," I declare.

Andy's eyebrows shoot up. "Really?"

"How many beers did you have?" Sadie asks, surprising the hell out of me.

"Plenty, but I'm not driving."

I leave it at that and walk away. Let her think whatever she wants. She wanted me out of her life; she doesn't get to know anything about mine.

29

SADIE

THE CELEBRATION last Saturday after the game was a total bust. I knew it would be hard. Anything that resembles a pub isn't really my scene anymore. Places like Tailgaters remind me of my attack, and then Nick had to show up. The arsehole who knifed me was someone like him. Drunk out of his mind.

But the main reason my evening was rubbish was because of Danny. I thought I could handle seeing him again. I was wrong. He wasn't happy to see me either. That much I could tell. Then he just left, and I spent the rest of the evening wondering how he got home. Did he Uber or have a jersey chaser lined up to give him a ride and later *ride* him?

I acted like a total psycho and stalked him on social media just to see if he hooked up with anyone after Tailgaters. Which was stupid as fuck. The whole point of ending whatever I had with him before it developed into more was to avoid drama and the heartache. But it didn't work out that way. I was blindly jealous and couldn't concentrate on anything on Sunday. Not even my one-hour run helped.

Monday morning, I head to class still feeling like shite. I'm glad it's an easy-breezy one, an elective about The Beatles. It boggles my mind that we're required to take classes that have nothing to do with our degree, but I've gotten a free ride, so I shouldn't complain.

No sooner do I sit down than I sense the obvious stares of my male classmates. They know I play football, so at first, I think they're just staring because I was brilliant last Saturday. But then the snickers follow, and I realize those stares aren't of appreciation. They're leery and mocking.

I get up from my seat and march up to the closest wanker to me. "What are you staring at?"

"Nothing." He hides his phone quickly, looking guilty as hell.

"Rubbish. Let me see your phone."

He leans back. "No way."

"They were looking at a list that popped up this morning on social media," a girl three rows down from us chimes in.

"What list?"

"It ranks all female athletes. Best ass, best tits, most likely to have a threesome, most fuckable, and so on. It's disgusting."

"What?" My voice rises to a shriek. "Who posted that?"

"No one knows. It's been shared a lot though. You were voted heavily in a few categories."

"Bloody hell." I turn and storm out of class. I need to get to the bottom of this.

In the hallway, I call Vanessa to ask if she's heard about it already.

"Yeah, I've seen it," she says before I even open my mouth.

"Do you know who posted it, because I'm going to kill whoever did."

"No, but I have my suspicions."

"Nick motherfucking Fowler," I grit out, trying my hardest to contain the red-hot rage going through my veins. And I haven't even seen the list yet. I'm sure I'll explode like the Tasmanian Devil when I do.

"He's one of my suspects, but there are more assholes on campus. I wouldn't put it past one of the frat boys either. They aren't saints."

"That's disgusting. We need to do something about it."

"Have you seen the list?"

I shake my head. "No. The wanker looking at it in class didn't want to show me. Probably a wise decision. I might have taken my anger out on him."

"He probably deserved it if he was reading it. I'm calling Coach Lauda, because this is something that requires bringing in the big guns. It's not only offensive but disrespectful to all women busting their asses to be the best athletes they can be. I'm sick of being sexually objectified."

Her mention of Coach makes me think about my dad. He has influence here, but I don't want him getting involved. Asking a man to help solve our problems doesn't feel right. Fuck the patriarchy.

"Let's meet after you talk to Coach. If we can't find out who created the list in the first place, we can't make the culprit pay."

"Oh, we *are* going to discover who the motherfucker is. And then I'm going to destroy him. I promise you that. Talk later, and try not to kill anyone before class is over for the day."

I can't make such a promise, but I don't tell Vanessa that, so I lie. "Sure. I'll be on my best behavior."

I return to the classroom, still fuming. None of the tossers who were staring before dare to look in my direction. I know I'm giving off crazy psycho vibes, and I'm not going to tone it down. But what was a pleasant class before becomes unbearable. I can't sit there and analyze a fucking Beatles love song when I want to murder someone.

My next class proves to be just as painful, and by the time

lunch rolls around, I'm coming out of my skin. I made plans to meet Joanne and Vanessa at the main cafeteria, but destiny would have it that I cross paths with Danny and Andy first. I know by the way they look at me that they've seen the list.

"Sadie, are you okay?" Danny asks in his usual knight-in-shining-armor manner, melting a little of my anger.

I don't know if it was the idea that he could have gone home with another girl last Saturday that's making my chest feel like it's bleeding out or that I simply just miss him so damn much.

God, I don't need to feel all mushy when some wanker on this campus needs an arse whooping.

"Not really. Do you know who posted that list?" I ask.

His blue eyes turn stormy. "No, but when I find out, he'd better run fast."

I shake my head. "Stay out of it, Danny. This isn't your problem."

"The hell it isn't!"

I wince at his outburst. Vanessa was definitely wrong when she thought Danny didn't have a temper. He's just better than most at keeping it in check.

"This isn't only your problem, Sadie," Andy butts in. "This jackass has disrespected our friends. Do you seriously think we'll just stand on the sidelines and do nothing?"

"He attacked us, not you. He didn't make a list asking people to vote for who has the biggest schlong or who is the ugliest football player on campus. I'm sorry if I don't see this as a general problem. It's an attack against female athletes, and it should be handled by us."

"So you're saying we aren't allowed to be your allies?" Danny asks angrily.

I can see that I'll never be able to get my point across, so to avoid an argument in front of the entire cafeteria, I back down.

"You know what? Do what you want." I spot Vanessa,

Joanna, and Melody across the room and use it as my escape route. "I have to go."

DANNY

"That was pleasant," Andy states dryly as soon as Sadie is out of earshot.

"It could have been worse. She reined in her anger."

"You sure didn't." Andy stares at me knowingly.

"That list was all kinds of fucked up. Of course I didn't. I don't care about what Sadie said, I'm getting involved."

"Don't be stupid now, Danny-boy. What are you going to do if you find out the person responsible for it is Nick Fowler?"

"Then he's dead meat."

"That's the whole problem, and I get why Sadie doesn't want you to meddle. If you touch Nick, even if it's justified, you'll get expelled, and there goes your dream of playing for the NFL."

I grind my teeth in frustration, knowing he's right.

"What if that list mentioned Jane. Would you be levelheaded then?"

"Hell to the fucking no. But again, my future doesn't depend on me graduating. Yours does."

"Your point is moot until we have a culprit. Who are we going to pressure to give up the intel?"

"Not Leo. He's too smart to blab." Andy pulls his cell phone out. "Ricky Montana it is."

I raise an eyebrow. "Do you think he knows?"

"Possibly. He has his ears to the ground. He deals in gossip."

Ricky Montana was in one of Andy's classes last year, and thanks to an exchange of favors, Andy took him under his wing for a while. But then shit happened, Jane came into the picture, and now Andy is no longer the king of parties on campus, so we haven't seen Ricky in a while.

Andy puts the call on speaker so I can hear it.

"Andy, my man. Long time no hear," Ricky's cheery voice comes through.

"Hey, Ricky, what are you doing right now?"

"I was about to grab some grub. Why?"

"Can you meet me at the main cafeteria? It's important."

"Sure can, homie. See you in ten."

Andy and I look for a free table, but it's prime lunchtime and the place is packed. While I'm looking for one, I spot Sadie playing with her food but not making a motion to eat any. I'm distracted and end up bumping into someone.

"Ouch, Danny. Look where you're going," Gwen says, followed by a giggle.

"Sorry. I didn't see you."

"Clearly."

I'm still looking in Sadie's direction like an idiot.

"You're probably wondering if what that list is saying is true."

Her comment makes me snap my attention to her. "What are you talking about?"

"You know, if the new Raven striker has had that many orgies. I mean, she's from England, and you know how European girls are."

I glower. "No, Gwen, I don't know how they are. My advice is to stop spreading rumors. It's a nasty habit, one I'm sure your sorority sisters would frown upon."

"I'm not spreading anything. Just making a comment. You're so touchy, Danny."

"Yo, Danny-boy. Are you coming?" Andy waves me over. He's found a table.

"Yeah."

I walk around Gwen, asking in my head for the thousandth time how I was able to date that girl. She's rotten.

I'm about to sit when my phone vibrates in my pocket. It's my mother. She never calls in the middle of the day unless it's important.

"Hey, Mom."

"Danny, sorry to bother you. Do you think you can swing by the apartment for dinner tonight?"

With everything that's going on, I really don't feel like paying her a visit. That thought makes me feel guilty as hell though.

"I'm a bit busy. Can I come later in the week?"

"I really need to speak to you in person, honey. It can't wait."

Shit. That puts me on high alert. A bunch of terrible scenarios rush through my head.

"Okay, I'll come over. Is everything okay with you, Mom?"

"Oh, I'm fine, honey. I'll see you at seven, okay?"

"Yep. I'll be there."

"Is everything okay, Danny?" Andy asks as soon as I put my phone away.

"I'm not sure. Mom wants me to come over for dinner tonight. She said it couldn't wait."

"Hmm, and you're worried it could be something serious, like she's sick or something."

"That's the first thought that crossed my mind. But she said she's fine."

"Maybe she's met someone." He wiggles his eyebrows up and down.

"Why do you have to do that?"

"Do what?"

"You know, let me know you're thinking dirty thoughts about my mother."

He scoffs. "I did no such thing. You're the one with a filthy mind."

"I'm getting food." I stand up.

"Grab me a burger, will ya?"

Usually I'd tell him to buy his own food, but once again I'm distracted. At least this time, I don't bump into anyone as I head to the food line.

30

DANNY

"Mom, I'm home," I call as I enter the apartment.

She appears in the living room a second later, wiping her hands on her apron.

"Hi, honey. You got here early."

"I didn't want to be late." I walk over and plant a kiss on her cheek. "Do you need help with dinner?"

"Oh no. I've got everything all set. I'm making ham and cheese lasagna."

"My favorite."

Mom returns to the kitchen, and I follow her, too anxious to find out what she wanted to talk to me about. I pull up a stool while she chops vegetables for the salad.

"So, I'm here. What did you want to tell me?"

She doesn't answer for a couple of beats, but I notice the new rigidness around her mouth.

"Mom? You're making me worried."

With a sigh, she stops chopping and looks at me. "It's about your father. He got in touch."

Suddenly, it feels like my world has gone off-kilter. I'm glad I'm sitting because I might have collapsed otherwise.

"I see. Why?"

A long time ago, Mom told me the truth about my conception and why my father wasn't in the picture. I pretended for her sake that I didn't care, but what eight-year-old wouldn't care that their father would rather he'd never been born?

"He's sick, and I guess he wants to make amends."

I laugh bitterly. "Oh, that's rich. So he only wants to connect with his son because he's on his deathbed?"

Her eyes fill with tears. "Honey, I know this is hard for you. It's not easy for me either. I almost fell off my chair when he showed up at Dr. Francis's office."

"What? He came by your place of work? The nerve!"

"He figured I wouldn't take his call. He was right. After I recovered from the shock of seeing him in the flesh after all these years, I wanted to toss him out. Of course, I couldn't cause a scene in the office."

"The bastard was counting on that."

"Yeah. He cornered me, and I had no choice but to hear what he had to say." She sighs. "Long story short, he wants to meet you."

"I don't care that he's dying. I want nothing to do with the man." I stand suddenly as all my years of suppressed anger come to the surface.

"I'll be behind any decision you make. I won't push you to meet him. But I also couldn't not let you know about it."

I pull my hair back, yanking at the strands. "I-I can't be here, Mom. I have to go."

"What about dinner?"

"Freeze it, will you?"

Her expression falls, but I don't want her to witness me wrestle with my conflicted feelings. I head out, forgetting to kiss her goodbye. My mind is going a hundred miles an hour, trying to reconcile the fact that I've always wanted to know my father and the truth that he only wants to meet me because he's dying.

The drive back to campus is torment. The radio is on, but no song that comes through helps with my dark mood. Traffic is brutal, and for once, I don't have the patience for it. I honk and curse, getting dangerously close to having a road rage episode.

This is hell.

After an eternity, I finally turn onto my street. But when I park in front of my building, I don't get out of the car right away. I'm not sure who is home, but I know I'm not in the mood to see or talk to anyone. I can't just sit here though.

Decision made, I get out and go for a jog. My head is full of thoughts, so I let my feet take me wherever they want. I run until my breathing comes out in bursts and sweat dots my skin. When I finally stop, I brace my hands on my knees to catch my breath. I have no idea where I am until I look up and see I'm in front of the library building. This is where Sadie and I used to meet every day for our morning runs.

I'm not sure why my subconscious decided to bring me here, but being reminded of what I lost is just adding insult to injury. I turn around, determined to get the hell out of here as fast as possible, even though my legs are beginning to protest. I stop when I see a familiar figure running in my direction, her blonde ponytail swishing with the rhythm of her pace.

She sees me and slows down, coming to a stop in front of me. She must have just started her run because she looks fresh out of the shower.

"Hey, I didn't expect to see you here," she says.

"Same."

She furrows her brow. "What's wrong? Did something happen?"

Am I that transparent?

"Why do you ask?"

"You don't look happy."

I rub my face, not knowing how to respond to that, then look out in the distance. "I went to see my mom today."

She steps closer and touches my arm. "Is everything okay?"

I try to ignore the goose bumps that form on my arm thanks to her hand there.

"No. But you probably don't want to hear me cry about my problems."

"Danny, you can talk to me."

I raise an eyebrow. "Can I? I remember vividly the last time we spoke. You didn't want anything to do with me. Friendship was off the table."

"I was wrong."

I want to yell at her, say she can take her friendship card and shove it where the sun doesn't shine, but I don't do any of that. That proves how low my self-esteem is that I'm willing to accept her crumbs. Pathetic.

Bone-tired, suddenly, I head for the steps leading to the library building and sit down. Sadie follows and drops next to me.

"My father contacted my mother. Showed up at her work."

"Without more context, I'm going to assume that's a bad thing."

I bring my knees up and hug my legs. "Sorry. I should probably explain why I never met him before."

"You don't have to, but I'm all ears if you do."

After our fight, Sadie should be the last person I'd want to unload my family drama to. But even after all these weeks without speaking, the feeling that I can tell her everything hasn't gone away.

"When he and my mother were dating, he neglected to tell her he was married. She only discovered after she got pregnant and he freaked out. Told her he wanted nothing to do with me and gave her money to have an abortion."

She touches my arm and squeezes. "I'm so sorry, Danny. That's total rubbish."

"Yep. And now he's sick, probably dying, and he wants to meet me."

"You must be feeling all sorts of conflicted emotions, aren't you?"

I nod once. "I am, and that's the problem. Why am I feeling guilty for saying I don't want to meet the son of a bitch? He told my mother to get rid of me. He never once in nineteen years reached out to ask how we were doing. And suddenly I'm supposed to meet him to make him feel better about his guilty conscience?"

"You're feeling guilty because you're not a horrible person like he is. You shouldn't though. You're probably going to think even less of me for saying this, but as far as I'm concerned, he's not your father. He's just a sperm donor, and you shouldn't feel an ounce of remorse for saying no to him."

"I don't think ill of you, Sadie."

She withdraws her hand from my arm, and I miss the contact.

"Why not? You should. I was a real bitch to you."

"A little."

"Not a little. Major cunt-ness. I think...." She pauses and sighs. "I think the reason I lost it was because I let you get too close. I never felt that way about anyone before, and I became overwhelmed and frightened."

My traitorous heart is racing as I turn to her. "What are you saying, Sadie? Did you fall for me?"

"Bugger. I shouldn't have said anything." It's her turn to hug her knees and look away.

"Too late now. You can't unsay it."

She faces me, glaring now. "It doesn't matter, does it? I

fucked up royally, and right now, I'm just trying to do the right thing and be a good friend, but I'm already messing it up again. Clearly I suck at relationships of any kind."

"Yeah, you're horrible. You can't even do a love declaration properly."

She opens her mouth, twisting her face into an expression of indignation. "Danny Hudson, you're such a concei—"

I reach for the back of her head, keeping her in place while I crush my lips to hers, ceasing her protest. She tenses for a split second before she returns the kiss with the same fervor. Damn it, I missed her taste, and the way being close to her makes me feel. This could be another mistake, but hell, there's no turning back now.

We break apart after a minute, and when I see Sadie's hooded eyes, my face splits into a smile.

"Why did you stop?" she asks.

"Because we're making out in front of the library."

"I don't care if people see us."

"You don't?"

"I want to kiss you whenever I feel like it. That is, if you want me to kiss you often."

I cup her cheek and run my thumb over it. "Damn straight I do. But I have one condition."

"What?" She leans back.

"No more friends-with-benefit BS."

Her eyebrows shoot up. "Wait. You want to date me?"

I chuckle. "Why do you sound surprised?"

"Because... well, in case you haven't noticed, I have issues."

"Who doesn't? I like you, Sadie. More than I thought I could like anyone again."

"What about us keeping our focus on our careers?"

"I say we were wrong about the whole thing. Being apart didn't help with my concentration."

She scrunches her nose in the cutest way possible, making me want to kiss her again. But I restrain myself.

"No, it sucked actually," she replies. "There's only a tiny issue."

"What is it?"

"How do you think my father will react when he learns you're sleeping with his daughter?"

Ah hell. I forgot about Coach Clarkson. But since I'm a guy, that's not what my mind focuses on.

"Are you saying sex is back on the menu?" I grin.

She narrows her eyes. "Based on your response to what I just said, maybe we should hold off on that for a little bit."

"Okay, okay. So let's stress about Coach Clarkson, then. That's way more fun."

31

SADIE

MY HEART IS BEATING like a drum, audible and fast as Danny and I walk side by side back to my car, his hand firmly clasping mine. When he said he ran all the way here from his apartment, I thought he was mental. Now I get to give him a lift back home, and I'm glad he felt the need to exert himself until he forgot his problems.

I'm giddy like a schoolgirl, and the butterflies in my belly are having a dancing competition. When we're both inside the car, it's like the air becomes supercharged with electricity. The sun has set, and the only illumination is coming from the streetlights.

Instead of turning on the engine, I turn to him. A second later, we meet in the middle for another hot kiss that sets fire to my body and melts my bones. His hand is resting on my waist, and mine has found its way into his hair. I twist my fingers around a strand as I tilt my head to the side, deepening the kiss.

I love the way his tongue dances with mine, taking and giving control. I can't believe I was stupid enough to walk away from this, from him. My body tingles all over as desire spreads through me like wildfire. I regret saying I want to take things slowly, because I'd love nothing more than to straddle Danny and ride him into oblivion.

But I don't want to mess things up again, so taking it slower —not slow—is the safest bet for us.

Danny bites my lower lip and then places open kisses across my jaw and neck. I arch my back, offering my throat for him to feast on. His hand has slid lower, and now his fingers dig deep into my hip. Would he think less of me if I begged him to move his hand between my legs? I'm so turned on that I'm beginning to lose my mind.

Breathless, I say, "I think I should take you home now."

"Yeah, I think you should," he whispers in my ear but makes no move to let go of me.

His mouth returns to mine, and it's another minute before I find the strength to ease off and keep him from following.

"If we don't stop now, I won't be able to drive at all."

He chuckles. "You know how hard it is for me not to make a sarcastic comment?"

"If you know what's best for you, you won't."

Still grinning, he rubs his thumb over my swollen lips. "Sometimes I don't, Sadie. You'd better keep me straight."

My core throbs as my dirty mind conjures up all kinds of kinky scenarios where I could keep Danny straight. And one of them involves taking our make-out session to the back seat of the car.

Reluctantly, I return to my side of the vehicle and turn the engine on. No surprise, all the windows are foggy. We've been kissing for a while.

I'm self-conscious when I pull out of the parking spot. Danny won't take his eyes off me.

"Uh, Sadie?" he says.

"Yeah."

"You forgot to turn the headlights on."

Ah, fuck. How can I get mad at him for making fun of my driving skills when I keep giving him ammunition?

"Stop distracting me."

"How am I distracting you?" I hear the hint of amusement in his tone.

"You're sitting next to me. That's plenty distracting."

"I'm not sure how I can solve that problem for you. Would you like me to move to the back seat?"

"And make me look like an Uber driver? No, thanks. Stay where you are."

He laughs. "Okay, babe."

"Babe? Is that going to be your nickname for me now?"

"You don't like it?"

"It's a bit generic."

"What would you like me to call you, then? Darling? Sweetheart? Sugarplum?"

I snort. "Sugarplum? I don't think I've ever heard that one before."

"Then it's settled. Sugarplum it is."

I peel my eyes off the road for a split second to glower at him. "You're acting sassy already and we've only been dating for a hot minute."

He gives me a boyish shrug. "What can I say? You rubbed off on me."

I open my mouth to reply, but Danny's phone interrupts. He fishes it out of his pocket and answers.

"Hey, Andy."

"Where are you?" he asks loud enough that I can hear from my side of the car.

"I'm on my way back home. Why?"

"I saw your car parked in front of the building and I was wondering. How was your dinner with your mom?"

"I'll tell you when I get home," he replies without the levity from before.

Curse Andy for reminding Danny of his shitty day. I know it's wrong to be annoyed with his roommate, but I'm a lioness when it comes to protecting the people I love.

I grip the steering wheel tighter. *Holy shit. Is that what I feel for Danny? I love him?* I knew I cared about him, and our fallout hurt me more than I thought it would. But I didn't realize I had fallen so hard already.

You'd better not say anything to him, Sadie, or he'll think you're a veritable psycho.

My thoughts are suddenly too loud, and I miss the next thing Andy says. All I know is that by the time I park close to Danny's building, he's gripping his phone in a viselike hold and staring out the window with his jaw clenched.

"What happened?" I ask.

He turns to me, looking too grim for my liking.

"We know who uploaded the list."

My spine becomes taut in a flash. "Who?"

"A freshman named Gary Hanson. Do you know him?"

"Never heard the name before. So not Nick Fowler?"

I can't help the disappointment. I wanted the dick to be responsible, so I'd have a reason to make his life miserable.

"As far as Andy knows, neither Nick nor anyone on the men's soccer team was involved."

"How did Andy discover who it was?"

Danny's eyes flash with guilt. "I know you told me to stay out of it, but I just couldn't, Sadie. We know a guy who's into every bit of gossip on campus. He asked around, and that's how we got to Gary."

"Do you think he could be covering for someone?"

"I don't know. Anyway, Andy passed the information to the school's administration and the coaches."

I squint. "When you say coaches, do you also mean my father?"

"I think so."

I turn away, leaning my head back. "Bollocks. I really wanted to keep my father from finding out or getting involved. I hate this."

Danny covers my hand with his. "Why are you so intent on keeping him out of your life, Sadie?"

I close my eyes, hating that his question makes my eyes prick with tears. "Because he let me down when I needed him the most."

"Come here." He reaches over, sliding his hand behind my neck and pulling me to him.

His lips are soft over mine, and the kiss is sweet and lazy. There's still the underlying raw need in it, but Danny isn't trying to sex me up right now. I can sense the emotion, his feelings in the way he worships my mouth. I melt into him, letting him erase the sadness from my heart.

He breaks the kiss too quickly, though, and presses his forehead against mine. "Come up?"

"I'm not sure I should," I breathe out.

"I promise to be on my best behavior."

"You're not the problem. I am."

"Come on, sugarplum. Are you saying you can't resist my charms?" He grins.

"No, I can't. You're my weakness, Danny Hudson."

"I'm not sure if I should take that as a compliment."

I capture his face between my hands and flatten my lips to his, no tongue this time. Then I push him back. "Get out before my knickers disappear."

He shakes his head, laughing. "You're one bossy woman. I'll call you later, okay?"

"Okay."

He gets out, and I watch him leave, unashamed to check his

fine tush as he walks away. The boy is so pretty it hurts. I can't believe I almost let him slide through my fingers. I was definitely dead from the neck up for the past four weeks.

No more. I'm gonna have my cake and eat it too.

My heart is soaring as I drive off. I plug in Anika's Spotify list and sing out loud to Spice Girls' "Wannabe."

Irrefutable proof that I've fallen head over heels for Danny.

DANNY

I have a stupid grin on my face when I walk through the door. Andy is in the kitchen baking something. Jane is sitting at the dining room table, typing away on her laptop, and Lorenzo is nowhere to be seen. My guess, he's in his bedroom.

Andy looks up and notices my happy expression, which prompts him to raise an eyebrow in question.

"What's with the I-just-got-my-dick-sucked face?" he asks.

Jane whips her head toward Andy, frowning. "I thought we talked about those comments. You're giving Lorenzo a bad example."

"He's not around, sweet cheeks." He winks at her, making her blush.

"This is not my post-BJ face," I reply good-naturedly.

"Something happened though. You were looking gloomy when you left for your mom's."

"Yeah. The conversation with her wasn't pleasant, but then I decided to go for a run, and I feel much better."

I wonder how long I'll be able to evade Andy's probing questions. I don't want to hide from him that I'm dating Sadie, but not telling him right away will surely drive him mad. I can't pass up the opportunity to yank his chain.

"What did she want to tell you?" Jane asks.

"Guess who decided to show up after nineteen years wanting to meet me?"

Andy stops whisking his mixture and stares bug-eyed. "Shut up. Your father?"

I nod, crossing my arms and leaning against the kitchen counter. "Yep. He's dying, and he wants to make peace with his shitty conscience or whatever."

"That's horrible. I mean, that he's dying," Jane says.

"Sure, maybe to the people he didn't abandon. I couldn't care less."

"So you're not going to meet him?" Andy asks, watching me intently.

"Nope."

"Danny, are you sure? This might be your only chance to get to know him," Jane replies kindly, but her words fuel the guilt I'm already feeling.

I like Sadie's reaction much better, and that's why I'm in love with her.

I stand straighter as the realization solidifies in my head. I suspected it, but after today, I know.

"So what if Danny never gets to know the douche? You can't miss what you never had," Andy retorts.

He's wrong about that. I can miss something I've never had. I realize it's not a real person I'm missing though but the idealization of a father figure.

"It doesn't matter. I told my mother I don't want to meet him, and that's that."

I turn around and head for my room.

"You still haven't told us why you looked like you were on cloud nine when you came in," Andy pipes up.

"Ah yeah. I was making out with Sadie in her car. Talk to you tomorrow."

"Wait, what?" he shouts. "You can't simply tell us that and leave."

Not stopping or looking back, I say, "Watch me."

Like the pest he is, Andy follows me. "Dude, you're with Sadie now? For real?"

I fall back in my bed and lace my fingers behind my head. "Yep. I bumped into her during my run, we talked, and, well... we decided to give dating a try."

"Do you think that's a smart idea considering what happened a month ago?"

I frown. "Why are you playing devil's advocate now? I thought you were Team Sadie."

"I'm Team Danny. I just want to make sure you're not jumping into a relationship because of the deal with your dad."

I'm torn between feeling moved by Andy's concern and annoyed that he'd think I'd use Sadie to forget my problems.

"That's not what this is about." I sit up, no longer relaxed.

Andy stares at me for a few seconds without saying a word. Then he grins a little. "I get it now. Well, welcome to the club, buddy."

32

SADIE

Even though I'm officially dating Danny, and we spent a couple hours on the phone last night, we didn't make any plans to meet today. So when Vanessa texted me, wanting to meet up for lunch, I said yes. The main cafeteria is always packed at lunchtime, but I don't have any trouble finding her in the sea of students. She's snagged a big table, and almost the entire team is there.

I head toward the buffet to grab lunch first, narrowing my eyes as I try to read today's specials from afar. Distracted, it's no surprise that when Danny throws his arm over my shoulders, I let out a yell and jump, startled.

He howls like a fiend.

"Bloody hell. You almost gave me a heart attack," I say, pressing my hand over my chest.

"Sorry, sugarplum. I couldn't resist. You were making love with your eyes at that menu board, and I got jealous."

My eyebrows arch. "You were jealous of food?"

He pulls me into an embrace, leaning down to kiss me

softly on the lips. In the middle of the cafeteria. In front of everyone.

Be still my heart. We are really doing this.

When he pulls back, he's smiling from ear to ear, and his eyes have a pleased twinkle in them. As for me, I'm dangerously close to combusting on the spot.

"Hey," he says lazily.

"Hi." My lips curl into a grin.

"Please stop making fuck-me eyes at each other. We're in the middle of the cafeteria for crying out loud," Andy complains.

I hadn't realized he was nearby. That's the effect Danny has on me. He makes me forget the world exists, which is a little scary. I'm not used to being so wrapped up in someone like that.

Danny glowers in his direction. "Like you and Jane are any different."

Andy tries to hold on to his annoyance, but the corners of his lips twitch upward. "Touché."

He gets in line, and Danny and I follow him. We're holding hands, and now everyone is staring, including Danny's ex, who's sitting not far from where we are. If looks could kill, I'd be dead on the spot. She doesn't care that I caught her staring. She maintains her hateful eyes on us. I do the only thing suitable in this situation: I step even closer to Danny and rest my head against his shoulder.

Eat your heart out, bitch.

"I didn't know you'd be here today. I made plans to sit with Vanessa and the girls," I tell Danny with regret. I wouldn't mind having lunch with him.

"That's okay. I'm not the possessive and controlling kind of boyfriend."

I lean back and look up. "What kind of boyfriend are you?"

He smirks. "The best kind."

"God," Andy groans. "*Stawp it.*"

Before either of us can reply, we're interrupted by a tall and lanky guy. "Hey, dudes. What's up? Oh, hello, dudette. I didn't see you there with Danny blocking the view."

"Hey, Ricky," Danny replies. "This is my girlfriend, Sadie."

"Nice to meet you, girlie. Hey, you were on that list."

Any goodwill toward Ricky evaporates into thin air. "So?"

"Such crappy bullshit. I'm glad I could help find the dickwad who uploaded it."

"Oh, it was you?" I asked, surprised, not connecting the dots until now.

Ricky nods. "Yep."

"Mr. Montana here is a master of digging up dirty on everyone," Danny pipes up.

"But anyway, I'm stoked that I bumped into you." He looks at Danny. "I got more news on that front."

Danny squeezes my hand a little tighter as his entire body becomes tense. Mine is too.

"What news?"

"Sadie, there you are." Vanessa joins us, interrupting the conversation. She spares a glance in Ricky's direction, and I notice the guy is now staring at her with open admiration.

The line moves, and we're forced to step forward too.

"Ricky was about to tell us more about that nasty list," I say.

"That's why I came here to get you. Gary fessed up about the whole thing after he was threatened with expulsion. It turns out he wasn't responsible for creating the list. The assholes from the soccer team did it, and that list was shared with all the fraternity houses for voting."

"Son of a bitch. I'm going to kill him," Danny grits out.

I pull on his arm, forcing him to look at me. "You're not getting involved. Let school administration handle it."

"Really? Are you saying you're not going to do anything yourself?"

"Of course she isn't," Vanessa butts in. "Right, Sadie?" She gives me a meaningful look.

"As much as I'd like to rip his nut sack off, I won't touch Nick as long as he's punished accordingly."

"He will be," Danny says with conviction.

His comment doesn't give me comfort though. He made it sound like Nick would get his punishment one way or another.

DANNY

We don't hear anything about Nick and the other nimrods responsible for the list for the rest of the day. Gossip about the situation didn't even spread through campus, which, to me, doesn't bode well. It meant school administration was trying to salvage the situation, perhaps give Nick a mild punishment such as academic probation instead of expulsion.

I tried to keep my frustration bottled up during practice, but I messed up a few passes and got yelled at by Coach Clarkson. It took everything in me not to seek him out afterward and ask if he knew anything about Nick, but I didn't want to make him suspicious of my interest. I was afraid he'd guess about Sadie and me. The fear itself was ludicrous. We weren't hiding from anyone on campus that we were dating; it wouldn't take long for the gossip to reach Coach's ears.

It's not until after dinner that my suspicions are confirmed by a text from Sadie.

SADIE: Nick and his wanker friends aren't off the soccer team!!!! I'm going to murder someone.

I call her instead of replying via text.

"What happened?" I ask.

"I don't know. All I know is the arsehole will only miss a few games and that's it. That's complete rubbish. What kind of message is the school sending? I want to break things."

My hands have already curled into fists. I'm with Sadie on the breaking things ideas, but mine is more specific. I want to break Nick's face.

"Do you want me to come over?" I ask.

"As much as I'd love to see you, I'm heading to Vanessa's place. We need to strategize and think of a way to convince whoever needs to be convinced that the only acceptable punishment for Nick Fowler and everyone involved is expulsion."

"Anything I can do to help?"

She lets out a heavy sigh. "Just... don't do anything to Nick, okay?"

"Why would you say that?"

"Because apparently, I'm the only one who knows about your temper when provoked. Everyone else thinks you're a levelheaded bloke." She chuckles.

Another person saying this might have pissed me off, but coming from Sadie, it's amusing.

"Are you accusing me of being a hothead?" I ask, not fighting the grin.

"No, just stating a fact. And that's one of the things I love about you."

My heart stops beating for a second, only to hammer against my rib cage in the next. A stretch of silence follows. I don't know how to respond to that. Did she mean to say she loves me, or should I take it as a meaningless expression?

"So you love things about me?" I ask finally.

She mutters a curse under her breath, and it sounds distant. She must have pulled the phone away from her face.

"Sadie?"

"Bloody hell. Yes, Danny. I love things about you. Don't let that go to your head."

"Too late now."

"You can be such a bellend sometimes."

"I bet that's one of the things you love about me," I tease.

"You're flirting with danger by taking the piss when I'm in a bad mood."

"All right, all right. I won't say another word, except that...." I pause, not knowing if I should confess what's on the tip of my tongue.

"Except what?" she asks, her voice softer, uncertain.

"Except that I love things about you too."

She doesn't reply right away, but her breathing has changed, turned shallow. With the way my heart is beating faster and my lungs are squeezing tight, I'm betting I sound the same.

"If you wanted me to turn into melted butter, you succeeded, Danny Hudson. I'll talk to you tomorrow."

The line goes dead before I can reply. It doesn't matter. I keep staring at my phone with a goofy grin. But then I remember the reason I called Sadie in the first place, and my amusement is replaced by anger.

I'm not going after Nick and getting myself expelled. I'm not a dumbass. But that doesn't mean I can't get involved. Practice is in the morning tomorrow, and I plan to arrive early to have a real talk with Coach Clarkson. If there's anyone who can apply pressure and force school administration to do more, it's him.

33

DANNY

When I arrive at the Rebels headquarters, the parking lot is empty save for Coach Clarkson's car and a brand-new beamer SUV I don't recognize. It's not unheard of for boosters to meet with Coach, so I don't think much about it as I head inside.

His office door is closed, but he kept the blinds open, allowing me to see that he's in fact meeting with someone. I sigh, regretting not calling him last night to ask for a time to talk. I veer to my locker to change into practice gear, hoping whoever is with him doesn't stay long.

It takes me all of two minutes to change. I could try to study while I wait, but I'm antsy and can't concentrate. I move closer to Coach's office instead, curious to see who is meeting with him this early. I can't see the visitor's face from my position, and if I step closer, Coach will spot me there, spying. However, I have a clear view of Coach's face, and his serious countenance makes me suspect whatever the topic of the conversation is, it's not pleasing him at all.

They aren't speaking now, just locked in a staring contest. If they were, I'd be able to eavesdrop since the walls and door are paper thin.

Finally, Coach shakes his head and says, "I can't help you with that. If he doesn't want to meet you, that's his decision, and I'll stand behind him."

A sense of dread drips down my spine. My chest constricts, and my heart begins to beat in a staccato rhythm.

"I'm sorry you feel this way, but I appreciate your time. If you change your mind, let me know."

The man stands, and Coach does the same. They shake hands, and when the man turns, I recognize him. It's Josh Fitzpatrick, an NFL legend. My stomach bottoms out, and I can't move a muscle. Shock prevents me from retreating. When he walks out, he catches me standing there, paralyzed like a statue.

"Danny," he says, clearly surprised.

I can't look away while my mind tries to process that this top athlete who filled our cheap TV screen while I was growing up is my father. Denial would be easier, but now that he's standing so close to me, I can see myself in his face. We have the same chin, the same eye shape and color. My hair coloring and curls, I got from my mother.

No, this can't be. This man, wealthy beyond reason, wouldn't let his son live in near poverty.

Coach walks out of the office and clears his throat. I shift my attention to him, and our eyes lock. The anguish in his gaze confirms what the bit of conversation hinted at. I take a step back.

"What are you doing here?" I force the words out, looking at my father again.

"Danny, please. I just want to talk to you."

My body is suddenly shaking with fury. I ball my hands into fists, clenching my jaw so tight it hurts.

"Who the fuck do you think you are to ambush everyone in my life? First at my mother's office, and now here?"

"I want a chance—"

"A chance for what? You had nineteen years!" I yell.

"You need to leave," Coach Clarkson tells him.

Josh gives him a scathing glare that tells me he's not used to people ordering him about.

"Very well. I'll go." He heads toward the exit but pauses next to me. "This isn't how I wanted our first meeting to go, son."

"I'm not your son," I grit out, taking a step to the side while fighting the sickness in my stomach.

My pulse is pounding in my ears, and for a while, it's all I can hear. I'm trapped in a personal nightmare, unaware of my surroundings. Then I feel a hand on my shoulder, which snaps me back to the here and now.

"Are you all right, Danny?" Coach asks me.

"What did that asshole want?"

Coach steps back and rubs his face. "He wanted my help to convince you to sit down with him."

"Did he tell you why?"

My stomach is twisted in knots. The idea that my father would air this secret to Coach Clarkson is mortifying. I feel dirty, unworthy, and I don't know why. I'm not the bastard who abandoned his kid.

"Yes, he did. Do you want to come in and talk?" He points at his office.

I shake my head. "No. I-I need to go."

Faster than lightning, I turn around and leave the locker room. I don't head to the parking lot though, counting on my father to be waiting outside to corner me again. Instead, I veer for the field, and then, I run.

SADIE

I wake up to the shrill sound of my phone ringing. Katrina moans from her side of the room and begs me to answer it. With my eyes still closed, I blindly search for it on my nightstand. When I finally have it in my hand, I open one eye and see it's my father calling. A week ago, that'd be an automatic send to voice mail, but today, I press the green button.

"Dad. Why are you calling me so bloody early?"

"Sorry, hon. It's about Danny."

As if a jolt of electricity went through my body, I sit up on high alert.

"What happened to him?" I ask, ignoring the fact that Dad knew to call me about Danny.

"He met someone he wasn't ready to this morning, and he didn't react well."

My stomach clenches painfully as an awful suspicion crawls into my brain. I don't voice it out loud though. I can't assume he knows about Danny's drama with his father. I won't betray his trust.

"Where is he now?"

"I don't know. He bailed before I could stop him. His car is still parked in front of the building. Wherever he went, he's on foot."

I jump out of bed and search for a pair of pants. "I'm coming over. Have you tried calling Andy?"

"Yes, he's also looking for him. I figured I'd try you as well since you and Danny have gotten so... close."

"He's my boyfriend, Dad."

Maybe the confession is ill timed, but he obviously suspected it already. Might as well let him know it's not a fling.

"We can talk about that later. Let me know when you have news."

"Sure. I'll keep you posted."

"What's going on?" Katrina asks in a drowsy tone.

"Nothing. Go back to sleep."

"Did something happen to Danny?"

Like I'd say anything so she can run her mouth and tell her sorority sisters about it. Fat chance of that. I walk out without bothering to reply.

In the hallway, there's a flutter of activity already. I may have been asleep, but the campus is wide awake. It's already past eight in the morning, and not everyone didn't have class early like me. I pull my cell phone out and call Danny, but it rings until it goes to voice mail. Either he doesn't have his phone on him or he's ignoring my calls too.

When I walk outside the building, I see Andy pulling in. *Shite.* If he's here, then he doesn't have a bloody clue about where Danny could be.

"Any word from him?" we both ask at the same time.

Andy curses. "No. I've looked everywhere I could think of."

"Dad said he left on foot. How far could he have gone?"

"If he was running, pretty far. I hate to do this, but we need to call for reinforcements," he says with his phone already in his hand.

"Who?"

"Puck and Paris for now. I wouldn't dare ask anyone else and risk gossip. Jane is out looking for him too. We'll split up to cover more ground."

"Good plan. Call me if you hear anything," I tell him as I head to my car.

"You do the same."

With my heart stuck in my throat, I get behind the steering wheel. I don't leave the car park right away; instead, I try to put myself in Danny's shoes. Where would I go if I wanted to disappear for a few hours? In the end, I drive to the place where he was last seen, the Rebels' headquarters. I spot Danny's car parked in front of the building. I get out, but instead of going in, I walk over to the wired fence that surrounds the training field. On the other side is the tree line and, hidden by the small forest, the Red Barn.

The entrance to the field is unlocked. No one is practicing outside now, which works for me. I run, covering its length in record time, barely breaking a sweat by the time I reach the other end. I slow down once I get to the forest track. The ground is uneven, and I can't risk spraining an ankle.

My heart is thudding loudly inside my chest as I approach the Red Barn. It looks sad and forlorn in the silence of morning. The door's unlocked, and when I push it open, the hinges creak loudly. I stop by the threshold and scan the open room. It's dim inside, but I can still see Danny sitting on the floor at the far end of the room, hugging his legs. His head is down, hanging between his shoulders.

"How did you find me?" he asks without lifting his gaze to mine.

"A hunch."

I walk over at a normal pace, which is hard when all I want to do is rush to him and pull him into my arms. When I'm near, I simply drop next to him and wait.

"Who told you?"

"Dad."

He glances up then. "Coach Clarkson called you? Why?"

"He knew we were close, and now, well, he knows we're together. I told him. I'm sorry."

His eyebrows furrow. "Why are you apologizing?"

"Because maybe you wanted to tell him yourself. He's your coach, after all."

"That was my plan when I went to see him this morning, but then...." He looks away.

"Your father was there." I finish the sentence for him.

"Yes. The son of a bitch wanted Coach's help."

"I'm so sorry, Danny."

"Did Coach tell you who he is?"

"He didn't say anything, only that you met someone you weren't keen to."

"My father is Josh Fitzpatrick."

The name sounds familiar, but it takes me a second to associate it with the person. When I do, I'm assaulted by a wave of anger. I'm mad at the man for not wanting to have Danny in his life until now, but I'm also angry at his mother for never telling him who his father was. It doesn't take a genius to figure out Danny's life was filled with hardships. He could have grown up like a king.

"Why didn't your mother ever tell you about him?" I ask.

"I don't know. Maybe because he wanted her to have an abortion. He wasn't a famous player when they were together."

Unable to keep my distance any longer, I place my hand on his arm. "Oh, Danny."

"Don't feel sorry for me."

His eyes are hard as they gaze into mine.

"I'm not sorry for you. I'm angry on your behalf. I want to punch your piece-of-shite father in the throat. I want to make you stop hurting so much."

He reaches over, cupping my cheek. "You being here is already helping me."

His fingers slide to the back of my head, tangling with a handful of my hair. He nudges me forward, leaning in to meet me in the middle. When he kisses me, it's soft and tender. It's a brush of lips that spells heartache. I let him set the pace, even though my entire body is yearning for more. I want to show him in any way I can how much he means to me. How much I love him.

He breaks the kiss before it deepens, then leans his forehead against mine. "I'm sorry I got everyone worried. That wasn't my intention."

"I know it wasn't. You wanted to be alone, to process what happened on your own terms without anyone interfering. And I ruined it for you."

"You didn't ruin anything, Sadie. I'm glad you were the one who found me."

I trace his full lips with the tips of my fingers, then his jaw. "You're the most beautiful man I've ever met. It's almost unfair."

He chuckles. "Have you looked at yourself in the mirror lately?"

Shaking my head, I say, "I'm not only talking about the exterior." I flatten my palm against his chest, feeling how fast it's beating. "Your beauty comes from within. Your face and body might have made it difficult to keep things platonic in the beginning, but it was your heart that won me over. I love you, Danny Hudson."

His beautiful blue eyes stay glued to mine, almost as if he's searching for the truth. Does he find it hard to believe I could love him?

His lips slowly curl into a grin as he reaches for my face again. "I'm going to kiss you now, Sadie. *Properly*."

When he says properly, he truly means business. I don't have time to be a little upset that he didn't say he loves me back because his possessive mouth has already made it impossible for me to think straight. The small distance between our bodies vanishes. We're both twisted in a way that brings our chests together, but soon I move to straddle him instead. I just need to be as close to him as possible.

Danny moves his feverish kisses to my neck, leaving goose bumps on my skin as his tongue brands me. I throw my head back, letting out a contended sigh. My fingers are in his hair, twisting and pulling as a manner to ground me somehow. It's impossible though. The warm feeling in my chest has turned me as light as a feather, and now I'm soaring high.

"Danny?"

"Hmm?" he hums in my ear.

"I'm done taking things slowly."

He leans back and looks into my eyes. "Are you sure? We don't need to put sex back on the table yet. I'm fine with waiting."

"I'm not. I said that because...." I lower my gaze, insecure suddenly. "Because I was afraid. I should know better than anyone that life is short and it can end at a moment's notice."

Danny runs his hand down to where my scar is. "Are you talking about this?"

I nod. "I was out celebrating with my teammates in London one evening. My friend and I were followed once we left the pub. The arseholes wanted to harm her, so I jumped in front of a knife to protect her."

His expression is one of wonder. He doesn't say anything for a couple of beats before he captures my face between his hands. "You're the most amazing person I've ever met. I love you so much, Sadie. So damn much."

I didn't tell the story behind my scar to get a love declaration from him, but damn if I'm not basking in it just the same. In an instant, we're kissing again, and then our clothes become superfluous. I don't care that we're in a public space. I just want to be with Danny again.

I pull my T-shirt off, making him freeze for a second.

"What?"

"You're not wearing a bra."

I glance down and then back at him. "I slept in this. When my father called me, I only worried about putting pants and shoes on."

"I really don't want to talk about Coach right now."

He shuts off my reply with his mouth while his hands find my tits. With expert fingers, he teases my nipples, turning them hard in an instant. I straddle him again, even though my sweatpants and his shorts are still in the way. I need the friction to ease the throbbing between my legs.

"Sadie... this is... fuck. We can't keep doing this or this party will be over before it starts."

"Fine."

I get off him and then jump to my feet.

"I didn't mean for you to get away from me."

"God. Blokes do live in hope and die in despair, don't they? Relax. I just need room to do this." I pull my sweatpants and knickers down my legs, then quickly step out of them.

Danny only freezes for half a second before he stands as well and gets rid of the rest of his clothes. He barely has a chance to remove his boxers before I'm on him like a bum on a hot dog. I run my nails across the expanse of his chest while I kiss the hollow of his throat. He makes a sound that's all male when my hand curls around his shaft. His mouth is on my neck now, licking and kissing as I have my fun with him below.

"Sadie, did you bring protection?"

"No. I'm on the pill now."

Unexpectedly, he lifts me and presses me against the wall. I wrap my legs around his hips, bringing my core flush against his erection. His lips slant over mine possessively, and with a precise thrust, he's inside me. I moan against his lips, not expecting the swift wave of pleasure that rolls down my spine.

We don't talk, too busy savoring each other. Our kisses are fiery and urgent, and they match the tempo of Danny's hips pumping in and out of me. This is the hottest thing I've ever done in my life. It's no surprise when I can't keep the climax at bay.

I bite his lower lip as I come hard, the feeling intensified by the increase of Danny's pace. He grows harder inside me, and then his entire frame is shaking. He groans loudly as he empties himself in me. I hold on to him for dear life, digging my nails in his shoulders. He doesn't seem to mind.

He keeps moving in and out even when his tremors subside. I lose track of time, but eventually we both still, and nothing can be heard save for our labored breathing.

Until the front door creaks again and a familiar voice says, "What the hell?"

Danny and I both turn into statues.

My father is here.

34

DANNY

Shit. Shit. Shit. What the hell am I going to do?

I stare at Sadie, seeing my panic mirrored in her eyes. Her face is pale too. Coach Clarkson just caught me in the most compromising position with his daughter, and the only thing I can do is pretend I'm made out of stone. My cock is still inside her, for fuck's sake. I just want a hole to open and swallow Sadie and me. Not even in my wildest nightmares had I pictured this. He's going to have my balls.

"Get dressed, you two, and meet me outside," he says.

The door bangs shut, and only then do I dare to look over my shoulder. He's gone.

"Bloody hell," she blurts out, unlatching from me.

I step back, still reeling from being busted. Quickly, Sadie gets dressed, and that spurs me into action as well.

"I'm so dead," I say.

"*You're* dead?" she shrieks. "What about me? This is so mortifying."

She shoves her arms through her T-shirt sleeves and then

pulls the fabric down with a jerky movement. Then she searches for her shoes. We finish getting dressed at the same time and then face each other.

"We'd better go before he comes back in here and drags us out by our ears."

"Has he ever done that to you?" I ask.

"No. But I think he's raving mad enough to do it."

"Great. Well, then, you'd better fix your shirt. It's inside out."

She glances down and curses. "Hell."

A minute later, we leave the Red Barn together, holding hands. A united front seemed like a good idea, but when Coach Clarkson's furious gaze lands on our interlaced fingers, I realize it was an error in judgment. But Sadie squeezes my hand tighter, signaling me to stay strong.

"Well, are you going to yell at us now?" she asks.

"Damn straight I will. What were you thinking? I called you to help me find my quarterback, not fuck him in public!"

I wince. "Sir, it was my fault. I wasn't thinking."

"No shit, you weren't thinking." He puts his hands on his hips and glares at us. "Do you have any idea what would have happened to your reputation if someone else had caught you instead of me? And in the wake of that horrible list, Sadie. Really?"

"Surprise, surprise. Only *my* reputation would have been smeared, right? Not Danny's."

Coach sighs. "You know the world we live in. It took me threatening to cancel football season to get Nick Fowler and everyone else involved with that list punished accordingly. Do you think the dean would have followed through if he found out about your tryst in the woods?"

"That's not fair," she replies, but without the usual spunk.

"Like I said, sir, it was my fault," I cut in. "Please don't yell at your daughter."

She pulls her hand from my grasp. "What the hell, Danny! I don't need you to take the fall for me. I can speak for myself."

I look at her, feeling way out of my depth now. *Shit.*

"Sadie, I didn't mean it like that."

Her gaze softens, but she won't take her words back. Instead, she glances at Coach. "We're both at fault. Blame it on hormones. We knew it was risky, and we went for it anyway. I'm sorry you had to see it, but I'm not sorry we did it. I have no regrets."

Coach stares at Sadie, motionless, but his eyes are shining with outrage. Damn, I've never seen him so incensed in my life.

Finally, he shakes his head. "What's done is done. I just wish I could bleach my eyes and unsee that."

Heat rushes to my cheeks. Mortification doesn't seem to cover what I'm feeling. I don't think I'll ever be able to look Coach in the eye again.

"Great. Can we go now?" Sadie asks.

"Let's." He turns around and heads down the path back to the training field.

Sadie and I give him a head start before we follow him. But now our united front is broken. Her arms are crossed in front of her chest, and she's pouting.

"I'm sorry," I whisper.

"For what?"

"For acting like a typical guy and forgetting you're more than capable of defending yourself."

"You did act a bit Neanderthalic."

"I know."

She gives me a side-glance. "I'm sorry I yelled at you. I know you had good intentions."

"When it comes to you, only the best."

She quirks an eyebrow. "Even when they're naughty?"

I glance at Coach walking ahead of us with tension in his

shoulders. He's still pissed, but hell, it can't get any worse. I step closer to Sadie and throw my arm over her shoulders.

"Especially the naughty ones."

When we approach the training building, Coach turns to us. "I'd like to see you in my office, Danny."

My stomach bottoms out. I thought yelling in the woods was it. I should have known better. Not only had I skipped practice, but I was caught railing his daughter in an empty building.

Yeah, I'm screwed.

"Yes, Coach."

I watch him disappear inside the building, then glance at Sadie. She gives me an encouraging smile.

"He won't be too hard on you."

"You don't know that."

"He likes you. I think he's just embarrassed that he saw us together."

My face feels warm again. "He's not more embarrassed than I am."

She grins. "You know, that'd be a fantastic story to tell our grandkids."

Despite my predicament, I smile in return, my chest expanding with emotion. I step closer and circle her waist with my arms.

"Grandkids, huh? I like that."

I lean down and nuzzle her neck. She shivers under my caress, moaning softly.

"You'd better go before he comes back out," she whispers without conviction.

"Right." I place a soft kiss below her ear and then step back. "Wish me luck."

She wrinkles her nose. "I don't think luck will help you at all. I'll pray for a miracle."

"Sadie!"

She laughs, skipping away. "Kidding. Call me later."

I watch her leave, and only once she steps through the wired fence gate do I go into the building. The locker room is empty, which is strange because practice was supposed to last a few hours in the morning. Guilt makes my insides feel like jelly. I'm queasy, dreading this meeting with Coach.

He left the door to his office open, but I knock on it anyway. He keeps his gaze glued to the computer screen as he waves me in.

"Shut the door," he says.

I swallow the huge lump in my throat and do as he told me. The click of the door shutting feels too loud and ominous. It's like I'm heading to the gallows.

I pull up a chair and sit down, keeping my gaze glued to his desk.

"I can't tell you how disappointed I am, Danny."

"I know, sir. I am truly sorry you had to see... that."

"No sorrier than I am."

I lift my gaze to his. "I want you to know that it wasn't a casual hookup. I'm in love with your daughter."

His eyes widen a fraction, but he quickly schools his emotions again.

"I see. This isn't an ideal situation. My reputation is based on me treating all my players with impartiality. You dating Sadie changes things."

"It doesn't have to. I'm still committed to the game, sir. I want to play in the NFL."

Coach regards me in silence for a couple of beats. "I wouldn't be doing my job if I didn't point out that your father being an NFL legend could open more doors for you."

His comment catches me completely by surprise.

"You said I had a chance before you knew about my father."

"And I wasn't lying. But I'm a big believer on taking responsibility, and if he's finally willing to shoulder his—"

"No! I don't want anything to do with that man. I don't need his handouts. If I make it to the NFL, it will be by my own merit."

"Fair enough. I won't mention him again. Now back to the subject of my daughter. I can't forbid you to date her, but I won't tolerate PDA of any form in front of me. Is that understood?"

Like I'd want to poke the beast with a short stick.

"Yes, Coach."

"I also expect no more meltdowns from you. I need to be able to count on my quarterback."

Shame washes over me, and the urge to avoid his gaze is immense. But I know Coach wouldn't appreciate cowardness.

"You can, sir. There won't be a repeat of what happened this morning."

When he narrows his eyes, I know he's not only thinking about me bailing after meeting my father. His mind is in the Red Barn again.

Shit.

"Good. You can leave now."

I jump out of my chair as if I was electrocuted. This has been the most excruciating talk of my life.

When I return to the locker room, I find Andy waiting for me, sitting in front of my locker.

"What are you doing here?" I ask.

"Making sure Coach left you intact." His eyes drop to my crotch. "I see he didn't rip your nut sack off."

I immediately put a protective hand over my junk. "What?"

Andy grins like a fiend. "I can't believe he caught you with Sadie. Classic, bro."

"How did you know?"

He quirks an eyebrow. "How do you think?"

"She told you?"

"She didn't mean to do it. I think she was a bit distraught. Don't worry, Danny-boy. Your secret is safe with me."

"It'd better be. No one can know, Andy. I'm serious."

"I know. My lips are sealed. However, I can't promise I won't tease you to no end."

35

SADIE

ONCE PRACTICE IS OVER, I can barely walk. Coach Lauda trained us harder than before. It was drill after drill, and now my legs are mush.

"Bloody hell. Do you think Coach was trying to compensate for something?" I ask Vanessa on our way out of the locker room.

"I think she's peeved that it took pressure from Coach Clarkson to get Nick Fowler dealt with."

"Yeah, I'm not happy about that either. Why couldn't the school do it from the get-go? It's bloody aggravating."

"Do you think he got involved because he's your dad?"

I clench my jaw tight, not knowing how to answer that. When I don't reply right away, Vanessa continues.

"Sorry. I didn't mean to put you on the spot."

"It's okay. I don't know. I.... We aren't close anymore."

"Shit. I had no idea, Sadie."

"It's okay."

My mood has definitely taken a swing downward. Dad

meddling in the Nick situation, plus what happened this morning is doing my head in. I don't know how to feel about him.

Vanessa, probably sensing the switch in my disposition, doesn't say another word. We continue the trek down the hallway in silence until we're out of the building and she nudges my arm.

"That ought to cheer you up," she says.

My head had been elsewhere, so I didn't see Danny standing in front of his car waiting for me. He's leaning against the door with his legs crossed and hands in his pockets in a casual stance. The pose has pushed his jeans lower, showing a hint of golden skin.

Damn it, now I'm drooling.

I was never one prone to big displays of affection in public, but I find myself running in his direction. He straightens before I jump into his arms and seal my lips to his. Laughing, he kisses me back with a whole lot of enthusiasm. We only break apart when Vanessa and my other teammates start wolf-whistling and making crude remarks in jest.

"Hi," he says, smiling from ear to ear.

"Hi. I didn't expect to see you here."

"I wanted to surprise you."

"I see you survived the meeting with Dad in one piece." I press my hip against his crotch.

"Barely."

"Was it that awful?"

"It could have been worse."

"What did he say to you?"

"He hasn't forbidden us to date, but he doesn't want to see any PDA in front of him."

I twist my face into a grimace. "Like I'd want to do that."

"I hope you aren't busy. I want to take you out on a proper

date." He reaches for a strand of my hair and rolls it around his finger in a distracted motion.

"I'd love to, but can this date be for takeout we get to eat in bed? I'm knackered. Coach worked us hard today."

"In bed, huh? I think that can be arranged." He kisses the corner of my mouth, making me melt on the spot.

"Get a room, you two," Vanessa hollers.

I step back from Danny's embrace and glower in her direction. "Piss off, Castro."

Danny laces his fingers with mine and tugs my arm. "Come on. I'll walk you to your car."

"Maybe drive me to it?"

He quirks an eyebrow. "Really? You can't walk? I thought you were a top athlete."

I hit his chest playfully. "Shut up. I was five minutes late today, so I had to park all the way in the back. And didn't you hear me when I said Coach Lauda destroyed us?"

He laughs. "I'm just teasing you, sugarplum. Come on."

It literally takes less than a minute to drive to where my car is parked. I get out quickly before I get too comfortable and decide I don't need to drive today at all. Danny waits so I can follow him. I blow him a kiss, and I'm still smiling when I face the side of my car and get the shock of my life.

The window is busted, and someone spray-painted "Cunt, you will pay."

The blood in my veins grows cold, and my entire body is paralyzed. I hear Danny's door open, but I can't take my eyes off those awful words.

"Sadie?" he calls, then says, "What the fuck?"

"I-I can't believe someone would do this," I say, disheartened.

"I'm going to kill him," he grits out.

His statement snaps me out of my shock. I look at him wide-eyed. "You don't think Nick Fowler did this, do you?"

"Who else, Sadie? You shot him down multiple times, and your dad got him expelled."

I shake my head, still in denial. "You won't do anything. Promise me, Danny."

His face is beet red, and the fury shining in his eyes tells me he has murder on his mind. I can't let him go after Nick and destroy his career. I grab him by the arms and shake him a little.

"Danny, please. If you love me, you won't go after Nick."

"How can you ask me that? He's threatening you."

"Let the authorities deal with him."

"Do you know how impossible your request is?"

"Fine. I'm calling on my favor, then."

His jaw drops, and the look in his eyes tells me he didn't expect that. "Are you serious?"

"Dead serious."

My heart is thundering in my chest now. I hadn't considered the implications of the words sprayed on my car until Danny pointed it out. I try to control the fear that's constricting my chest, but the familiar panic is rising. I let go of him and hug my middle.

He pulls me into his arms and hugs me tightly. "I won't let anything happen to you, Sadie. I promise you."

I bury my face in his chest, curling my fingers around his T-shirt while I try to force my heart to slow down. Being surrounded by Danny's strong arms does help to keep my fear at bay. I want him to take me away, but not until we deal with this situation properly.

"We need to call campus security," I say.

A car pulls up behind Danny's. It's Vanessa. She lowers her window and sticks her head out.

"What's going on?"

I ease out of his embrace to reply, "Someone vandalized my car."

"What?" she shrieks.

She's out of the car in the next second and staring at the damage.

"Son of a bitch. Do you think this is Nick Fowler's doing?" she asks.

"Who else?" Danny replies angrily.

Vanessa has her phone out and glued to her ear before we can say anything else. She calls Coach Lauda first, then campus security. I let Danny steer me to his car and wait for everyone to arrive at the scene inside and away from prying eyes.

My teammates are the first ones to see the damage, but then Coach Lauda appears with my father in tow. Great. I hadn't considered that she would call him too. Both stare at my car for a brief moment before they exchange words in hushed whispers.

"I'm going to talk to them," Danny tells me.

"Okay." I sink deeper in the seat, crossing my arms in front of my chest.

I should be the one speaking to them, but I'm still reeling from the ugliness of the situation. I know once I'm over the shock, anger is going to take control, and the thirst for retaliation is going to light my veins on fire.

I probably spaced out, because I get spooked when Dad knocks on the window. Clenching my jaw, I lower the barrier.

"What?"

"Are you okay, honey?"

"I'm fine."

He frowns, obviously not believing the lie.

"Do you want to stay at my place for a few days?"

I swallow the huge lump in my throat. I don't know why his offer makes me want to cry. It's like I've reverted to my six-year-old self who would love nothing more than to let her father protect her.

"I want to stay with Danny," I reply.

Dad's jaw clench tells me he's not happy about my answer, but what can he do?

"All right. We'll get to the bottom of this, sweetheart. You don't have to worry, okay?"

"I'm not worried."

It takes another fifteen minutes to be done with the circus. I have to answer the campus security questions, but my testimony isn't that helpful. Sure, we all suspect Nick Fowler, but without eyewitnesses, there's nothing they can do.

On the way to Danny's place, my mood switches from stunned to aggravated. When he parks in front of his building, I want to smash things. My hands are balled into fists, and my nails are digging into my palms' soft flesh.

"We're here." Danny covers my hand with his.

"I know."

"Tell me what I can do to help."

I look at him and wrestle to find the right answer. I don't want him to pick up on my murderous vibe. It took a while to calm him down and dissuade him of the idea of kicking Nick's ass.

"How about that date?"

He stares at me as if trying to read my thoughts. "Anything you want."

I touch his face. "I want tacos, a silly movie, and you."

He takes my wrist, turning my hand around to place a kiss on my palm. "That can be arranged."

36

DANNY

WE'RE lucky that we have the apartment to ourselves. Lorenzo has a school function, which will buy Sadie and me a few hours of privacy. Andy must have his phone in silent mode or he would have blown mine up already, just like Puck and Paris have. News about what happened to Sadie's car has already spread like wildfire through campus.

"Do you have any preference where you want to order tacos from?" I ask.

"I thought maybe we could make them ourselves."

I rub my neck. "I'm sure we have taco shells and salsa, but I'm not really good in the kitchen."

She smirks. "Lucky for you, tacos are my specialty."

Unable to resist, I pull her closer, caging her in against my body. "Oh yeah? Are you trying to win me over through my stomach?"

"Isn't that how it's done?" Her smile broadens.

"It's a perk, but I'd be yours even if you were the worst cook in the world."

She blinks fast, and I swear her eyes seem brighter. I lean forward, ready to steal a kiss, but she steps back, breaking free from my embrace.

"I'm famished. I'd better get started before you meet my hangry version."

"Is it worse than your angry version?"

"Of course, dude. It's a compound feeling."

I make the sign of the cross in jest. "Then no, I don't want to see that side of yours."

Sadie shakes her head before she turns around and veers for the fridge. "I hope you have some type of protein."

"Andy always has meat handy. He and Lorenzo are carnivores."

"Me too. How about you?" She pulls a tray of ground beef from the fridge.

"I eat meat, but I won't die if I go a couple of days without it."

She gives me a scathing glance. "You'd better not be a closet vegetarian, Danny. That would seriously not work in your favor."

"Oh, so you're saying if I'm not ravenous for blood and rotten flesh, I'm not good for you?"

She twists her nose, making her look more adorable than what's fair. It's hard to stay on my side of the kitchen island.

"Who's eating rotten flesh?"

I point at the tray of meat in her hand. "That's rotten flesh right there."

"Gross. Stop putting images in my head."

I pull up a stool and sit down. "All right. I'll stop."

"Where do you keep the taco shells?"

"I think there's some in the pantry. I'll get them."

I stand again and go look for the dry ingredients to make dinner. In the pantry, I also find a margarita mixer bottle. It's the middle of the week, but hell, after what happened today, we both could use a drink. I bring everything to the kitchen and set it on the counter. Sadie eyes the margarita mixer and raises an eyebrow at me.

"Are you trying to get me drunk, Danny?"

"Not at all. But we can't have tacos without margaritas. That's against the law."

She chuckles. "Is that so?"

"Yep."

"Are you even old enough to drink?"

My jaw drops. "How dare you bring up that pesky detail?"

She shrugs. "Don't you know this already? Antagonizing people is my favorite pastime."

I circle around the island and walk over until she has nowhere to go. I place my hands on each side of the counter to cage her in.

"Do you want to know what my favorite pastime is?"

She lifts her chin and looks into my eyes. "Flirting with danger?"

I grin. "Flirt? Nah, I've moved on to making sweet love to danger."

My mouth covers hers before she can get another sassy remark in. I keep my hands on the counter, trying my best not to invade her space. I just want to savor her lips for now. But Sadie is a wicked little thing. She hooks her fingers around my belt loops and tugs me forward. My hands immediately find her face, and what was meant to be a sweet kiss becomes hotter than tamales in a split second.

Her hands are in my hair now, pulling hard enough to toy with the line between pain and pleasure. I lift her onto the counter, nudging her legs apart to press my hips against hers. We break apart to help each other out of our shirts. Sadie is wearing a sports bra though, which is a fucking pain in the ass to deal with.

"Why couldn't you be a feminist and refuse to wear these contraptions?" I ask as I attempt to unclasp the hindrance.

"Try to run while your tits are bouncing left and right and come back to me on that."

She runs her tongue down my neck while her nails scratch my chest. Desire shoots down my spine, and my patience leaves the building.

"Fuck, I give up." I forget the clasp and curl my fingers around Sadie's waistband. "These need to go."

"Here? Your roommates can come in at any moment."

"They won't."

I tug her pants down, and unlike her sports bra, they come off easily, even with her sitting on the counter. I'm on my knees and between her legs in the next second, dying for a taste. I lick her through the thin layer of her underwear first, making her jerk forward. Letting out a loud moan, she grabs a lock of my hair and twists it around her fingers.

Spurred on by the sexy sounds she's making, I slide her panties to the side and sweep my tongue over her clit, loving her sweet taste.

"Danny, oh my God." She yanks my hair back, making it hurt a little.

Pain mixes with desire, creating a potent cocktail that makes my cock grow harder. Damn it, I can't come in my pants. That would be unacceptable. I clench my butt cheeks, trying my hardest to ignore the tightness of my balls. This is all about Sadie. I want her to fall apart on my tongue first.

I focus on how she reacts to each of my caresses. She likes when I circle my tongue around her bundle of nerves, and when I suck her clit into my mouth, she jerks forward again. I grab her hips to keep her in place, digging my fingers into her skin as I begin to fuck her pussy with my tongue. Her little moans turn louder, and then she screams my name and trembles under my touch. I insert two fingers inside her and milk her orgasm until her body relaxes and she grows quieter.

Her hand is still in my hair, but she's no longer pulling at the strands. Now she's running her fingers through my curls, sending ripples of pleasure throughout my body. I look up, finding her leaning her head against the cupboard. Her eyes are closed, and her breathing is a little uneven.

I uncurl from my kneeling position and kiss the hollow of her throat.

"Only you could distract me from tacos," she says.

"I hope you're not hangry yet." I bite her earlobe softly.

"Not hangry. Only hungry... for you."

Our gazes lock, and the heat I see in her eyes is almost enough to make me lose the tight control I have over my body. I pick her up, earning a little squeak from her, and then run to my bedroom.

"Danny, what are you doing?" she asks through a laugh.

I drop her on the mattress and get rid of my jeans as fast as I can. She's still giggling when I join her in bed.

"Stop laughing, woman. This is a serious matter." I kiss her neck while grinding my hips against hers.

She opens her legs for me, hooking them behind my ass. "Yes, very serious," she whispers against my lips.

I claim her mouth as I thrust forward, sheathing myself in her. There's no going slow because she already drove me to the point of no return in the kitchen. I can't think of anything besides pounding into her and making her scream my name again. I was ready to explode a minute ago, and it takes less than that for me to lose it and climax inside her. Another minute goes by before I stop moving and collapse half on top of her.

"Holy shit," she says. "You were really on the verge."

I glance at her. "Did you...?"

She smiles. "Not this time. I couldn't keep up with you."

Not what I wanted to hear. "I'm sorry."

She touches my face. "Danny, don't apologize. You made me come in the kitchen, and that was hot as hell."

"Give me a moment and I'll make it up to you."

She leans on her elbows. "There's nothing to make up for, silly boy. But you can have your way with me *after* dinner."

I kiss her arm softly. "Fine. After dinner, then."

37

DANNY

MISSION ACCOMPLISHED. I think. When I drop Sadie at her dorm the next morning, she no longer has the haunted look in her eyes. I'm not an idiot to believe she isn't worried about the threat anymore. Hell, it was hard for me to pretend I wasn't thinking about it while I was with her.

But I can't let her worry about me on top of everything else. I promised I wouldn't take matters into my own hands, and I won't break my vow. Keeping Sadie's trust is more important than revenge, but that doesn't mean I'll let my guard down.

Vanessa volunteered to drive her to practice, and since I can't skip training twice in a row, I had to accept that I can't be around Sadie twenty-four seven.

I'm determined to not think about how much I want to hurt Nick Fowler for putting fear in Sadie's heart. There's no doubt in my mind that he wrote those disgusting words on her car. Thinking about football helps a little, but when Coach asks to talk to me before we head to the field, my concentration evaporates into thin air.

I didn't expect to have another one-on-one meeting with him, but here I am, once again, in his office.

"What happened now?" I ask, not trying to hide my irritation.

His grim expression doesn't comfort me.

"Nick Fowler wasn't responsible for the vandalism to Sadie's car."

"The hell it wasn't him," I blurt out. "Who else would have the motivation to do something like that?"

"We don't know. The investigation is still in progress. Nick, however, isn't the culprit. He was already in Alabama when the vandalism happened."

"Then maybe it was one of his former teammates."

Coach clenches his jaw. "All soccer players were accounted for when it happened. It wasn't a retaliation."

I rub my face. "If those assholes didn't do it, who is trying to harm Sadie?"

"I don't know. Maybe she pissed someone off. You know my daughter has a temper."

I shake my head. "She hasn't mentioned anything."

Coach sighs, leaning against the back of his chair. "When you look at me, it's probably difficult for you to picture me as anything other than your coach. But I was once a young football player like you, and even back in my time, girls were vicious trying to catch our attention. Could the attack be attributed to an envious girl you dissed in favor of Sadie?"

My spine goes rigid in an instant. "You think this was motivated by petty jealousy?"

"I can't rule out anything."

I pass a hand over my face. "I haven't led anyone on. Sadie is the only girl I've ever wanted to date since I got here."

The moment the words leave my mouth, my stomach coils tightly. I hadn't dated anyone at Rushmore before Sadie, but my past has caught up with me. Gwen has given enough proof that she isn't over me like she claimed. I can't tell Coach about my suspicion though. He's already unhappy that I'm dating Sadie. If he thinks our relationship is putting his daughter in danger, he'll order me to stay away.

"Well, it goes without saying that I need to make sure Sadie is safe, Danny. She won't let me protect her, but she trusts you, which means I have to trust you too."

"Sir, I won't let anything happen to her. You have my word."

He nods. "Good. You can join the team on the field now. I'll be there shortly."

I put my game face on and head out. I can't let him see the guilt that's now swirling in my chest. I barely see anything in front of me. My mind is still stuck on the possibility that I'm responsible for the target on Sadie's back.

It's no surprise that I play like shit, getting sacked more times than I can count and making erroneous passes. At one point, Andy has to pull me aside for words.

"What the hell is wrong with you?" he asks.

"I'm worried, okay?"

"I get that, but you can't allow your personal problems to interfere with the game. Nothing is going to happen to Sadie."

I shake my head. "You don't know that."

"Yes, I do. Coach Clarkson would never let anything happen to his daughter. You don't think he has campus security following her around?"

"She'd hate it if that was true."

"Well, she can't hate it if she doesn't know about it." He shrugs.

"She's going to stay with me until we find out who's responsible."

"I know that, dumbass. And I wouldn't have it any other way. Now can you please focus? We need to win this week's game."

My blood freezes when I realize we aren't playing at home this weekend.

"What's with that horrified look?" Andy asks.

"We have an away game."

His eyebrows arch. "Ah, fuck. Well, I'm sure the girls aren't playing at home either this weekend."

I press a closed fist against my chest, trying to ease the sudden tightness there. I have to figure out who vandalized Sadie's car before the weekend or I'll go nuts.

"Yeah, probably," I reply, distracted.

He claps my back. "Come on. Let's see that golden arm shine."

SADIE

I can't say learning from Couch Lauda that Nick Fowler wasn't the douche who vandalized my car didn't affect me. I was sure it was him. Now I have no clue. But there's nothing I can do besides try to move past that.

The referee's whistle stops the game, and it takes me a second to realize it was because of me. Charlotte is lying flat on her back after I fouled her.

"Are you all right?" I offer her my hand.

Grimacing, she lets me help her up. "I hope so. But what the hell was that?"

"I'm sorry."

"Sadie!" Couch Lauda calls.

"Bollocks," I mutter and then run to the sideline. "Yes, Coach?"

"What were you thinking? You bulldozed Charlotte."

"I'm sorry. I didn't mean to."

"Is this about the incident yesterday?"

I want to deny it, but I don't think lying will help me. "In a way. I'm really mad that the only suspect has an airtight alibi."

"There's nothing we can do about that. I'm relieved that Nick Fowler isn't behind it. It's possible this was a bad-taste prank."

I bite my tongue, not wanting to dig a bigger hole for myself.

"Yes, probably."

"I should bench you until you cool off, but we can't really afford that. Our next game will be tough. I need my best players sharp, Sadie. Can I count on you?"

I nod. "Yes you can, ma'am."

"Good. Now get back there and try not to maim your teammates."

Being chewed out by Coach Lauda helps. I hadn't realized before that I let my anger take control. I'm still aggressive, but I'm careful not to hurt anyone. By the end of practice, Coach is no longer watching me with disapproval. No surprise, considering I scored two goals against Steff.

In the locker room, Vanessa stops next to me. "Do you have any plans tonight?"

"I'm going back to Danny's."

"Really? You two went from zero to a hundred faster than a Tesla."

I smirk. "I can't deny that. I'd be on cloud nine if it weren't for that bloody graffiti on my car. I'm annoyed that we're back to square one."

Vanessa leans against the locker, crossing her arms over her chest. "It's possible some jealous bitch did that."

I frown. "Seriously? That's extreme."

She shrugs. "Bitches be crazy. You're the hot freshman who snagged the most eligible bachelor on campus. I know a bunch of girls who are eating their hearts out now."

"Any of them psychos?"

"Possibly. I'd have to ask my sister if any of her cheerleader friends have a crush on Danny."

"Do you think she'd tell you?"

"I think she would, but to be honest, I don't think this was done by a cheerleader. Doesn't Danny have a jealous ex?"

I groan. "Fuck me. I didn't even consider her. I was too focused on blaming Nick."

Joanne walks over. "What are you talking about?"

"We're trying to discover who trashed Sadie's car. We may have found a new suspect."

Joanne arches her eyebrows. "Oh, that crazy sorority chick. What's her name again? Gwen?"

"How do you know she's crazy?" I ask.

Joanne's face turns a shade redder. She rubs her neck, looking sheepish. "Uh, well, I was hanging out with one of her sisters at their house and overheard a conversation."

At first, I don't get why Joanne would be embarrassed about that until it dawns on me. "Oh."

"What did you hear?" Vanessa asks.

"I heard her saying that Danny deserved better than European trash."

"What the fuck?" I snap. "Man, I knew she was a cunt."

"Yeah, I got into her face and got kicked out," Joanne adds.

"Why didn't you tell me?"

"I didn't want to upset you."

Right. She didn't want me going berserk on Gwen's ass. But I can't fault her for thinking I would. I did kick Nick in the balls, after all.

"I'm glad you told us now, Jo," Vanessa chimes in. "Gwen does sound like a person who would threaten Sadie because of a guy."

"But how do we prove she did it?" I ask.

"The ChiO and Theta houses are having a joint charity event party on Thursday," Joanne replies. "We should crash it and try to get information then. You know how trashed people get at those parties."

Or drugged.

I shake my head, trying to forget my bad experience. "Count me in. If this bitch Gwen is responsible for my car, then she needs to pay."

"Sadie...," Vanessa starts.

"In the right way. I'm not touching her. I'll let the school handle it."

"Are you gonna tell Danny about your suspicion?" Joanne asks.

"Not without proof."

"Good idea. He may think you're picking on Gwen because you're jealous of her," Vanessa says.

I glare at her. "Like I'd be jealous of that girl."

Vanessa lifts both hands in a sign of peace. "Sorry. Forget I said anything."

I look away, pretending to be very interested in the contents of my locker. Anything to hide the fact that I am suffering from major retroactive jealousy. Danny did date the bitch, despite her odious personality. Everyone has a past, but that particular one is hard to swallow.

38

SADIE

VANESSA DROVE to the sorority party, and now we're standing on the corner of Greek row, waiting for the rest of the gang to arrive—Joanne, Charlotte, Steff, Phoebe, and Felicia. I'm surprised when Melody approaches us, still using crutches to move around.

"What are you doing here?" Vanessa asks.

"Do you seriously think I'd pass up the opportunity to mess with those Greek whores?"

"Whoa. I didn't know you drank the Greek hatorade too," I say.

"Melody pledged to ChiO. She didn't make it." Vanessa smirks, earning Melody's death glare.

"I only pledged because I'm legacy and I was trying to please my mother," she grits out.

"I'm sorry. That sucks," I say, trying to keep the peace.

If Melody wants to help bring Gwen down, I won't send her away.

A moment later, Joanne walks over with Charlotte, Steff, and Phoebe, and Felicia in tow.

"All right, what's the plan?" Joanne asks.

"We should split up. Some of us can mingle and try to fish for information from the drunks while I head to Gwen's room and try to find incriminating proof," I reply.

"What kind of proof are you hoping to find?" Charlotte asks.

I shrug. "I don't know. Something useful."

"I know which room is Gwen's, but please don't get caught," Joanne pipes up.

I pull a half-empty bottle of tequila from my purse. "Don't worry. I came prepared. If I get caught, I can always claim I was drunk out of my mind and got lost."

Vanessa shakes her head. "Why I'm allowing you to do this is beyond me. We could get in serious trouble."

I toss my arm over her shoulders. "You're doing it because some skank trashed my car, and family sticks together."

She sighs. "Of course you would remember that."

"We're looking too suspicious standing here. Let's go already," Melody says, irritated.

We let her hop ahead of us. Vanessa and I fall behind the group, and when the noise from the party gets loud enough, I say, "You don't need to stick with me. I'll go snoop in Gwen's room alone."

"No way. I'm coming with you. If we fall, we fall together."

A warm feeling spreads through my chest. I didn't expect to find friendship here at Rushmore so quickly, especially considering how awful I can be. The fact that my teammates are willing to risk punishment to help me fills me with emotion.

God, I think I'm getting choked up. For fuck's sake.

We're swarmed by people the moment we step inside. I

didn't expect the place to be so packed on a Thursday, but I guess the weekend does start earlier on most college campuses.

Joanne turns to me. "Gwen's room is the third door to your left. I hope it's not too late and it's occupied."

Melody's gaze sweeps the room. "If it's occupied, it's not by her. She's over there." She nods in Gwen's direction. "We should go before she sees you, Sadie."

"Wait, you're coming with me?"

She gives me a droll look. "I can't be seen here. There's a reason why I didn't make it through pledge week."

Shit. Now I really need to know what Melody did. However, now is not the time to satisfy my curiosity.

We head to the stairs, hoping no one will notice three non-sorority girls going up to the second floor. We're lucky no one pays attention to us. As we move down the hallway, we hear giggles from some of the rooms we pass.

"I guess some bimbos already found their dicks for the night," Melody mumbles.

"You really don't like them, do you?" I ask.

She looks over her shoulder, frowning. "What's to like?"

I know better than to answer that. Besides, we've reached Gwen's room, and all my focus is now on the search.

"Damn, what's that smell?" Vanessa wrinkles her nose.

"Eau de bitch?" I reply. "Okay, I'll take the closet. Someone take the room and...." I push a third door open. "And the bathroom. Wow. I didn't know these girls had en suites."

"ChiO is the biggest sorority in the country, which means a lot of wealthy alumni," Melody replies.

Inside the closet, the sickly sweet smell of Gwen's perfume is strong enough to make me gag. I search through her clothes quickly, sticking my hand in pockets and looking inside her purses. I also touch the back of the wall, hoping to find a secret compartment. I lose track of time, but I know I've spent too much in here.

"Girls, I found something," Melody calls from the bathroom.

"Me too," Vanessa says.

Since Vanessa is closer, I go see what she found first. She has a huge box on Gwen's bed, and inside are several pictures of Gwen with Danny and mementos of their relationship.

Jealousy and nausea hit me at the same time.

"Oh God. I think I'm going to be sick," I say.

"Man, if she's holding on to all this crap, then she definitely isn't over Danny," Vanessa observes, picking up a homemade Valentine's Day card that says "Gwen and Danny forever" in glitter letters.

The door opens suddenly, and in comes the fucking bitch and the last person I'd expect to see with her: Danny.

DANNY

"You didn't tell Sadie where you were going tonight?" Andy asks from shotgun.

"Nope. She has plans with her teammates, and I don't plan to linger at the party."

"Bro, she *will* find out."

I clench my jaw tight. "I know. I'm not trying to keep this a secret, but I figured telling her after the fact is better. Do you seriously think Sadie would agree to let me come here without her?"

"If she can't trust you...."

I rub my face. "It has nothing to do with trust. I wouldn't be happy if she went to a frat party without me either."

Andy chuckles. "Relax, Danny-boy. I'm just teasing you. I'm like that too. Territorial as fuck."

"Don't I know it? Besides, the whole point of coming

tonight is to find out the truth. Gwen won't confess if I show up at her sorority party with Sadie on my arm."

Andy shakes his head. "It's your funeral."

"Can you please be a little more supportive?"

"I *am* supportive, and that's why I'm telling you your grand idea is stupid as hell."

I park on the street parallel to Greek row and get out of the car. I'm aware of the risks, but I have to find out if Gwen is the one threatening Sadie. It's my job to make sure she's safe, especially if the danger is my ex.

Andy follows me but keeps his piehole shut as we stride side by side to the ChiO house. The bulk of people in attendance are Greeks, but because it's a charity event, the crowd is more varied than usual. People I barely know turn to me to shake my hand or clap me on the back as if we're old friends. I follow along with the charade, pretending not to be bothered that strangers are so familiar with me.

In the entry foyer, I stretch my neck and look for Gwen. I find her in the middle of an open room to our right, chatting with her sisters, red Solo cup already in hand.

My stomach twists. Now comes the hardest part—playing nice with her. Sadie once told me I was a terrible actor. I hope she's wrong.

"Found her. Wish me luck," I tell Andy.

I make a beeline to Gwen, conscious of all the stares following me through the party. When she notices my approach, she walks away from her group of friends, beaming from ear to ear.

"Danny, what are you doing here?" she asks.

"This is a party for charity, isn't it? You know I'm a sucker for good causes." I force a smile, hoping I don't look like a deranged psycho.

"I'm glad you came." She looks over my shoulder. "Are you alone?"

"Nah, Andy is here somewhere."

My reply makes her smile harder. She steps closer, touching my arm. I have to fight the urge to increase the distance between us.

"Can I get you something to drink?"

I take the cup from her hand and drink from it, making sure I keep my eyes on hers as I do so. It's cranberry juice and vodka, Gwen's favorite. It could have been something worse. As flirtation goes, I think I'm doing a good job. Her eyes sparkle with delight, and her smile is still firmly in place.

I don't finish her drink, returning the cup to her after a couple of sips.

"I think I'm okay for now," I tell her.

"You always liked to share red Solos."

"Yeah, and you didn't forget."

She moves closer, making it harder to not take a whiff of her drunken breath.

Okay, I'm officially queasy.

"Oh, Danny. You know I'd never forget anything about you, about us."

Unable to endure her closeness, I step back. But to keep up the pretense, I take her hand and say, "I want to talk to you in private."

"Let's go to my room, then. No one will bother us there."

Fuck me. This will look bad. I can already picture Sadie receiving a text with a picture of me and Gwen. This act better deliver results.

I let Gwen steer me through the party and up the stairs. On the way there, I spot a couple of Sadie's teammates. I lock gazes with Joanne Barnes. Her murderous expression tells me she came to the worst possible conclusion. I shake my head, hoping to convey that this is not what it looks like.

Surprisingly, she doesn't make a move to stop me. Then I see Andy heading her way. There's nothing I can do but hope he can explain to Joanne what I'm up to and that she'll believe him.

A sliver of dread drips down my spine as I walk down the corridor. How am I going to keep Gwen's hands off me long enough to get a confession from her? I really didn't think things through. I'm such an idiot.

Still lost in my thoughts, I don't see the situation I'm stepping into until Gwen opens her bedroom door and my gaze connects with Sadie's.

Fucking hell.

39

SADIE

It takes a moment for the rest of my body to catch up with what my eyes are seeing. At first comes the sharp pain in my chest, the ache of betrayal. Then comes the anger surging through me like a tidal wave.

"What the hell are you doing in my room?" Gwen shrieks.

Despite the shitstorm that's coming from her, I can't take my eyes off Danny.

"Sadie... it's not what it looks like," he says.

"I'm calling the cops," the bitch continues. "This is home invasion."

Melody rushes out of the bathroom, holding something in her hand. "Go ahead. Call them. I'm sure they'd love to know about the stash of Rohypnol I found hidden inside your toilet tank."

She waves a clear plastic bag with small glass vials inside.

"What the hell!" Danny takes the bag from Melody and stares at its contents.

"That's not mine!" Gwen's eyes widen in fear.

Suddenly, the truth about the night I was drugged comes rushing through me. We'd never thought to turn our suspicions to a female party.

"Did you spike Sadie's drink at the Pike party?" Danny takes a step toward his ex, looking possessed.

My anger at him diminishes. Maybe he had a valid reason for coming to Gwen's room. I can't jump to conclusions, not when it comes to him.

"How dare you accuse me of something that despicable?" Gwen retorts.

Melody takes the bag from Danny. "I bet we'll find your fingerprints all over these vials."

"You bitch. Give me that." She jumps on Melody, surprising everyone.

Melody loses her balance and ends up falling with Gwen on top of her. The act of violence triggers something in me. I react on impulse and shove Gwen off Melody. She lashes out like a feral animal, scratches my face with her nails, and we become tangled in a catfight. She pulls my hair and tries to bite my hand.

For fuck's sake. This is insane.

Despite the situation, I hold back. I could do some serious damage to her, but if I break her nose with a punch, it'll be hard to explain to Coach Lauda.

Vanessa and Danny manage to break us apart. Vanessa is the one holding me, but I don't offer resistance. Danny, on the other hand, has to put some muscle into restraining his ex. Man, she's a total psycho.

"Let me go!" She tries to shake free.

"Stop it, Gwen," he demands.

We must have made too much noise, because the room quickly fills with more people. I see Andy and Joanne. The other newcomers all seem to be Gwen's sorority sisters.

"What's going on?" one of the girls asks.

"I found these bitches in my room," Gwen accuses us.

A tall brunette takes a step forward, looking directly at Melody. "*You*. I told you you weren't welcome at ChiO house."

"I wouldn't be here if one of your sisters hadn't threatened a Raven."

The girl looks at Gwen. "What's she talking about, little sister?"

Ugh. Do they seriously call each other that? Barf.

"She's lying. They're all here because Danny ditched their friend for me."

Danny's expression contorts in disgust.

My hands ball into fists. "You lying cunt. We're here to find proof you vandalized my car, but instead we discovered you drugged me at the Pike party."

"What?" Joanne says. "She's the one who spiked your drink?"

"Son of a bitch." Andy passes a hand over his face.

"All lies!" Gwen shrieks again.

"Settle down, Gwen. It's over," Danny tells her.

"You need to leave now. This is a matter for the ChiO," the brunette says.

"Fine. We'll go. But we're taking the proof with us." Melody shows everyone the bag with the drugs.

"That's not mine, Caroline. I swear. The bitch must have planted it in my bathroom," Gwen whines.

Melody shrugs. "They won't find my fingerprints on them, that's for sure."

Caroline pinches the bridge of her nose, sighing loudly. "Whatever. Just go, and take your proof with you."

Danny finally releases Gwen and shortens the distance to me. She sits on the edge of her bed, hugging herself, and starts to cry in earnest. Crocodile tears.

"Are you okay?" he asks me.

"Yeah."

He touches my face where Gwen scratched me. "You're bleeding a little."

"I'll probably need rabies shots."

He shakes his head and then pulls me into a hug. "You're crazy, girl. What were you doing here?"

"What I said I was. Looking for proof that your ex trashed my car."

His body becomes tense against mine. He pulls back and looks into my eyes, ready to reply, when Andy taps him on the shoulder and motions us to follow him out. Yeah, we shouldn't linger here in case Gwen decides to pounce on me. Fucking crazy cunt.

Danny takes my hand, and we don't stop moving until we're outside the ChiO house and away from the front door.

Then I stop and force him to look at me. "What were you doing with that bitch?"

"Same thing as you were. I figured if I led her on, I could get her to confess she damaged your car."

I pull my hand from his and cross my arms. "So you flirted with her?"

"A little."

He didn't even need to reply. His eyes look guilty as hell.

I bite my tongue. Getting into a fight because of Gwen would be giving her too much power over our relationship.

"You're not going to say anything?" he asks.

"Not right now."

I can see he has words lodged in his throat, but our friends walk over, so whatever they are will have to wait.

"What are we going to do now?" Vanessa asks.

"We need to hand this over to the police." Melody shakes the plastic bag.

"Damn. I can't believe Danny's psycho ex was the one who drugged you, Sadie," Andy pipes up.

"Yeah, me neither. It makes me wonder what her endgame

was." I hug myself, hating that because of her, Nick motherfucking Fowler got his hands on me.

"Guys, I don't want to be the one to rain on your parade, but most likely, the police won't be able to do anything with that evidence," Joanne butts in.

"What do you mean?" I ask.

"They could only use it against Gwen if they had been the ones who found those drugs."

"Hell, you're right," Andy replies.

"So we can't do anything against her? She'll just walk away free?" I ask.

When no one replies, I have my answer. All this drama and humiliation for nothing.

I throw my hands in the air. "That's just spit-on-your-neck fantastic, innit?"

"Maybe she'll get kicked out of her sorority?" Charlotte suggests.

"That would be a heavy blow to her ego," Danny replies.

I glare at him. "Yeah, because that punishment is severe enough for drugging me and almost getting me sexually assaulted by Nick Fowler."

Danny winces at my remark, right before his gaze turns murderous. "Don't remind me of that."

"Why the hell not? It's the truth."

"Sadie...," Vanessa starts.

"Don't 'Sadie' me. I have to go." I turn around and stride away from the ChiO house.

"Sadie, wait up," Danny calls after me.

That makes me walk faster.

He jogs to catch up and then blocks my path. "Stop, please."

"Why, Danny? What do you want from me?"

He runs his fingers through his hair, sighing in frustration. "I don't want you to leave angry with me. I'm sorry I didn't tell you what I had in mind beforehand. When Coach Clarkson asked me if a jealous girl could have been responsible for your car, I only had one suspect in mind."

"And you thought seducing the information out of her was the way to go?"

He frowns. "Are you telling me your way was better?"

"At least it didn't involve getting near an arsehole and pretending to like them."

"I'm sorry, okay? I couldn't think about anything besides making sure you were safe." He takes me by the shoulders and steps into my space. "I love you so damn much, Sadie. I'd do anything for you."

Suddenly, my eyes prickle. What the hell? I never cry. But here I am, on the precipice of bawling my eyes out.

"You're an idiot." I grab his shirt and pull his mouth to mine.

His arms slide to my back, pulling me closer while his tongue takes possession of mine. My cheeks become hot and wet, and I curse whatever broke in me that turned me into a puddle of emotions.

He pulls back, cradling my face in his hands. "You're crying."

"You'd better get a good look at it, because this is a rare sight."

He wipes the moisture from my cheeks with his thumbs. "Did you drive here?"

"No."

"Good. Let's get home, then."

40

DANNY

"I LOVE THIS." Sadie sighs in my arms.

"Me too." I kiss the top of her head and then hug her tighter.

She's snuggled nicely against my chest, and our legs are tangled together. Our breathing has finally returned to normal after our "good morning" sex marathon.

"I wish we could stay like this forever." She kisses my chest, then rests her cheek against me.

"I don't want you to go back to your dorm."

"And you think I do?" She chuckles. "But I can't simply stay here indefinitely. This apartment is already a full house."

I open my mouth to suggest we look for our own place but then bite my tongue. It might be too soon to suggest that. We just started dating, after all. I can't help the way I feel about her though. The idea of not waking up next to her every day is grim. But besides the fact that I don't want to rush things and scare her, I'll never be able to find a rental as cheap as what

Andy charges me. And I can't ask him to let Sadie move in with me. This apartment *is* already at full capacity.

Both our alarms go off at the same time.

I groan. "Peace broken. The world intrudes."

She leans on her elbow and reaches for her phone on the nightstand. "We missed our morning run."

I pull her against me and nuzzle her neck. "I prefer the type of cardio we did."

She giggles, and it's like music to my ears.

"So do I. But I don't think doing the horizontal tango will help us win games." She sits up, throwing her legs to the side of the bed. "Coach Lauda wants us in top shape for Saturday's game."

"I got the same speech from Coach Clarkson."

"I think I'm going back to my dorm today," she says on the way to the bathroom.

I get up suddenly. "What? Why?"

She stops and looks over her shoulder. "We know who trashed my car. I don't think your psycho ex will do anything to me now that everyone knows she was behind it."

My chest becomes tight. Drugging Sadie and leaving a threatening note on the side of her car are the craziest stunts Gwen has ever pulled. I can't help but to be concerned. Unhinged people don't care about consequences.

"Just because we know she did it doesn't mean we should let our guard down."

Sadie furrows her brow. "I'm not going to live in fear, Danny. If I let her get into my head, she wins."

I walk over and stop in front of her, placing my hands on her arms. "Just promise me you'll be careful."

"Of course I will. That applies to you too." She rises on her tiptoes and gives me a quick peck on the lips. "I'm going to shower now. Stop worrying so much."

"I'll try. Want company?"

"Tempting, but no. I can't be late for class."

I drop my hands and watch her disappear inside the bathroom.

The feeling of doom is still swirling in my chest despite my promise to not worry. I won't have peace of mind until Gwen is gone from Rushmore and this city.

SADIE

Telling someone I won't let a deranged person get me rattled is easier said than done. I didn't want Danny to stress about me too much, so I had to put on a brave face. But my stomach has been coiled tight the whole morning. I'm not sure if it's because of Gwen or that her despicable acts simply triggered my PTSD again.

I'm so jumpy that when someone taps me on the shoulder while I'm in line to buy a snack, I jerk back.

"Relax, Sadie. It's just me," Jane says.

"Blimey, girl. You almost gave me a heart attack."

"I heard about what happened yesterday. How are you?"

"Jittery as fuck, as you just witnessed," I blurt out, and then regret it. "Please don't tell Danny I said that. I don't want him to freak out."

"He's already concerned."

"I know."

"But I think everything will be all right. A girl in one of my classes is a ChiO. Danny's ex was kicked out of the sorority, and school administration is investigating the claims against her."

"They are? We didn't tell anyone what we found in her bedroom."

Jane shrugs. "Someone did. Anyway, I thought you'd be happy to know."

"I'd be happier if she had been expelled already."

"I know. It's possible she'll only get academic probation. Better than nothing, right?"

"Not really" is on the tip of my tongue, but I keep my retort bottled in. Jane has been nothing but kind to me. I shouldn't bite her head off because I don't like her news. Don't shoot the messenger and all that.

I plaster a fake smile on my face and say, "Sure."

"It's your turn now." She nods toward the counter. "I have to run to my next class. See you later."

"Yeah, see ya."

I buy an orange juice and a protein bar, then rush out of the cafeteria. I lost track of time, and now I only have five minutes to cross the park and get to the Humanities building. I'm about to break into a run when someone yanks my arm.

"Hey!" I turn, coming face-to-face with the psycho. "What the hell? Let go of me."

"You think you won this war, don't you?" she asks, still clutching my arm in a vise grip. "You're sorely mistaken. Danny and I are meant to be together, and no one will come between us, least of all some European trash like you."

Goddamn it. The crazy in her eyes is real. My heart is racing as I pull my arm free from her grasp.

"You're delusional and belong in a psych ward."

My words have no impact on her as she continues her tirade. "This is your final warning. Stay away from Danny or you'll regret it."

She whirls around and walks away while all I do is stare at her gobsmacked. My pulse is pounding loudly in my ears, and my chest is tight.

For fuck's sake. She did not just put me in a state of panic. I should have done something, but save for punching the bitch in her throat, there was nothing I could do. My speech to Danny this morning flashes in my mind mockingly. I told him I doubted she'd do anything to me now that everyone knows what she did to my car. What a fucking joke. No one can predict what deranged people will do.

I pull my cell phone out and look at the time. I'm already late for class, but hell, I'm in no condition to sit through a lecture.

If Gwen thinks she can simply threaten me and get away with it, she's mistaken. It's time I speak with the dean's representative. If he can't help me, then I'll use every resource I have.

That crazy fucker needs to go.

41

DANNY

THIS WHOLE DEAL with Gwen has taken up too much space in my head. The first thing I do when I return to the locker room is check my phone for messages from Sadie. There's only one, and it's just a bunch of goofy emojis. It brings a smile to my face, which is erased in the next minute when an email notification pops up on my screen. It's from the dean's office.

My mood turns bitter after I read the message. The dean would like to speak to me about Gwen at my earliest convenience. It doesn't come as a surprise, but I know if I want him to take the matter seriously, I have to tell him everything about my past with her.

With a deep sigh, I send a quick reply with my availability. The sooner I get this over with, the quicker they'll act. At least, I hope so.

On my way out the building, I call Sadie. It rings until it goes to voice mail. I'm hoping I can convince her to stay another night at my place. My gaze is down as I leave her a quick voice message.

"Danny Hudson?" a male voice asks.

I look up and find a teenager standing in front of the building.

"Yeah."

He doesn't say anything for a couple of beats, but his stare is unnerving.

"Can I help you?" I ask.

He shoves his hands in his pockets. "I'm sorry. I didn't expect this to be so hard."

Chills run down my spine. I look at the kid closely. *Do I know him?*

"You lost me," I say.

"You look a lot like him."

A sudden lump forms in my throat, and my stomach feels like it turned into lead. I finally figure out why he looks familiar. He resembles the jerk who fathered me.

That means....

"My name is Josh Fitzpatrick, Jr. I'm your—"

"Brother. You're my brother."

He nods. "I'm sorry to show up like this out of the blue. I wouldn't have come if it wasn't important."

His face is solemn, and suddenly I realize he's hating having to be here. He didn't come to meet his half brother; he came to plead for his father. The knowledge should make me angry, but all I'm feeling in this moment is sadness.

He's as much a victim in all this as I am. I won't send him away like I did his dad.

"If you want to talk, walk with me."

I head to my car, not bothering to wait for his reply. He does follow me, but he doesn't say a word until I stop next to my vehicle.

"You must be wondering why I came here," he says.

"I'm fairly certain I know why."

He watches me through slits. "I didn't know you existed until a month ago."

"Somehow I don't think that would change anything between us. You wouldn't have sought me out before you felt you had no choice."

He lifts his chin. "That's right. I wouldn't. I hate the fact that you exist."

I try not to wince at his words, but only a cold-blooded person wouldn't react to that statement.

"I have no interest in pursuing a relationship with your old man. I don't want any of his money either."

His eyebrows shoot up to the heavens. "Do you think I hate you because I'm afraid you'll make a dent in my inheritance? I don't care about the money. All I care about is my mother, and your existence is a constant source of pain to her."

Ah shit. Way to make me feel bad about something I didn't do.

"I can't help that. I know you didn't come here to wish me gone, so go on, say what you want and leave."

His nostrils flare, and his hard swallow is audible.

"I know my—*our* father isn't the best person in the world. But for some twisted reason, my mother loves him more than life itself. I don't know what will happen to her if he dies. So I'm here to ask you to help him, not for him but for my mom."

"Help him how?"

My question seems to catch him by surprise. "You don't know?"

"I never gave him the chance to say a word. I only know he's sick."

Josh passes a hand over his face. "He has leukemia. I'm not a match, so we're hoping you are."

Clarity rushes over me. My father didn't come to reconnect with me because he's dying. He came because he had no choice. That makes me feel ten thousand times worse.

"I see." I look out in the distance, seeing nothing.

"The doctors say it's a long shot, but will you at least find out if you're a match?"

There's so much sadness and resentment in my brother's voice that it makes my chest constrict. Bitterness washes over me. I'll never be able to have a relationship with him. I think if the situation wasn't so wrapped in hurt, we could have been friends.

I glance at him again. "Of course I will. I didn't know that's what he wanted. I'm not a heartless bastard."

His lips curl upward, dispelling the animosity for a moment. "You didn't take after him, then."

"No. And my guess is you didn't either."

He shakes his head. "The jury is still out on that. I'll let his assistant know you're willing to help. He'll handle everything."

"Sounds good."

He nods and then walks away.

SADIE

I left the meeting with the dean's assistant feeling discouraged. He was dismissive as fuck about my concerns. He obviously never watched *Fatal Attraction*.

Women can be psychos too, buddy.

His assurance that he'd look into the Gwen matter felt hollow to my ears. Since I'm not going to sit around and wait for her to come at me with a knife, I decide to use the last trump card I have up my sleeve.

I drive straight to the Rebels' headquarters. Danny messaged me an hour ago, so I know practice is over for the day. It means Dad will be in his office, watching tapes until past dinnertime—that is, if his habits haven't changed.

The car park is almost empty, but his car is there. Not willing to take risks, I dig in my purse and fish out the can of pepper spray I bought after the encounter with Gwen. I'm on edge as I stride across the car park, paying close attention to my surroundings. I hate that the bitch did this to me.

My heart is racing when I enter the building, and it doesn't slow down until I see Dad in his office. A wave of relief washes over me. Deep down, I know he'll never let anything happen to me. I don't fight the feeling like I would have a couple of months ago. My resentment with him has lessened considerably, and I think Danny is responsible, in part, for it.

His door is open, but he's facing away from it, watching the TV screen. A football game is on. Most people would notice someone lurking behind them, but not Dad when he's in the zone.

I knock on the doorframe. "Hey, Dad. Got a minute?"

He turns so fast that he almost falls out of his chair.

"Sadie. What are you doing here?"

I enter and then shut the door. "I need to ask you a favor."

He gets up and drags his chair back to behind his desk.

"If it's anything within my ability, I'll be glad to help."

I pull up the chair opposite his and sit down. He follows suit. Immediately, an uncomfortable silence descends.

For fuck's sake. This is horrible. And I know I'm to blame for it.

"I'm not sure you're aware that a sophomore transfer was responsible for trashing my car."

His eyebrows furrow. "I'm aware. She wasn't simply a random student. Danny told me it was his ex."

"He did? I didn't know he had."

Dad nods. "He told me before practice. Even though I appreciate his transparency on the matter, I can't say I'm happy about it."

Oh boy. He's not going to like what I have to say, then.

"Please don't blame him for the actions of his psychotic ex."

"I'm not blaming him, but I can't help thinking if you hadn't gotten involved with Danny in the first place, none of this would have happened."

I take deep breaths, trying to control my temper. "If he hadn't come into my life, I wouldn't be here talking to you."

Dad's eyes narrow, but I don't give him the chance to offer a rebuff.

"Danny is the best thing that's happened to me since I discovered football. He's helped me so much, Dad."

He leans against his chair. "You really love him, don't you?"

"Yeah, I do. So I need you to promise me not to get angry with him once I tell you what happened."

"If your news is anything along the lines of Madonna's 'Papa Don't Preach,' you can forget me not getting angry."

I choke on my saliva. "God, Dad. I'm not pregnant!"

Relief is evident on his face. "For heaven's sake, Sadie. Don't scare me like that."

Glowering, I cross my arms over my chest. "You scared yourself by jumping to conclusions."

He rubs his face. "Fair enough. What's the favor you want to ask me, then?"

"Gwen accosted me earlier today."

He sits straighter. "What did she do?"

"She spewed garbage. Talked a bunch of nonsense about Danny belonging to her and told me I'd regret it if I stayed in her way."

"She threatened you?"

"Pretty much. I had a meeting with the dean's assistant, but I don't think he took me seriously."

"That guy is a moron. I'll go straight to the dean. He *will* take this matter seriously. You have my word."

"Thanks, Dad. That's all I need from you."

He nods. "Of course, honey. I wish you'd have come to me as soon as it happened though."

"I wanted to go through the proper channels and not pull the 'I'm the coach's daughter' card."

"But you *are* the coach's daughter. There's nothing wrong with using your connections to keep you *and* Danny safe."

His comment drops like a ball of glass shards in my stomach. I had been so concerned about Gwen coming after me that I didn't consider she might hurt Danny too.

"I think her beef is only with me," I reply without conviction.

"Are you back in your dorm? I don't like the idea of you staying there while this woman is still around campus. Maybe you should stay with me for a few days."

The refusal is on the tip of my tongue, but then I think about Danny. What if by staying with him, I'm painting a target on his back too? If I stay with Dad for a few days, she'll think her threats scared me.

"I can do that."

His eyebrows shoot to his hairline. "Really?"

I smirk. "You were expecting me to say no, right?"

He rubs the back of his neck and looks at his computer screen. "Absolutely. But I'm glad you said yes. It'll be like old times."

My smile wilts a fraction. I'm not sure it will ever be like the old times between us, but I don't tell him that.

42

SADIE

No sooner do I step foot inside my father's house than my phone pings with a message. I check right away, guessing it's from Danny. I missed his call earlier, but I didn't want to talk to him before I had taken care of the Gwen situation.

DANNY: I need to talk in person. Can I come over?

My stomach coils tightly as worry consumes me.

ME: I'm at my dad's.

DANNY: When will you be home?

I bite my lower lip. Maybe I should just call him.

"Sadie, what type of food do you feel like? Italian, Mexican, Chinese?" Dad asks me from the kitchen.

"Anything you want. Hey, can Danny come over?"

He joins me in the living room, frowning. "Did something happen?"

"I'm not sure. He says he needs to talk in person."

Immediately, Dad's expression darkens, but not in a way that makes me think he's unhappy about my request. I think he's worried about Danny too.

"He can come over, honey. As long as you don't...."

"Get within six feet of each other?" I raise an eyebrow.

He shakes his head. "If he's coming over, I'm ordering Chinese *and* Mexican. That boy can eat."

My smile broadens. "Really? I've never seen him pig out. He's super conscious about his diet."

Dad gives me a droll look. "You haven't seen him after a game."

"You've got me curious."

I text Danny back, still smiling.

ME: I'm spending the night. Come over for dinner? We're ordering Chinese and Mexican.

DANNY: Are you sure it's okay?

ME: Yup.

DANNY: Okay, see you in ten.

DANNY

During the short ride to Coach's house, I almost changed my mind several times. Having dinner with him and Sadie has the makings of a terrible idea. But I do need to talk to her about meeting my half brother today and what I agreed to do. Since I have to disclose that decision to Coach too, might as well kill two birds with one stone.

The thought doesn't give me comfort though. I'm a nervous wreck as I ring the doorbell. This is the first time Sadie, Coach, and I will be together under one roof after he caught us in the Red Barn.

Thankfully, Sadie is the one who opens the door.

"Hey." She smiles, rescuing my mood from the pits of despair.

I step closer and lean down to kiss her on the lips but

change my mind at the last second and kiss her on the cheek instead.

"What was that?" she asks.

I look over her shoulder to make sure Coach isn't in the vicinity, then whisper in her ear. "Can't risk igniting your father's wrath again."

Shaking her head, she laughs. "He's not going to bite your head off if you kiss me on the lips."

"Don't count on that," Coach grumbles, coming into the living room with a mug in his hand.

I jump away from Sadie, my body as rigid as a board. "Good evening, sir."

He takes a seat on the couch and brings the mug to his lips while staring at me. That's not the man I got to know on the field. That's a pissed-off father who knows I'm sleeping with his daughter.

Hell. I shouldn't have come.

"Would you like something to drink?" Sadie asks me.

"Water, please."

She walks toward the kitchen, leaving me alone to deal with her dad.

Great.

"Have a seat, son. I won't bite."

"Are you sure? You're looking pretty feral to me, sir."

My stupid reply only makes Coach Clarkson glare harder.

Fuck me.

Sadie returns with a glass of water in hand but stops in her tracks when she notices my stiff stance and her father's angry expression.

"Blimey. You promised you wouldn't do that, Dad."

He looks at her innocently. "Do what?"

"Act like Danny is the devil."

With a semi-guilty face, he turns to me. "I'm sorry, son. Please sit down. I'll try to behave."

I take a seat on the opposite chair, and when Sadie hands me the glass of water, I drain the whole thing in a few gulps. Nervousness made my throat dry.

She joins her dad on the couch, and now both are looking at me expectantly.

"What's on your mind, Danny?" Coach asks.

"I met my half brother today."

"What?" Sadie sits straighter. "When? Where?"

"After practice. He was waiting for me outside the building."

"What did he want?"

"To ask for my help. I never gave my father the chance to talk. It turns out he has leukemia, and I'm his last chance to find a donor in the family."

"Wow. That's awful," Sadie replies. "What did you say to him?"

"That I'd do the test to see if I'm a match."

"That's very noble of you, son," Coach says.

I drop my gaze to the coffee table in front of me. "I still don't want anything to do with the man, but I'm not going to turn my back on him like he did to me."

Sadie gets up and, to my surprise, sits on my lap, looping her arms around my neck.

Jesus. What is she doing? Her dad is sitting right there.

"You're a wonderful person, Danny."

She hugs me, resting her cheek on my shoulder. I look at Coach, panicked. His eyes are narrowed, but he doesn't seem as pissed as I thought he'd be.

"What's the recovery time if you're a match?" he asks.

"I don't know. I haven't really looked into it yet. I guess I'll take one step at a time."

Sadie leans back and, thankfully, gets off my lap. "No need to worry before we get the results back. When are you taking the test?"

"It's just a blood test. Tomorrow morning."

Coach stands. "We *do* need to worry about it, Sadie. I'm sure donating stem cells isn't a simple procedure. We have to account for Danny's recovery time. It might take weeks."

Shit. I haven't considered that possibility. Guilt makes me gloomy again.

She puts her hands on her hips. "Dad, can I talk to you in the kitchen?"

I sink farther into the couch and barely notice when they leave the room. I don't want to disappoint Coach Clarkson or let the team down. But I also can't tell my father's cancer to wait until it's a convenient time for me.

The doorbell rings, pulling me back to the here and now. Since Sadie and Coach are still in the kitchen, I answer the door. It's a delivery man with a food order. I take the bags from him and apologize for not having any tip on me.

"It's cool, man. The tip was included in the online payment. Good luck in Saturday's game."

"Thanks."

And just like that, my guilt doubles. I hadn't considered the Rebels' fans.

"Is that the food?" Sadie returns to the living room.

"Yeah."

"Which one?" She looks inside the generic bag.

"No clue."

"Mexican," she says after a couple of seconds. "Come on, we can dig in while we wait for the Chinese delivery."

I follow Sadie to the dining room, where there are plates and utensils set up already. A minute later, the doorbell rings again, and Coach goes to answer it.

"What did you tell your father?" I ask in a low tone.

"Nothing."

"Sadie... I don't want to antagonize Coach Clarkson more than my presence here is already doing."

"You're not. Trust me. Dad gets tunnel vision when it comes

to football. I was just reminding him that his players aren't robots and that personal problems shouldn't be dismissed. If you have to take weeks off to recover, so be it."

"It's not that simple."

She glares. "It *is* that simple. The world won't end if you miss a couple of games."

I watch her through slitted eyes. "Oh yeah? Was that your attitude when—"

Ah hell. I can't believe I was about to mention her attack. Sadie's face blanches. I didn't stop soon enough, and she got where I was going.

She swallows hard. "No, but I learned from it."

"I'm sorry."

She shakes her head. "It's fine. Let's eat."

Coach joins us and seems oblivious to the sudden tension in the air. We eat in silence. I have to force down the food because my appetite is gone.

I never thought I'd pray for time to go faster while in Sadie's company, but I can't wait to leave. The thought makes me guilty. It's not her fault I'm so damn conflicted about my decision.

"Well, since the mood is absolutely rubbish, I might as well hammer the nail in the coffin," Sadie announces.

I frown. "Did something else happen?"

She exchanges a meaningful glance with her father, which makes me even leerier.

"Gwen threatened me again."

"What?" I grit out.

"She found me on campus today and told me to stay away from you or I'd regret it."

My hands curl into fists while rage runs free through my veins. I knew she wouldn't simply go away quietly. She's a fucking nutjob.

"You have to tell the dean. She can't be allowed to stay at Rushmore."

"I have a meeting with him first thing in the morning," Coach replies. "But I've asked Sadie to stay here until the matter is resolved."

I feel partial relief, but that's quickly replaced by a sharp pain. I turn to her. "You could have stayed with me."

Remorse seems to shine in her eyes. "I know, but I felt like a mooch. Besides, I haven't really spent any time with Dad since I moved to California."

Now I feel like a jerk. *Way to go, Danny.*

I rub the back of my neck and stare at my plate. "Yeah, I get that. Forget what I said."

Coach clears his throat. "Anyone want dessert? I have ice cream."

I shake my head, getting up. "None for me. I'll help with the dishes."

"I'll join you," Sadie says.

Together, we clear the table and then head to the kitchen. Coach doesn't follow us. I set all the dirty dishes in the sink, and when Sadie finishes disposing of the trash, I pull her into my arms and hug her tightly.

"I'm sorry this was so weird," I say.

"Me too. I should have told you earlier why I was staying at Dad's."

I ease back and look into her eyes. "Why didn't you tell me about Gwen earlier?"

"Because I didn't want you getting involved."

"Sadie, I *am* involved. She's going after you because of me."

"Exactly. I knew if I told you, you'd seek her out. I don't want her near you. That bitch is crazy. I wouldn't put it past her to kidnap you."

I want to tell Sadie she's exaggerating, but that'd be a lie. In truth, I don't know how far Gwen would go.

"I wish I could do a better job of protecting you."

She smirks. "You're doing a fine job, mister. I promise I'll come over after my game Saturday."

"You know we aren't playing at home, right? We won't get back until late."

She loops her arms around my waist and rises on her tiptoes.

"And I'll be waiting for you. In your bed. Naked."

A loud groan makes her jump back. We turn to see Coach Clarkson perform the quickest pivot of all time and walk away.

"Do you think he heard me?" Sadie asks.

"Oh, he heard you."

And he's going to flay me alive tomorrow at practice. Fucking great.

43

SADIE

"THANKS FOR LETTING me tag along to say goodbye to Danny, Dad."

He scoffs. "I didn't think I had a choice."

"You're not wrong." I laugh.

"Jesus, you've only been apart for a few days."

"So?" I take a large sip of my iced chai latte.

Those days were hard. I thought staying at Dad's until the Gwen situation got resolved was a good idea at the time. I didn't think about the practicality of it. With school, practice, and Dad suddenly expecting me to be home in time for dinner, I barely saw Danny.

"Nothing," he grumbles, clutching the steering wheel tighter until his knuckles turn white.

"Anyway, I appreciate you forgetting for a second that you don't like the idea of me dating one of your players."

He sighs. "It'll take me longer than a week to get used to it, Sadie. It's not because Danny is one of my players."

"Oh?" I raise an eyebrow.

He passes a hand over his face. "I haven't seen you grow up, honey, and it kills me that I've missed so much. I know you're a young woman now, but to me, you're still my little girl."

My eyes prickle, filling with tears as I become overwhelmed with emotion that seems to overflow my tight chest. Crossing my arms, I look out the window, hiding any rogue tear that I don't manage to keep from escaping.

"Did you ever regret not asking for custody of Dom and me?" I ask through the lump in my throat.

"Every single day, Sadie. Giving you up was the hardest thing I've ever had to do in my life."

"Why did you, then?"

He doesn't answer for a couple of beats. "It wasn't an easy decision. Your mom loves you and Dom very much, sweetie. She wouldn't have been able to handle being apart from you."

"But you could? How is that fair?"

"She wasn't well."

"What do you mean?"

He grows quiet, and I fear I already know the answer to my own question.

"She was depressed, wasn't she?"

"Yeah. I didn't want to give her a reason to.... Well, I thought it was best for everyone if I didn't ask to share custody."

A lonely tear escapes the corner of my eye, and I hastily wipe it away. "All this time I thought you simply didn't love me enough."

"Honey, how could you think that?"

There's so much hurt in his question that it's almost impossible to keep from bawling like a little girl.

This is ridiculous. I never cry, for fuck's sake.

"I wasn't a very smart six-year-old. Besides, I was hurting too much with the separation. I needed to blame someone."

"No, I think you were too smart. You sensed your mother

couldn't cope with more grief, so you chose me to channel your anger."

I sink farther in my seat, feeling so small that I might have turned into Frodo.

We finally pull into the car park in front of the Rebels' headquarters, where the team's buses are waiting. Some of the players and cheerleaders have arrived, including Danny, Andy, and Heather, Vanessa's twin. I'm glad the cheerleaders and the players aren't interacting—*yet*.

This is the first time Danny is playing an away game since we became official, and I'm getting a little jealous that the cheerleaders get to tag along and I can't. It's damn stupid since the reason I'm unable to attend Danny's game is because I also have to play today.

Is being love-drunk making me stupid too? God, I hope not.

Once Dad parks his car, I turn to him. "Okay, I'm going to say hello to my boyfriend now. It will involve major PDA."

Twisting his face into a grimace, he says, "I'll look the other way."

I smirk, then get out of the car. Danny doesn't know I planned to come to see him off, so he doesn't look in my direction until I'm almost on top of him.

His eyes widen. "Sadie?"

"That's my name, don't wear it out."

I jump in his arms, needing to soak up his essence as much as I can. He hugs me tight, nuzzling my neck in the process. Bollocks. He really shouldn't have done that. Now I want to take him inside the locker room for a quickie.

Must not entertain these thoughts.

"I had to come and wish you good luck in person," I say.

"We don't need luck," Andy chimes in.

"Ignore him," Danny tells me, then leans down to kiss me. He stops suddenly, then glances over my head. "Where's Coach?"

I curl my fingers around his shirt. "Relax. I've warned him already. He's not going to look." Then I pull him the rest of the distance until our lips collide.

He kisses me hard and deep, much to Andy's chagrin, who is pretty vocal about his annoyance. We ignore him and snog like the two horny teenagers we are.

"Coach is coming," Andy warns us, and we jump apart, only to discover the bellend lied.

"Dude, you suck," Danny tells him.

He shrugs. "I'm not even a little bit sorry."

More people start to arrive, so Danny and I refrain from kissing, but we remain attached at the hips until Dad does make an appearance and tells everyone to get into the buses. Danny gives me a quick peck on the lips and jogs after Andy. Since I came with Dad, I'm taking his car back to the house. I don't have to be at the stadium until later.

I remain standing in front of the Rebels' headquarters until all buses depart. I can't help the morose feeling that sweeps over me.

Ugh, get a grip, Sadie.

My phone rings, and I thank heavens for the timely distraction. It's Vanessa.

"Hey, girlie. What's cracking?" I ask.

"Have you heard?"

"Heard about what?"

"That psycho bitch. I was with Couch Lauda when the dean called half an hour ago to let her know Gwen has been expelled."

"Shut your face. For real?"

"Yep. I thought you should know as soon as possible."

I pump my fist into the air. "Fuck yeah. Thanks for letting me know. The dean must have called my father too, but he already left with the team."

"I'm sure he did."

The sound of a car accelerating draws my attention to the street. I turn and see a black sedan coming straight at me. What the hell?

There's no time to do anything besides jump to the side, hoping to not be turned into roadkill. I roll as I hit the ground, glad for my hoodie's protection.

The car misses me by a couple of inches, but it keeps barreling straight ahead without slowing until it hits the wired fence, punching through it. It finally comes to a halt, but that doesn't give me comfort. Whoever is behind the wheel wanted to kill me.

"What the hell was that?" Vanessa asks, and I realize I'm still holding my phone.

"Someone just tried to run me over with a car," I shout through the fear that's made my heart beat loudly in my chest.

My pulse is drumming in my ears as I get up on shaky legs. I have to get out of here.

"What? Oh my God. Are you okay?"

"N-No."

My panic is rising, the devastating emotion taking control of my muscles. The driver gets out, and there's no surprise on my part when I see Gwen, bleeding from a cut on her forehead, her deranged eyes set on me.

"Sadie, are you there? Sadie!" Vanessa shouts. "Shit. I'm coming over."

I should run, should tell Vanessa that Gwen was the one who tried to kill me. But terror already took my ability to think, to speak. I'm trapped by my own mind at the mercy of a psychopath.

"You fucking bitch. Did you think you'd get rid of me that easily?" she taunts me, slowly walking over.

It's like she knows I can't move. Or maybe she wants me to run so she can chase me like in those slasher movies.

"I bided my time, waited patiently for Danny to finally see

that I'm the only one for him. Then you had to come along and ruin everything I've worked for."

For fuck's sake. I can take her now that she isn't inside a three-thousand-pound car coming at me at sixty miles an hour. That is until she flips open a switchblade. Nausea takes over me. Shakes wreak havoc throughout my body. My scar throbs as if my body remembers the pain of a similar blade piercing my skin.

No. No. No.

This is a nightmare.

I have to run.

The mental command finally breaks through my paralysis. I take off toward Dad's car, and Gwen comes after me.

"Where do you think you're going, Eurotrash?"

I don't look back. I just need to focus on running as fast as the wind.

I'm able to cross the car park in the blink of an eye. She won't catch me before I'm safe inside my vehicle, but when I try the driver's door, it's locked. I glance over my shoulder. She's almost on me. I won't have time to check the other doors. *Fuck.* I dash between the cars, hitting the side mirror of one in the process. I barely notice the pain.

The sound of an engine approaching distracts me. I glance at the street and see one of the buses came back. That second of distraction costs me, and now she's right behind me. I turn, raising my arms to deter her attack. The knife slashes my palm open, and I cry out in pain. She pulls her arm back to stab me again.

"Gwen! Stop!" Danny screams.

It was his bus that returned. My heart soars with hope and then plummets in despair in the next second when she turns her murderous attention to him.

"You betrayed me! You promised we would be together

forever!" she shouts like a maniac, waving the blood-coated knife.

I should get out of her range now that she's distracted, but sudden anger overrides my survival instincts. I reach for her wrist and try to wrestle the weapon from her. My hand is burning as if acid was poured over it, but I push through the pain, fueled by adrenaline.

She's taller than me though, and freakishly strong, which works to her advantage. With a shove, she breaks from my hold. I stagger back, colliding with a parked car. She intends to finish me off, witnesses be damned.

Suddenly Danny and my father are there, restraining her. Dad applies pressure to her wrist, and the knife falls to the ground. He kicks it away for good measure.

Shock is quickly taking over again. My breathing is erratic, my pulse beating too fast. But when Danny pulls me into his arms, the wave of panic that was rising slowly recedes. He's my fortress. He's home.

I bury my face against his chest and finally allow myself to cry.

44

SADIE

I'VE BEEN SITTING in Dad's office for over an hour. The police were called, and Gwen was arrested. I gave my statement to them, and to the dean, who came personally to see how I was doing. Now I'm clutching my second cup of coffee while Danny rubs my back in a soothing way. Dad is talking to the dean outside, and even though the door is open and I can hear the conversation, I'm not paying attention to what they're saying.

"Are you sure I can't get you anything to eat, sweetheart?" Danny asks.

I shake my head. "No, I'm okay. You should get going or you'll miss your game."

"The bus left half an hour ago. I spoke to Coach. I'm sitting this game out."

I whip my face to his. "What? You have to play."

"I don't. Do you think I can concentrate after what happened? My fucking ex almost killed you in front of me."

My chest becomes even tighter. I was only thinking about my trauma and didn't stop to consider Danny's.

I touch his cheek. "I'm so sorry. Do you want to talk about it?"

He gives a pained look. "God, no. You're the victim. I'm the one who should be offering you comfort, not the other way around."

"Danny... come on. That monster put us both through the wringer. I'm not made out of paper, you know. I can be your rock too."

"You are my rock." He leans forward and kisses me gently.

A knock on the door interrupts our moment. Couch Lauda is there.

"How are you feeling, Sadie?" she asks.

"Better than an hour ago."

She nods. "That's good. I just want you to know that if you want to sit today's game out, it's okay."

I jump out of my chair. "Are you benching me? I can play. I *wanna* play."

Her eyebrows shoot up. "You just experienced a traumatic event. No one will judge you if you miss one game."

"You don't understand. I need to play. It's the only thing I can control right now. Please, don't make me sit on the bench."

Coach Lauda's expression is filled with doubt. I don't know what else I can say to convince her that I'm not going to fuck up if I play.

"If Sadie says she can play, she can play," Danny pipes up.

She turns to him. "You aren't playing today."

"No, but I'm not Sadie."

I glance at him. Is he saying I'm stronger than he is?

Coach Lauda sighs. "If that's what you want, then I'm not going to stand in your way. But if I suspect at any point that you aren't well, I *will* bench you. Understood?"

"Yes, ma'am."

She leaves, and a minute later, Dad comes in. "How are you, kiddo?"

"I'm okay. My hand is throbbing a little, but thank goodness I'm not a goalie."

"Coach Lauda told me you're playing today."

I frown. "Please don't try to change my mind."

He rests his hands on his hips and stares me down. "I'm not, but I wouldn't be doing a good job as a parent if I didn't ask if you're sure."

"I am."

His lips form a thin flat line while we engage in a staring contest. After a moment, he sighs. "All right. I'm heading to San Diego in a few. I wish I could stay but—"

"The team can't lose their QB and coach at the same time," I finish for him.

He nods. "Right."

"I'll take care of Sadie, sir. I promise," Danny says.

"I know you will, son."

Vanessa, Joanne, and Melody crowd the entrance to Dad's office. They've been here a while, but with the aftermath, we didn't have a chance to speak yet.

Dad looks over his shoulder and says, "I guess I should let your friends talk to you now. I'm done being on the receiving end of their death glares."

He walks out, and then they come in.

"How are you feeling, Sadie?" Joanne asks first.

"Bloody awful, but I told Coach I want to play."

Vanessa and Joanne trade a worried glance, but Melody watches me through narrowed eyes. "How angry are you right now that you let that bitch bleed you?"

"Melody!" Vanessa exclaims.

I smirk. "Fit to be tied."

"What's that?" Vanessa cocks her head to the side.

"It means I'm bloody pissed off."

"I feel sorry for the other team. This game is going to be epic." Melody smiles from ear to ear.

DANNY

I wasn't sure if Sadie would be able to handle the pressure of a game after this morning, but I kept my worries hidden for her benefit. In the end, my concerns were all in my head because she kicked ass. Melody's earlier comment was spot on. Sadie was able to funnel her anger toward decimating their opponents. She scored two goals and assisted on the third.

Seeing her thrive in the field softened the guilt I had been feeling for bailing on my team today. It was the right decision for me though. I wouldn't have been able to focus, and maybe the Rebels would have lost by a landslide and not the four-point difference. It sucks that we didn't win, but it's the beginning of the season. We can recover.

The highlight of staying behind was being on the sideline when the whistle announced the end of the game, and Sadie ran into my arms. Best thing ever.

I couldn't follow her into the locker room, but I'm waiting for her in front of the building when she gets out.

She says goodbye to her teammates and walks over, beaming. I take the duffel bag from her shoulder, and surprisingly, she doesn't put up a fight.

"You're so gentlemanly today."

"Only today?" I raise an eyebrow.

She shrugs, smiling in the sassy way I love.

"*You* are quite amenable," I add.

She loops her arm around my waist, hugging me sideways. "What can I say? Sometimes I like having a strong man doing manly things for me."

"Uh-huh. I smell a trap here."

"No trap. I just want to be taken care of for a change."

I turn her around to look in her eyes. "I'll always take care of you, sugarplum, even when you tell me to go to hell."

Silently, she rises on her tiptoes and kisses me. I pull her closer, deepening the kiss and quickly running the risk of devouring her out in public. My pulse quickens, and chills of desire roll down my spine. I pull back, already breathing hard.

"If you need me to do manly things to you, I have a few ideas in mind."

She bites her lower lip, tempting me even more.

"We'd better crack on, then."

45

SADIE

MONDAY MORNING after the attack was strange. Lots of staring and gossiping. By Tuesday, no one gave a crap that I almost became another blonde casualty in a horror movie. Gwen is still behind bars. It's likely her lawyer will plead insanity. As long as she's locked up, I don't care where she winds up. Prison, psych ward—it's all the same to me.

I'm finishing a paper in the library when Danny finds me. He drops into the seat next to mine and kisses me soundly on the cheek.

"Hey, sugarplum. Are you done?" he asks.

"Nearly. I need another minute."

"What's the paper about?"

"An analysis of the lyrics of 'Julia' by The Beatles."

"I don't think I know that one."

"It's less popular for sure. It's the only one in their entire catalog recorded by John Lennon alone. It's supposed to be an ode to his mother."

"Ah, gotcha."

I'm just about to hit the Save button when Danny's phone pings. A few seconds later, I see from my periphery the sudden tension on his face.

"What's wrong?" I turn to him.

"I just got the test results from the lab." He looks up. "I'm not a match."

Hell. With everything that happened, I forgot about the bloody test. Judging by the stunned glint in Danny's eyes, the results were not what he was expecting.

"We knew it was a long shot," I say. "How do you feel about it though?"

"I'm not sure." He runs his fingers through his hair and looks away. "He's a piece of shit for what he's done to my mother and his wife, but after meeting my half brother, hearing his plea, I feel bad that I can't help the douche."

I cover Danny's hand with mine. "At least you tried. Maybe they'll be able to find another donor."

"Yeah, maybe." He stands suddenly. "I need to see my mother."

"Isn't she working today?"

He shakes his head. "She has Tuesdays off."

"Do you want me to come with you?"

His forehead crinkles. "Don't you have class after lunch?"

I close my laptop and get up too. "Eh, I'm still too traumatized. I can't be arsed."

Danny's furrow deepens, and I guess he didn't get my joke.

"Oh, for fuck's sake. I was taking the piss. What I meant to say is that you're more important than some stupid lecture."

He cracks a tiny smile. "Oh, okay, then. And yes, of course I want you to come."

I collect my things, and we leave the library together. His arm is around my shoulders, possessively, and I confess it feels so bloody nice. I don't care about feminism when it comes to him. I love being claimed by Danny.

He texts his mother as we walk to the car, getting an immediate reply.

"She's asking what you'd like to eat for lunch."

"Anything, really. I'm not that picky, but ask if she has cookies."

He chuckles. "Don't worry. She'll have cookies."

"Oh, I almost forgot to tell you. I spoke to my mother before class this morning. She and Dominic are coming to visit me at the end of the month."

"That's great. You must miss them a lot."

I bob my head up and down. "I do. You know Mum was frantic when she learned about Saturday's incident. It was hell convincing her that she didn't need to drop everything to come see me."

"I think you've told me that story a few times, babe."

I hit his chest with the back of my hand playfully. "Bellend."

He laughs, making it hard to pretend to be angry at him.

"Who will be hardest to impress, your mother or your brother?"

I snort. "You'll have Mum wrapped around your finger in a second. Dom will be a bit trickier, but the worst of the lot is definitely Dad."

"Hopefully I'll return to his good graces once we give him grandkids."

A fuzzy and warm feeling spreads through my chest. I love hearing Danny talk about our future. Getting married and having kids were never part of my vision board. It's crazy how one person can make you see the world in a different light. Now I can't imagine my life where he's not in it.

I glance at him and notice that, despite our easy banter, there's tension around his mouth. His arsehole father must be still weighing heavily on him. To take his mind off the wanker during the ride, I purposely keep the chat light. We talk about our favorite shows, movies, and songs. We rank Will Ferrell's movies from best to worst, then disagree about Hermione and Ron's pairing in *Harry Potter*. He thinks she should have ended up with Harry, and I'm a total shipper of Hermione and Draco. I earn an "are you mad?" look from him for that one. In fact, the discussion lasts until we arrive at his mother's.

The delicious scent of freshly baked cookies reaches us out in the hallway. My stomach grumbles loudly in appreciation. It's already past one, and I only had an apple for breakfast.

"You're not going to judge me if I go straight for dessert, right?" I ask.

"Are you kidding? I'll totally judge you."

He opens the door and calls for his mother. She appears in the living room, holding a tray of cookies.

"Hello, darlings. I hope you're hungry."

"Famished," I say, following the tray with greedy eyes.

She sets them on the coffee table and says, "Lunch is ready. Go wash your hands."

"What are we having, Mom?" Danny asks.

"Pasta carbonara. I hope it's okay, Sadie."

I grin. "Oh yeah. I love Italian food."

She beams and then heads to the kitchen.

Danny veers off the corridor, and no sooner does he give me his back, I step closer to the cookies.

"Don't even think about it. Wash your filthy hands first, piggy," he says without looking over his shoulder.

"Joy killer," I mumble.

I follow him into the bathroom in the hallway. He washes his hands first, then watches me with keen attention as I wash mine. I glare at him through the reflection.

"You'll pay for this, *Potter*," I say in my best Draco impression.

He spins me around before I get the chance to dry my hands and kisses me so passionately that I forget why I was annoyed with him in the first place. The temperature is rising at alarming speed, and if we don't stop, we'll both need a cold shower before we can face his mum.

As if I summoned her with my thoughts, she calls us from the living room. Danny ignores her and deepens the kiss, pressing his erection against my belly.

Bloody hell. What is he trying to do here? With regret, I push him back.

"Danny, stop it."

His eyes are at half-mast, eating me up. "Sorry, I couldn't resist."

"Please don't say my Draco impression caused this."

Twisting his face into a scowl, he steps back. "You had to ruin the moment."

With a smug grin, I walk out of the bathroom and quickly make my way back into the living room. I can smell the pasta now, but I still throw a longing glance at the cookie tray.

"Come on now, Cookie Monster." Danny throws his arm over my shoulders and steers me to the kitchen.

The apartment is small and doesn't have a formal dining room. The table is tucked into a corner, and the food is served on the kitchen counter. There's a big bowl of steaming pasta, plus garlic bread and salad.

"Go on. Grab a plate. It's self-service here," she tells me.

We all fill our plates and head to the table. I moan loudly after the first bite. Danny's mum smiles proudly while Danny raises an eyebrow.

"That good, huh?" he asks.

"It's so, so good."

He smirks. "Aren't you glad you didn't stuff your face with cookies?"

I nod, since I just took a huge bite of garlic bread. Not ideal for kissing later though. Oh well.

We eat in silence for a few minutes, and only when Danny is about done does his mum speak.

"What's on your mind, Danny?"

He sets his utensils down and glances at her. "I'm not a match."

Her brows shoot up, and then sadness sweeps over her eyes. "Oh, honey. I'm sorry."

"Don't be sorry. It is what it is."

"Don't try to downplay how the news is affecting you, Danny. You're my son. I know you better than yourself."

"Yeah, yeah." He picks his piece of garlic bread apart.

"At least you've met your half brother," I chime in, trying to be helpful.

"I don't think he wants to get to know me."

I shrug. "His bloody loss, innit?"

"I didn't expect the news to affect me so much. I mean, I was resigned that he would die, and I didn't care. Then my brother showed up, and it changed my perspective of things. Now that I can't really do anything, I feel helpless."

"Why do you feel helpless, honey?" his mum asks. "We knew the chances you'd be a match weren't great."

Eyes downcast, he replies, "I know."

"Maybe he'll find another donor and you can develop some kind of relationship with him," his mother adds.

Danny's spine goes rigid. "I still don't want anything to do with him. I haven't changed my mind about that."

"All right." She gets up and turns to me. "Are you all done?"

"Oh, I can take my plate to the sink," I protest.

"Nonsense, sweetie. You're a guest. You go get your cookie while I clean up and take Danny with you. He needs something sweet to wash off that sourness."

"I'm not sour," he retorts.

I nudge his arm with my elbow. "Come on, sourpuss. Let's get some well-deserved sugar."

Danny trudges behind me, and he doesn't crack a smile even when I feed him a cookie.

"I thought coming here was supposed to make you feel better," I say.

"Yeah. I guess not even my mother's cooking can get me out of my funk."

"Anything *I* can do?"

There's a slight upturn of his lips. "Yeah." He steps closer, invading my personal space. "We can go wash our hands again."

"Danny Hudson, you're horrible. Your mum is right there." I point at the kitchen.

He kisses me below my ear, sending shivers down my spine. "She knows I'm not a virgin anymore."

I shake my head despite the desire that's weakening my resolve. "I'm not going to shag you in your mother's bathroom," I grit out.

"Fine. Wanna come see my old room?"

I narrow my eyes. "Is that a trick?"

He widens his eyes, playing the innocence card. "I'd never trick you, babe."

He's definitely up to something, but I *am* curious about his bedroom. "Okay."

His face splits into a radiant smile that could light up an entire stadium. He glances over my shoulder and hollers, "Mom, I'm showing Sadie my room."

"Okay."

He takes my hand, looking too pleased with himself.

Yeah, super dodgy behavior there, mate.

I expect him to jump on me as soon as we're alone, but he doesn't. Instead, he watches me as I take his room in.

When I don't say anything for a whole minute, he asks, "What? No comment?"

I look at him, smiling. "You've always been a hopeless romantic, haven't you?"

"What makes you say that?"

I point at the *Howl's Moving Castle* poster on the wall. "Dead giveaway."

He reaches for my hair and tucks a strand behind my ear. "I'm not ashamed of that."

I throw my arms around his neck. "You shouldn't be. It's sexy as hell."

His eyes twinkle with delight as he curls his lips into a crooked smile. "I'd like to point out that you're the one who's starting it this time."

"I know. Does your door lock?"

46

DANNY – Three years later

I'VE BEEN SITTING in my car for the past ten minutes, trying to gather the courage to ask Coach Clarkson the most important question of my life. My hands are clammy, and it feels like I've swallowed a dozen bees that are now buzzing in my stomach.

A text message distracts me from my rising panic. I glance at the phone. It's from Josh, my half brother, congratulating me for my NFL contract with the Tampa Bay Buccaneers, which was announced yesterday. We kept in touch despite our rocky beginnings. Despising the same man bonded us.

The prick found a bone marrow donor after his plea in the media and made a full recovery. He never tried to reach out to me again. It was clear that he only contacted me out of desperation. It took me a long time to accept that he would never be anything besides a sperm donor, and that wasting time feeling sorry because the piece of shit didn't want to be part of my life was pointless.

I text Josh back, thanking him for his message, and then get out of the car. My pulse accelerates, and my body tingles all over with anticipation. It's akin to pregame jitters, but the stakes are much higher. I force one leg in front of the other, not stopping until I'm standing outside Coach's office. The door is closed, so I take a steadying breath before knocking.

"Come in," he says.

"Hey, Coach. Do you have a minute?"

His face splits into a grin as he waves me over. "Of course, son. Come in."

I shut the door and pull up a chair. He's watching me expectantly, almost as if he knows why I'm here. I suppose he could have guessed. I've been dating Sadie for three years, and I've never hidden from anyone that she was the one for me. Eventually, Coach Clarkson got over his annoyance with me dating her. But now that I'm standing in front of him, seeking the ultimate approval, I feel puny, almost unworthy.

"Well," he probes, "what can I do for you, Danny?"

I clear my throat. "Sir, you know how I feel about your daughter. I'm crazy about her."

He nods. "I know."

"Well, now that my future is settled, I'm ready to take the next step in our relationship."

He leans back, lacing his fingers together and resting them over his stomach. "Go on."

"I'd like your blessing to ask Sadie to marry me."

His expression reveals nothing. His face could have been made of marble. I swallow the huge lump in my throat while I endure his stare. I can't flinch, can't show that I'm terrified he'll say no.

Finally, after what feels like an eternity, he cracks a smile. "Of course you have my blessing, son. I couldn't have hoped for a better match for my daughter than you."

A wave of relief washes over me, and I sink lower in my chair, releasing the breath I was holding.

"Thanks, sir."

"I planned to torture you longer, but you were looking a little green there, and I didn't want you throwing up in my office."

"Now I know where Sadie gets her mean streak from."

He shakes his head, laughing. "Oh no, Sadie is a whole new level."

"Well, I'd better get going." I stand up.

"Do you know already how you're going to pop the question?"

I grin. "Yeah."

SADIE

"Did you eat that entire Ben & Jerry's carton already?" Vanessa asks with her hands on her hips.

I lick the spoon and then answer, "I did. And don't give me that look. These containers are tiny."

"Tiny but loaded with calories. Are you sure you want to pudge up now that your beau is moving across the country?"

I glower. "Bloody hell. Don't remind me of that, okay? Why do you think I inhaled all that ice cream?"

She takes the empty carton from my hand and sets it on the coffee table. "Get up. We're going for a ride."

Like a petulant child, I cross my arms. "Why? I'm perfectly fine sitting here on your couch."

"Because I'm already sick of you moping around."

"I've only been here for two hours!"

"Long enough. Come on. You need to burn all those calories you consumed. Let's go for a run."

She's right, I shouldn't drown my sorrows in food. I'm beyond happy that Danny achieved his goal, but I'm also terribly sad that we'll be apart in only a few months. I've been trying not to think about it or show it in front of him. I don't want to put a damper on his excitement.

"Fine."

Vanessa turns on the radio, and when "Hips Don't Lie" by Shakira comes up, she sings along too loudly for my ears.

"Oh God." I pinch the bridge of my nose for a second. "You're determined to annoy me today."

After a few minutes on the road, it occurs to me to ask where we're going.

"You'll see." She smirks.

"You're acting super dodgy. What's going on?"

"I'm not acting dodgy."

I narrow my eyes. "Right."

After another ten minutes, we arrive at the Rebels' training field.

"Why are we here?" I look out the window and search for Danny's car in the parking lot, but I don't see it.

She shrugs. "I figured we could run on the boys' turf for a change. Come on. I'll race you to the Red Barn. The last one there buys dinner."

The pest gets out of the car before I can protest her stupid bet. We're well matched in speed, so what will determine the winner is whoever has a head start. I run to catch up because she doesn't wait for me once she hits the grass. Bitch.

She speeds ahead, and as hard as I pump my legs, I can't take over the lead. All that ice cream I ate is sitting heavily in my stomach, and it's slowing me down. Bollocks. She laughs as she reaches the door of the Red Barn, then disappears inside.

A few seconds later, I follow her and stop. Danny is standing in the middle of the room, wearing his best jeans and my favorite T-shirt, and holding a little box in his hand. My heart leapfrogs to my throat, getting stuck there. Suddenly, "A Picture of You" blasts from the speakers. It's the song that was playing when I gave him a ride to Ikea. That was when I began to fall for him.

I walk over, extremely aware of how fast my heart is beating now. My throat is tight, and I can't believe I'm actually shaking.

"Danny, what is this?" I choke out.

"Sadie, you came into my life like a thunderstorm. Loud, fierce, and so damn beautiful. I couldn't help being enthralled by you, even though I wasn't looking for love."

"Danny...."

My nose burns as tears slowly fill my eyes. I'm still not a crier, but I'm not made of stone either.

He drops to one knee and opens the box, revealing a beautiful diamond ring. "You're the best thing that's happened to my life, sugarplum. Please say you'll marry me."

Unable to speak, I simply nod.

"Is that a yes?" he asks.

"Of course it's a yes. Now get off your knees and kiss me already."

"Hold on. He needs to put the ring on first," Vanessa pipes up from behind the bar.

I look over my shoulder. "How long have you known about this?"

"Nearly three years!" She laughs. "I called it, didn't I?"

Danny takes my hand, and I forget Vanessa. He slides the ring on my finger and then finally pulls me into his arms to kiss me like he did the first time.

Thank you for reading *Heart Starter*! Curious to know what's the deal between Paris and Vanessa? Read their story in *Heart Smasher*.

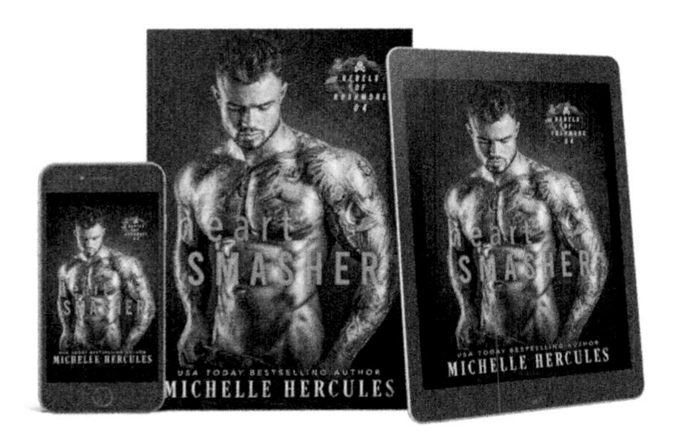

I thought my last year at Rushmore was going to be epic. The Ravens were kicking butt and taking names. As the captain of the team, I took special pride in that.

Until one wrong decision sent me spiraling down a dark void. I didn't think I'd ever find the way out.

Then he came along. The last person on earth I thought would help me, Paris Andino, a linebacker for the Rushmore Rebels.

We've never gotten along before, mainly because he had a girlfriend who hated my guts.

Now he's single and determined to make up for all the times he acted like a jerk.
The last thing I need is a knight in shining armor with a guilt conscience—especially one who can smash my heart into pieces.

One-click HEART SMASHER now!

ABOUT THE AUTHOR

USA Today Bestselling Author Michelle Hercules always knew creative arts were her calling but not in a million years did she think she would become an author. With a background in fashion design she thought she would follow that path. But one day, out of the blue, she had an idea for a book. One page turned into ten pages, ten pages turned into a hundred, and before she knew, her first novel, The Prophecy of Arcadia, was born.

Michelle Hercules resides in Florida with her husband and daughter. She is currently working on the *Blueblood Vampires* series and the *Rebels of Rushmore* series.

Join Michelle Hercules' Readers Group:
https://www.facebook.com/groups/mhsoars

Connect with Michelle Hercules:
www.michellehercules.com
books@mhsoars.com

Printed in Great Britain
by Amazon